First Printing, 2022

CHAMPIONS OF THE GARGOYLE

Champions of the Gargoyle

YULE TIDINGS

Lukas Allen

Contents

1

I opened the book back up.

Ahh... Hanatrix the Dominatrix, by Nevaeh Shinto... I loved how she wrote, the magical, fantasy races all living together, the adventurous spirit of Hanatrix... and most importantly... the beautiful *romance...*

"Hana! Get your nose out of your books and get ready for school!" my mom yelled up the stairs.

I placed my bookmark, and got ready for school. I took a shower, brushed my pitch black hair, made much too much of a fuss on my outfit, and put back on my glasses.

I went downstairs. My dad was drinking coffee and smiling to me with his smile with an extra incisor. My super thin mom was humming and making pancakes, and turned to me and said, "Good morning, Hana. You're not wearing that on your first day of school, are you?"

"What? Are the straps coming undone again? I hate when they do that..." I said, checking my clothes.

"...It's just... aren't your clothes... a little... spiky? And I don't think you can call that a shirt, maybe more of a metallic bralette... And high heels are not the best shoes to wear when walking around from class to class all day..." my mom said.

"You like my pure black pants at least?" I said.

"Very fashionable. Well, sit down for breakfast, and you can take the dragon to school." my mom said.

"Really?? You never let me ride him!" I said.

"I want you to have a magical experience today. It's your last year, and you should try and go out with a bang." my mom said, and served pancakes and bacon with maple syrup on a plate for me to eat.

I chowed down on the food. My dad just drank coffee and read the local news. I asked him if anything interesting was happening, and he told me about the local projects they were starting. I couldn't wait to visit that animal shelter when it was finished.

I finished my breakfast and waved my parents goodbye. "Good luck, Hana!" my mom said, and I went out back to the dragon.

"Morning, Hana." the dragon said, who was finishing his breakfast of a big carcass of a cow.

"Morning, Dragon. Let's get this day started!" I said, and jumped on his back.

He grinned, and we went roaring into the sky, flying through the abyssal black darkness of my hometown, which happened to be in the lowest pits of Hell. Yes, I live in actual Hell. It's really not as bad as it sounds, because the people are so nice.

I went to my first class, and I tried hard to please Mr. Beleth, the Demon of Music, my lifelong music teacher, on the flute, but he still seemed to be in pain.

"...I don't think you've been practicing over the summer like you should've been, Hana." Mr. Beleth said.

"But- But- How can you tell?" I said.

"It is very easy to hear a note that hasn't been strengthened. You sound mushy, like soggy cereal, and not crisp like you should be." he said.

"Oh... I really want to make you proud, but maybe I should just quit the flute..." I said.

Mr. Beleth smiled gently, and said, *"Anyone is capable of making music if they practice. I have high expectations for you, Hana, and I think you can do better than what you've been showing me."*

"Ok. I'll try again-" I said, putting the flute up to my mouth.

Mr. Beleth quickly said, *"Er, I think you've played enough for now. Remember our lesson today, and keep practicing."*

I packed up my flute, and went to the rest of my classes.

I tried to pay attention to my demon teachers... but man, most of these teachers didn't get stuck in Hell because they were great at their jobs. I flew through the bodily mutilation course, always just had a knack for it I guess, as I practiced mutilating my teacher. I asked him how his summer was, and we exchanged pleasantries, and then I made him scream. Afterwards, he wiped the sweat off his brow with what was left of his arm and said, *"Well done, Hana! You're going to get that torture scholarship for sure!"* I liked the demonology lesson the most, where Mr. Faustus taught us all he knew about ritualistic summoning, pagan magic, and the hierarchy of Hell, with Mr. Beleth and some other demons I knew being archdukes and lords of Hell, but all serving the Queen at the top.

I was sitting with my friends at lunch, and they invited me to skip the rest of the day with them, but I declined since I knew if my mother found out I was skipping... there would be all Hell to pay. When you're the daughter of the Queen of Hell like me, you don't fear reprisal from bologna teachers and silly school authorities... you fear the one who cares for you most.

My friends teased me and laughed at me, and left anyway. I didn't really mind, because I knew they were just stupid demons who had no life of their own...

It was a good day, all in all, but I still sometimes wish I could've been transferred to a school that wasn't in a literal pit.

I went to the local park after school, and walked through the stinging flowers down the burning river of fire. It was such a peaceful day...

The bloodsucking vampire bats swarmed me cheerfully, and I let a few of them playfully nip me. They were so nice. I loved being in and around nature.

I waved to the sinner who had just committed suicide again on the big, dead oak. His neck was broken and he was twitching, dancing the hangman's dance, but he still lifted a hand up and waved to me. I liked that people also loved and cared for the park like I did. We had a good community.

I sat on a bench made of bones, and let the wind scream past me in a gale that sounded like a thousand people dying. It was so quiet out here, and the perfect place to read. I took the book out of my bag and continued where I left off.

Ahh... Hanatrix, you dirty dog... She had finally enslaved the entire kingdom, and forced them all to be her sexual servants... She was so cool, and I loved that my parents named me after such an awesome story.

But wait... instead of what I expected, she wasn't satisfied in the least with the nationwide orgy, where the peasants all had endless sex in praise to their new Queen, the kids all laughed at the silly adults, and Hanatrix...

She had wandered away into the forest, leaving unimaginable pleasure behind.

And she moaned out in agony for the love of her life who was dead, the dashing dragon slayer.

That was so sad! But I couldn't stop reading.

I gasped, as I read the next part, where drawn to her bloodcurdling scream of anguish, the dragon slayer comes back from the dead, revealing himself to her... in astounding ghostly nudity!

The next descriptions of their love made my head swim, and I shut the book to save it for later, when I could be in private and properly enjoy it...

I smiled to myself after I shut Hanatrix the Dominatrix at home. What a great ending! I still felt sort of sad though, because the journey with her was over.

Nothing to do but start another journey with a brand new book!

I went into my mother's library. I passed by the many infernal grimoires and dark tomes of secret knowledge, and looked for another good adventure story.

The big, burning book on the pedestal in the center was whispering to me, like it always did, but I ignored it trying to tempt me to learn its forbidden lore. All I really wanted was a sequel to Hanatrix... but, oh well.

The burning book said, *"You'd like a sequel, wouldn't you... Well, I can tell you what happens next..."*

"Nah, Nevaeh Shinto really wrapped up everything quite well. Having a sequel would be nice... but it isn't necessary." I said.

"...But don't you want to know what will happen to the protagonist? Hanatrix goes to... and then she... I don't think I can explain it all, it's so great. Just take a look under my covers and see for yourself..." the book said.

"Hmm... My mother told me never to read you, but I suppose one little peek couldn't hurt..." I said.

I approached the book, which stopped burning for me, and I opened the book.

I gasped as I read the first sentence.

This wasn't a book of Hanatrix. This book was the actual Devil.

The Devil tempted me with all sorts of fantastic stories, adventures that were wonderfully described, and would keep me interested for the rest of my days, with my eyes chained to the book and reading until I was a withered corpse. I was completely enthralled, and I couldn't stop reading line after line, page after page...

But I frowned, and shut the book.

"...What's wrong?" the book said.

"Just seems too good to be true. Finally, I found a book that never ends and always keeps me interested, but..."

"Isn't- Isn't that what you want??" the book said.

"I don't want a story that is perfect. Nothing is as good as you describe, and it's actually kind of disappointing that it's so wonderful. I live in Hell, for Christ's sake. I prefer when people's imperfections shine, when their mistakes define their life and force them to make actions against their will. It's just called being human." I said.

"I should still be the ruler of Hell. A human has no place conquering my dominion, and trapping me in the pages of a damned book. How will the story of the Bible continue if God doesn't have an eternal antagonist anymore??" the book said.

"That story was interesting, but had *way* too many sequels. It needed a definitive end, and I think my mother finished that sad story quite well." I said, "Well, I think I'll read this book about the Nameless Knight, if that's ok. I haven't read that one yet." and I picked up a book on a shelf.

"But- But-" the book said.

"See ya, Devil. Maybe I'll use you as a paperweight one day." I said, picked up the Nameless Knight, and went to my room as the burning book screamed in anger.

2

I had been begging my parents for this since forever. But now it was finally going to happen.

We were going to get a puppy!!

We looked at all the damned hellish creatures. The rotting kittens were so adorable! They mreowled up at me, and I pet their mangy fur.

I didn't know which animal I wanted! They were all so nice and cuddly, although I had been really wanting a puppy to train and be my constant companion. But I couldn't decide on any of these great creatures! I was even thinking about getting that evil parrot who kept calling me a cunt!

But then I saw him, the biggest dog ever, snapping and growling with his three heads.

"Aww! What happened to this guy to be left here?" I said, looking at Cerberus chained up and barking at me.

My mom said, "Well, he *is* the guardian of Hell, and I had a hard time just subduing only one of his heads when I invaded."

I unlocked the lock on Cerberus's chains, and immediately he jumped on me, looking like he was going to rip my throat out with his three maws! I laughed and cuddled him.

As Cerberus was trying his hardest to maul me to bits, I asked my mom, "I thought animals didn't go to Hell? How come there are so many of them?"

"Actually, these 'animals' are people who've abused animals in their past life. Now, they're trapped in the forms they've tortured, and now know what it feels like to be unable to fend for yourself as a starving puppy dog." my mom said.

"Hmm… These animals all seem pretty happy though, if adorably vindictive." I said.

"I decided to change some things when I took charge. That's why we've got an animal shelter even at all. Felt right to also let these sinners know what it feels like to go to a good home." my mom said.

"Can I keep Cerberus?? I'll feed him, and brush him, and walk him and clean up his poops of flaming fire too!" I said.

"Alright. But he better not chew up the sofa, or I'll have to give him away to someone who can tame him properly." my mom said.

Cerberus nearly bit me again, but I got up and said in a commanding tone, "Cerberus! Shake!" and the three headed dog whined a bit, and raised his paw to shake. I shook it, and said, "Good boys! Now roll over!" and the three headed dog rolled over and I scratched his belly.

We took him home, and I knew I had a friend for life.

I went cruising on the dragon, and looked down on the beautiful burning city beneath me. The flames flickered and roared, probably going to consume the entire city in fire again, and then happen again and again for eternity. It was a magical sight, and I think I even heard a few tortured screams.

I stopped by my boyfriend's house, and jumped off the dragon.

I knocked on his door. My boyfriend left me waiting for a long time, probably ignoring me just to toy with me again, but eventually I saw a succubus sneak out the back and run down the alley, so I knew he would come to the door soon.

He opened the door, tried to straighten out his shirt that was all ruffled after that succubus had defiled him, and said, *"Er... Hana! How nice to see you. I thought I broke up with you."*

"Oh, I know you were just kidding, Asmodeus. Whatcha doing?" I said, and let myself into his apartment.

"Well, I was just having passionate lust with a woman who fell to Hell for me... but I suppose I can do the same with you if you want-" Asmodeus said.

"Oh, you silly goof. You know I want to wait until I'm married." I said.

"Right... the Princess of Hell wants to wait until she's married... Er... You want to watch TV then?" he said.

I nodded, and we sat on the dirty, stained couch and watched the shows of Hell.

We laughed at all the silly people getting horrible vengeance on each other! They were so diabolical, and I admired their creative ingenuity of getting revenge. We watched a horrible snuff film that never seemed to end, and cried together. That poor person was going to go through that forever and ever in Hell... I just felt so proud of him for being able to film his suffering for others to enjoy. That takes guts, like the guts spilling out of him, and really showed a passionate, artistic soul. Some people really put their all into their art!

I gave Asmodeus a hug before I left. It was starting to get late, and I didn't want to miss dinner. It was the best meal of the day, sitting down together with my family. "Thanks for hanging out with me, Asmodeus!" I said, and waved him goodbye. He didn't wave back, and slammed the door in my face. He knew just what a girl likes!

I saw the succubus sneak back into his apartment as I was flying on the dragon, and I waved to her and she froze. My boyfriend was cheating on me! I was happy that he even had the time to spend on me, if he was also seeing someone else.

I ate dinner with my family at home, as Cerberus ate three giant steaks with his three heads under the table, and told them all about my day. My dad said, "What? Your boyfriend... is Asmodeus? The Demon of Lust? I thought he was some poor guy who committed suicide, and would soon be going to Purgatory to make amends... And Asmodeus is *cheating* on you even??"

"Yeah! But don't judge him all bad! He's a really down to earth guy, even though we never talk and only watch TV." I said.

"...Dina, do you really think... that this is the best place for Hana to continue her life?" my dad said to my mom.

"Don't worry about it, Zax. She's got a great, positive view of life from living in Hell with us." my mom said.

"You do seem like you've grown up into a good woman, Hana, like those damn twisty roses here which always bite me on my way to work, but... maybe... you need to see what is outside of Hell, like... actual life." my dad said.

"But..." my mom said, "I was going to groom her to take charge for a while, so we could take that vacation we've been wanting for so long..."

"I know. But I think Hana should be transferred to a nice school, a school on Earth, so she can broaden her horizons." my dad said.

"A foreign exchange program?? That sounds like so much fun!" I said.

My dad smiled, and my mom said, "Ok... I suppose that is the right choice. We'll be here for you when you get back, Hana, and we'll always love and care for you-"

"I'm going to start packing!! I can't wait! Thank you so much!" I said, and rushed off to my room to gather my things.

I packed up a whole bunch of different books... but I felt sad for the one that I was going to leave behind.

I looked at that burning book, still trying to get me to read it, and couldn't ever imagine a worse fate than a good book not being read. I said to it, "You're not really my taste, but maybe I can try to at least get through a few chapters of you."

"Yes!! Just skip through the lines even and not notice any of the intricate details! That's what I've been wanting for so long!!" the book said.

"Alright. But don't burn my stuff." I said, and the book stopped burning as I put it in my big backpack.

<h1 style="text-align:center">3</h1>

"It'll take a lot of walking, so be prepared to be tired down the road. Did you eat a hearty breakfast?" my dad said.

"Yep! Can't we just take the dragon?" I said.

"Er- No, Hana. You see, when your mother took over Hell, she made sure that Hell stayed in Hell. We can't take a demonic dragon into the living world." my dad said.

"Oh… Can we at least take him to the edge of Hell? I finally get to ride him, and now I'm not even going to anymore. I guess Cerberus has to stay too?" I said.

"Yes, Cerberus has to stay. We can take the dragon to the edge of Hell, if that's what you want." my dad said.

"Ok. Remember that Cerberus likes three meals a day for three mouths, a walk around the Seventh Circle, and he really hates it when you tell him to si-" I said.

My dad smiled, and said, "Don't worry about it! I think I've figured out a few tricks from watching you. See, watch this. Sit, Cerberus!"

Cerberus stood up from laying down, and began growling at my dad.

"Uh… Good dog?" my dad said.

Cerberus barked and gnashed his teeth at my dad, making him jump back. I smiled. It looked like my dad had everything handled by the way he was shaking, and Cerberus seemed to love my dad just as much as I did.

I hugged Cerberus, and said, "Be good boys, Cerberus, and keep Mom and Dad safe." Cerberus licked my cheeks with his three tongues, each head vying to give me the most attention.

My mom gave me a big hug goodbye, and said, "Learn a lot, Hana. I love you."

I rolled my eyes, but mumbled, "Love you too, Mom…"

I put on my walking shoes, shouldered my backpack, and we rode the dragon to the edge of Hell.

I looked down at all the waving demons, and I shouted out, "Bye, everyone! I'll see you all again when I graduate!"

They roared up at me, chanting,

"The Princess of Hell goes to Earth!

To force the people into the dirt!

To conquer them all with her horrible will!

The Princess of Hell will kill, kill, kill!"

They were all so nice. I was going to miss them. Especially Asmodeus, but he didn't deign to tell me goodbye.

We got to the river Styx, dismounted the dragon, and we paid the ferryman a single coin each to take us to the living world.

It was spooky on the river, as the ferryman didn't say a single word, but he did look a bit surprised. He cleared his throat, looked like he was about to say something, muttered, and was silent again.

At the end of the long, spooky journey, my dad said, "Thanks, Charon. You've gotten even smoother at steering than before."

Charon nodded, and pressed the coins back into our hands.

"But…" my dad said.

"You don't- You don't pay to get out of Hell. This one's on me." Charon said.

"Oh! So this is for the return trip?" my dad said.

"You won't get a return trip, Zaxazaxar. Goodbye." the ferryman said, and left on his boat, leaving us with a chill in our bones.

"What did he mean by that?" I asked, as we hiked up the long, winding stairs.

"Um… People here can be a bit cryptic without meaning to… Let's just forget about it, and focus on the brand new journey you're going to have! Yeah…" my dad said.

After what took a really long time, we eventually got to the top. Actually, you would usually just climb those stairs forever if you tried to get out of Hell, but my dad said the trick was to, "Think positive, and let your soul be as light as air again." Seemed like a pretty easy trick to get out of Hell to me, but I suppose some people really did have trouble thinking good thoughts, especially if they're suffering.

I wondered what this so-called sun would look like? I had lived my entire life in Hell, and I wondered if it really had a big, happy grin like the stories I've read. Of course, I also knew it was a giant ball of flaming gas, but the books always described the sun "smiling" on you, so I didn't really know what to believe.

My dad budged open the giant sealed stone portal, impervious to all but the absolute strongest, the legends said. I thought my dad must really be a strong guy! But he said, "True strength is not raw muscle. True strength comes from facing adversity, and overcoming it."

Then the sun shone through the crack.

I wandered out, and gasped. There was… green carpet everywhere… Grass? And big trees that weren't dead. And the wind didn't scream at me, and seemed so quiet.

"Welcome to life, Hana." my dad said, and smiled.

"It's beautiful… but I sure wish it wasn't so bright up here." I said.

"You'll get used to it. Actually, up here light and darkness alternate, day and night, so you'll see both sides of life." he said.

"Hmm... So the duality of life is really just shades of light? Poets always moan and groan about that sort of thing, but it's so simple looking at it as just night and day." I said.

"Um... Kinda. But there are some people who are as good as actual angels up here, and some more wicked than the most evil demons of Hell-" my dad said.

"Demons aren't wicked. They just made a few mistakes." I said.

"...Yes. That is a good way to put it." my dad said.

We went through this beautiful... *day...* and walked to my new school.

4

We stopped for a rest by a river that wasn't burning like it should be. We walked for sooo long… I was exhausted, and my dad lit a small fire with a flint and tinder as we rested. "Won't it never go out, then?" I asked.

"No, it's not like hellish fire. Fire up here can be tamed, and will go out eventually if it doesn't have any fuel." my dad said.

"Tamed? Like Cerberus? Fire. Be bigger." I said.

The fire seemed to ignore me, and was still a small little power source.

"Why isn't it listening?" I asked.

"Er… Hana, to make a fire bigger, you need to feed it fuel. Like this." my dad said, and threw a log on the fire. It licked up and down the log, just like I had seen fire do to sinners in Hell.

"Oooh. How do you make it smaller?" I asked.

My dad went to the river, cupped his hands in the water, and took it to the fire. He then poured it on the fire, and it started making a horrible sizzling sound and got smaller!

"Poor fire…" I said, "I like it better when it listens to me, and burns unrestrained."

"You need to be careful with fire, Hana. It is very dangerous, and could hurt you or someone." my dad said.

"But they'll just hurt for a while, right? Then they get back up and are as joyful as ever after their pain." I said.

"...No, Hana. When people get hurt here... sometimes they don't get back up again." my dad said.

I opened my eyes wide, and said, "You mean like... *death??* I thought that was just fiction."

"It is a very real occurrence, and is the passage everyone- most people, take after life." my dad said.

"You mean my pet goldfish from the living world... when she fell asleep forever... Hm. I feel like I want to see this mystical death some more. You make me wonder about it. Is it really a skeleton that takes you away on a pale horse?" I said.

"...Trust me, you never want to see the pain of death. Try to focus on life instead, and the majesty it can bestow." my dad said.

So I listened to life, these birds chirping around us, the quiet wind through the living trees, and the trickle of the not burning river going past. I wanted to hate it, but it felt peaceful in a way.

I took out my flute, packing it because Mr. Beleth told me to practice, and played it for the peacefulness. But I just seemed to scare the peacefulness off, and my dad said, "...How about we continue walking, Hana." He put out that poor fire with that non flaming water, and we went walking down the path of life.

We walked for a long time again, but I was getting used to the pain. It was nothing like my walks with Cerberus in eternal Hell. Seemed shorter in a way. I asked my dad if this school was really as good as he said, and he said, "My old friend, Lux, a robot, runs it, but he really has more life experience than all of us combined, and will be a good mentor for you. Plus you get to talk to the other kids and learn from them, as well."

"What's a robot? I've read about them, but I'm never quite sure how to picture them." I said.

"A robot is a very advanced machine. Humanity went a long way, in the living world, and figured out how to replicate life with technology. It's kind of like a TV, but much more intelligent." my dad said.

"More intelligent than a TV? This robot must be able to show me all sorts of suffering and torture then! What fun! I can't wait to learn from him." I said.

"...Mostly he'll teach you how to prevent that, so keep your mind open for new experiences." my dad said.

"Oh yeah, because of that death thing. Alright, I'll learn all I can from the robot." I said.

"Good. We're nearly there. Do you need to rest?" he said.

"No way! I can't wait to go to my new school! I'm all super excited!" I said.

We kept walking, and I whistled a fine tune, nearly out of the forest with plains approaching.

But someone heard me, and a man came out from the bushes who was shaking terribly. He said, "Give me your money. I don't want to have to hurt you." and pointed a pistol at us.

Oh, he must be some sort of bandit. So cool! Remembering a book about a cowboy I read, I said, "Put down your gun, pardner, if you don't want to lose your head."

He shakily aimed the gun at me, as I was pulling an imaginary pistol from my imaginary holster, and my dad stepped in front of me.

And the man shot my dad.

The man ran away into the distance, as my dad bled on the carpet grass.

"Are you ok? Please, get up and quit making that sad expression." I said, kneeling before him.

He could barely speak, but said in a voice that had a deathrattle, "I... love you, Hana..." and then he...

He died.

I screamed as I realized that my father was dead.

But he would just go to Hell, right?? He would be back with my mom and everything would be fine-

But a short man came driving up to us in a pale car, rumbling down the distance on the plains. He stopped before us, got out, and knelt before my dad. The short man was wearing a white hoodie, and had angel wings and a halo on him. I said to this strange person, "Please help my father!!"

The angel man smiled, and said, "I will. Zaxazaxar has earned his eternal reward."

Then the angel took out a gentle, white fire from my dad's chest... and I could see my dad *get out* of his body, take the man's hand, and go to the car.

I screamed out, "Don't leave me, Dad!!"

My dad looked sad, as he got into the backseat, and the man started up the car.

So I opened the passenger door, jumped into the passenger seat, and got into the car.

"What?? You're not supposed to be able to do that!!" the short driver said as I tried to strangle him.

"Leave my dad alone!! Don't abduct people who are dead!! Who the hell do you think you even are??" I said.

"I'm the angel of death for Zaxazaxar. My name is Max." the short man said, trying to fight me off as we drove down the road and soon were ascending to the sky.

"Hana. It'll be ok." my dad said in the backseat.

I stopped trying to strangle this driver, and said to my dad, "But you felt death now!! And this guy's not even letting you be dragged down to Hell!! Something is wrong."

"Technically... Spiritually... this man is Death, Hana. And he wants to take me to Heaven." my dad said.

"No one wants to go to Heaven! All my friends gave up on that ages ago! You have to go through Purgatory, and yada yada, and it's just a giant pain in the ass! It's way cooler in Hell!" I said.

The short driver, Max, said, "Much hotter. In Heaven you get just the right temperature-"

I said, "Turn this car around! I'll kill you if you let my dad suffer a death he doesn't want!!"

"I do want this, Hana." my dad said.

I turned to my dad, and said, "...What?"

"I love you and your mother, but I truly did hate Hell. You and her were the only ones who made it bearable, and I only bore it for you two. I can accept an afterlife I would be proud to have." my dad said.

"But then you're giving up on our family!!" I said.

"I invited Dina to join me in Heaven, with you, a long time ago. She would rather try to build her own creation, than suffer through any other's. She'll change her mind eventually, and we can finally live in peace. It's not like I have any choice now, anyway, since God has spoken through this angel." my dad said.

"I don't give a shit if he's a fucking angel! God has no right to tear apart my family! You'll never go to Heaven and leave us!" I shouted.

"We're already here, guys." Max said.

I looked out the window again, and saw giant pearly gates beckoning to us, swinging forth for my father.

My dad got out, as I protested, then I got out and chased after him, and he stopped walking and held my hands before he could be accepted into Heaven.

I was crying, because I would miss him eternally if I could never see him again.

But he smiled, and said, "We'll meet again, Hana. I have faith that you'll be here too. Relax, and enjoy the beauty of life."

I was sobbing, and I could see my dad would've held my hands, just outside of Heaven forever, instead of seeing me suffer.

So I let him go.

My dad hugged me, kissed me on the cheek, and said, "Remember to pray, Hana. I love you."

"I love you too, Dad." I said.

Then he walked through the gates.

I cried even more, as the gates shut again.

I went to the driver, Max, who was leaning against his car, and said, "Take me back to Hell. I never want to see this horrible life."

"If that's what you really want..." Max said, and we got in the pale car.

I was silent, but this annoying angel of death kept on trying to make conversation.

He said, "So you really don't want to go to school with the living? I hear Lux's school is the top one today, and he could really teach you a lot."

"I just want to learn to kill and mutilate, and then people be fine again after I do." I said.

"...I think you've been living in a hellish bubble, Hana. You should try to see what's outside, see some sights, and not get too accustomed to one thing."

"Then teach me how to take people away. I want to take people to Hell, where everything is fine under my mother's reign."

"Are you asking for an apprenticeship? I don't think I've ever heard of such a thing, a child of Hell learning from an angel of death..."

"Yes. That's exactly what I'm asking. If you don't teach me, I'll kill you."

He just laughed, and said, "You don't even know what death is, Hana. It's not some joyful experience where you go to Hell and be happily tortured forever. It's the end of life."

"So teach me. Show me what it means to be truly dead, and I can see what it means to live."

"...Hmm... That's not a bad idea... showing a child of Hell her place... even just someone who's wrong what's right... I accept your begging, and accept you as an apprentice. We'll start tomorrow morning, *early* morning, so don't be late."

"Really?? I'm not begging. I just want to beat you."

"That's as desperate as it's going to get, going against God's will. Well, we're here, Hana. Enjoy your life."

"...But this isn't Hell."

"Nope! This is your new school in life. Enjoy it while you can... because one day, someone may snuff you out for good. Have a good time, and tell Lux I said hello!" Max said, opened the passenger door, and pushed me out of the car.

I fell flat on my face in the mud, breaking my glasses, and Max laughed and drove off.

Stupid angel. I lifted myself up, put my broken glasses in my pocket, and walked to the school.

5

"...He says hello? Well that's as disconcerting as it's going to get, having an angel of death greet me..." the robot with a crystalline eye said in his office, looking at the skull on his desk.

"So what. Teach me what you know and get it over with." I said.

"...It's not that simple for humans to sponge knowledge into themselves. You're going to have to take lessons, painstaking tests and learn through trial and error... It will be a long road for you, Hana." the golem said.

"Grrr... I just want to kill people and let them go to Hell... I don't want to spend a life having to learn new shit that doesn't make sense!" I said.

"...Ok. I would teach you how wrong that viewpoint of the world is, but I think you've had a rough day, as your clothes are muddied, you look tired, if I had to guess I'd say you are nearsighted and can't see without glasses, and your father... So I'm going to let another student show you to your room. Sara! Please show your new friend to her bed!" the golem shouted out down the hall, and a girl with big muscles grumbled and came into Lux's office.

Sara said, "Why do I always gotta do this shit, Lux? I help one idiot kid, and then I'm the welcoming committee for every sap that wanders in here."

"I just think you have a truly welcoming soul. You take the time, and care for the other students, no matter what their strange origins. And Hana here has some *very* strange origins." the robot, Lux, said.

"...Well... I'm not a fucking welcome mat. But thanks." Sara said, and beckoned me to follow her down through the school. She said, as we passed through the long, narrow halls, "They're coed dorms, since we only got so much space we got, so don't worry if one of the guys tries to peek in sometimes. If they do, do what I do, and punch 'em in the dick, and he'll put those eyes elsewhere. Just watch out for some of the guys who want to claim the new girl."

"I will make them suffer with the wrath of Hell if they try it. I'm seeing Asmodeus, the Demon of Lust, and I am ever so loyal to my boyfriend." I said.

"...I guess you're probably seeing him right now too, hallucinating... but that's alright. I've met weirder bitches than you Wiccans. Micah used to be a damn cannibal! Took her forever to stop shaking every second, after Yule rescued her from that life..." Sara said.

"Yule?" I said.

"She's just a cool scavenger and looter and stuff. Always finds the neatest things out in the wastes. Sometimes she finds people who need help, and brings them back to us too." Sara said.

"Interesting. I don't understand why Micah needed help if she was a peaceful cannibal... but interesting..." I said.

"Uh... Well! Here's your bed in the corner here. Micah sleeps right next to you there, and I'm lucky to have the one far away from you... Micah snores... but you probably find that comforting. Have fun... new chick." Sara said, and quickly ran away from me out of the room with five beds in it.

I looked at this girl, Micah, who had a horrible deadeye stare staring at me from the bed beside mine and shook a lot at random times, but...

it did sort of remind me of the sinners on TV. I took off my muddy clothes with my broken glasses in my pocket, put on my pajamas, got into bed, and soon listened to her snores in the night which were like the peaceful, roaring winds of the underworld... I fell asleep imagining I was in beautiful damnation...

I stretched awake from an awesome nightmare... Gosh, it was so early... It was as dark as Hell...

Then I gasped, and remembered I needed to meet with my new master.

I quickly got dressed, and ran out the doors of the school, looking for the pale car. I saw it parked just outside of the school, and I ran to it, hoping I wasn't late.

Then the car started up, and started driving away.

No!! I needed to have this angel's power!! If I could, then everyone would be happy in Hell, and not be torn away from each other in Heaven!!

I ran to that car, chasing along after it, sprinting at full speed behind it...

Then the car stopped, and I whammed into its brake lights.

I rubbed my head on the ground, and Max came out and said, "I didn't think you were going to show up! But then I saw you still chase after me as I was driving, and then I knew..."

"You kept driving even after you saw me?" I said.

"Call it a first test. I'm not going to teach just *anyone* the power to take souls away... Here, let me help you up." Max said with a grin, and offered his hand.

I refused the offer, and got up myself.

"Suit yourself. But we should really try to be friends, if I'm going to be your teacher." Max said.

"I need no friends, I only need knowledge. I learned all I could without worthless teachers and their petty lectures. I learned from books." I said.

"Those books were written by someone, you know. But get in, you're going to have a first lesson." Max said.

I quickly ran to the car and got in, as Max got in as well, and we drove off.

6

We flew through the early morning sky in the pale car, and it did look sort of pretty with all the stars and weird moon thing, with the sun coming over the horizon as well. "I never get tired of this sight. I'm glad I can spend a little bit of my eternity in the living world." Max said.

"Who are we going to kill? Jesus, maybe? He'd be a good practice, since he'll just come back to life anyway. I hear he had to walk through Hell after he died, but then he left! But I suppose I would understand if I wanted to go see my father in Heaven like him too..." I said.

"We aren't going to kill anyone, Hana. It's more the soul moving that I do. Each angel takes on a specific job after their death. Some become angels of war to continue God's merciful battle, even though the war technically ended because of your mother, some angels become caretaker's of Purgatory to help the lost and confused sinners make amends for their mistakes, a few of the extremely rare chosen become seraphim to protect God's throne, and some become angels of death like me. There are numerous other jobs in the hierarchy of Heaven, but you don't need to learn about every single one of them right now." Max said.

"A lot of demons used to be lost and aimless, fighting eternally for their scraps of Hell and claiming themselves as lords of Hell under Satan's reign, but now under my mother's rule a lot of them continue the jobs they've had in their past life." I said.

"...So they're all lawyers, then?" Max said, and grinned. I didn't know if he was making a joke or something. People can be evil no matter what their job, and I applauded them for being so diverse. Max's grin slowly faded, and he coughed, saying, "We'll do something easy, first. You can watch as I help a nice, old man through to the next passage after life. It's been his time for ages now... but he has such a kind soul, and it would've been a shame to let him go without seeing this beautiful sunrise one more time."

"How's he gonna bite it? A fall in the shower? Choking on a chicken bone? Or... like my dad, and killed by a bullet..." I said, and grew kind of sad.

"He will breathe out one last time, and pass as his body fails from natural causes, old age, sitting on the bench that he first saw the love of his life on in the park of the town he grew up in, as the sun finally is completely over the horizon." Max said.

"Sounds kinda dumb. I'd want to die properly, screaming in anguish as someone squeezes my last breath out of me, after they had just been done flaying my skin off and eating it. I saw such a thing on the TV in Hell, and she won an award for her horrible suffering." I said.

"...I think I've seen that too... It takes a lot to just be an angel of death and show mercy to the dying and suffering, and not be an angel of war and end those who made them suffer..." Max said, and gripped the steering wheel hard.

We landed in the park, and Max told me to stay put in the car, but I ignored him and walked up to the dying man sighing in contentment at the rising sun. Max stuttered in protest at me and chased after me, and I sat beside the smiling old man and said, "You're going to die now."

He blinked, and started panicking, saying, "But I still have to go to church and volunteer at the breakfast! I-I... The sun's not even out, and I haven't said my prayer for my wife! Are you going to kill me??"

"No, he is." I said, and pointed at Max, and Max sighed.

"N-No! I have to say goodbye to everyone! I need to listen to my granddaughter's recital, she's been practicing so hard! I n-need to go there!" and the old, withered man got up off the bench, and tried to shamble quickly away at his slow, old pace with his walking cane.

The old man then tripped, and hit his head on a rock.

The old man was trembling on the ground, blood spurting from his forehead, and Max calmly went up to him, rested a hand on his shoulder, and he stopped trembling.

Then Max picked out a white fire from the old man, and I was so excited to talk to the old man and ask him what it felt like to die that way, but Max just put the fire in his hoodie pocket, and told me to get back in the car.

I did, and said, "...Can you let him out so he can enjoy the ride with us?"

"No, Hana. You've made this poor soul very confused, and I'm going to keep him safe in my pocket, *without* letting you harass him some more. I'm taking you back to your school, and you can continue your learning *without* learning from an angel of death." Max said, as he started the car and we ascended again.

"You're not going to teach me anymore? But why?? This was only our first day!" I said.

"You obviously don't have the kindness to allow the dying peace. This was a foolish idea..." Max said.

"But- I can be really nice! Please give me another chance!! I'll do everything you say! I'll just sit in the car and let you kill people yourself! I'll never do anything stupid like that again! I just thought he would want to know it was his time, is all!" I said.

"It is a terrible burden knowing when you have to give up life. Most people are better off if they don't see it coming. Otherwise they try to grip onto life even more, and end up spoiling it because they're squeezing too hard. I thought you would know that, living in Hell and hanging around all those demons..." Max said.

"I'm *so* sorry! See, I'm learning a lot already! Please don't give up on me!" I said.

"...This is against my better judgement, but maybe this is God's will, since I still don't understand how you even got in the car and saw the gates of Heaven before your time..."

"So you'll still teach me??" I said.

"Yes. But you need to keep to your word, and do *absolutely everything* that I tell you. If you don't, a mistake could be made, and something terrible could happen." Max said.

We continued on in the sky in silence, me wondering what that exactly meant.

7

I continued the rest of the day at the school, very tired. I took a shower in the girl's locker room, had a short breakfast in the cafeteria as a lot of the boys stared at me, and I then hummed to my first class, which was a current events class. I knew a lot of the stuff they told me from my parents, that my father, Zaxazaxar, created unlimited energy for the world using demonic electricity, which is power harvested from a demon's soul, as he imprisoned Satan himself and harvested him, but Satan escaped and caused all sorts of suffering on Earth. They didn't seem to know that Satan had been defeated eternally by my mother, however, and was now trapped in a book in my bag.

Although, they kept on talking of my father like he was some super villain!! They said he corrupted the world, and that's why everything is so disordered, lawless, and terrible today!! I had seen my father actually go through Heaven's gates! I was very frustrated by this class, and wanted to tell them all off, but only fumed in my seat...

I wish he actually was as evil and horrible as they pictured, because then he would still be in Hell with me and Mom...

We all had lunch in the cafeteria together, and these kids were very nice, although it seemed like a lot of the boys were trying too hard to be too nice.

They would fight over who got to sit with me, giving me gifts of their dessert cakes, and soon I had a whole pile of cake sitting on my plate. I said to them, "Thank you all so much! But I really don't like angel's food cake."

"I-I got a bag of chips I've been saving! Want that?" a boy said. I shrugged, and he shakily took out a bag of chips, looked down on it one last time, sighed, and gave it to me. I thanked him, and ate the chips. They were very spicy.

I threw all the cake into the trash, and the boys all gasped.

I eventually went to my last class, which Lux was teaching himself.

"You are all familiar with circumferences from our math lessons by now, and you all know the first thing you want to know about calculating a circumference is the entity called pi. Pi is a set value that won't ever change, but when calculated it continues to show new digits that continuously don't follow a pattern, and its exact value is unknowable to us. I've tried to calculate every digit for a long, long time, yet it still surprises me. Pi never ends apparently. We are going to discuss the history of pi, and how it was first discovered by the mathematician known as Archimedes, and how he-" Lux said.

"So pi never ends? Is it like a Circle in Hell?" I said, and the other kids laughed.

"Um, I suppose. Some believe it will show a definite pattern or an end to it, but probably not until the world collapses to dust-" Lux said.

"I admire pi's longevity. I sure would give anything to have an eternal cherry pie, but then I'd have to calculate its never-ending circumference..." I said, and the other kids laughed some more.

"Yes, yes, humans love to eat. Anyway, Archimedes-" Lux said.

"Archimedes must be like my mother, and must have eternally conquered his enemies with the power of eternal pi. I'd like to meet Archimedes at some point, and tell him he is doing a wonderful job at being eternally dominating." I said. The other kids were silent, and someone coughed.

"...Anyway, let's get back to the lesson. Archimedes..." Lux said, and told us about some dead guy who I wasn't sure I had seen before. Maybe I missed him in Hell, or maybe he escaped Hell's grasp and got to Heaven. I don't know. Demons were never really that good at teaching history of the living world, and honestly most of them sounded like they were just making stuff up.

The classes were all pretty enjoyable, although there wasn't any sort of my favorite subject, demonology, and I felt like something was missing in this school. They had no demonic religion to practice! I decided to start a club.

I handed out cute little fliers for people, inviting them to learn demonology, voodoo, and black magic with me. A lot of the kids just threw the fliers on the ground, which I picked back up again, but Sara picked up a flier I was about to pick up, looked at it, looked at me, and said, "...So you really are some sort of witch. This Asmodeus must be quite a handsome devil, if you're literally worshipping him..."

"Oh, no. I don't worship him. We just watch TV together. But you can learn so much evil magic with me! Sure, most of it is just tricks and lies, but that's what makes it so fun!" I said.

"...Hm. So I can curse that one bitch who keeps on badmouthing me behind my back? I sure would like to see her have warts like a toad's..." Sara said.

"Of course! The toad curse thing is actually only biological warfare in a witchy form, but I can curse her, if you like!" I said.

"Cool. Well, I *guess* I'll see what you're offering and try to keep an open mind." Sara said, smiled, and walked away and crumpled the flier and put it in her pocket.

The boy who gave me the chips nervously accepted my flier, and said, "D-Did you like those chips? I had been saving them for a special occasion, because they're so good and rare."

"I sure did! They made my tongue feel like it was bleeding! Thanks for the chips… Chip!"

"Uh-Uh no problem. I'll come to your club." Chip said, and basically ran away from me clutching onto the flier.

Lux noticed me handing out my demonology club fliers, and I gave one to him. He looked down at the flier and said, "…Ever since demons actually did invade creation, things like this aren't looked favorably on by most people…"

"Oh, it's just good fun, is all. And you know demons were all dragged down to Hell again by my mom! What's the harm?" I said.

"I suppose. As long as you do not practice any harmful practices, no sacrifice, no ritual laceration, and explore your interests only in theory." Lux said.

"Oh. Ok… That'll work, I think." I said.

"Good. Enjoy yourself, Hana! We definitely need more clubs in school." Lux said, and walked away with my flier.

The frog in my pocket wriggled again, and I guess I would have to let him go, instead of sacrificing him to Marbas, the Demon of Knowledge…

8

We had our first meeting on the stroke of midnight, the witching hour, in a secret location in the library. I noticed someone following me in the dark corridors, and I invited her to come along instead of stalking me in the shadows. Micah stared at me with that deadeye stare, wiped a bunch of drool off her chin, and continued to follow me in the shadows.

We sat in a corner of the library, hidden between bookshelves in a very boring part that was all old math books, shrouded in darkness. I began speaking in a sinister voice, as the three other dwellers in the darkness listened to me preach. I whispered, "There is great power in the unseen. The world is filled with magic signs and mystical occurrences… and they have much to teach us. I will be teaching you what I know of the world in darkness, of how to command the very fires of Hell, and so we will become greater with our conjoined knowledge, and see even further than what's beneath the veil…"

"Spooky." Sara said, "What exactly are we looking for beneath the veil?"

"…I don't really know, actually." I said.

"Really? I thought you would've seen whatever is beneath the veil already." Sara said.

"…Well, no, not technically, but I have lived in actual Hell, and my mother has seen what's beneath the very surface of existence." I said.

"Oh! So she taught you a lot about magic and the dark arts, then, right?" Sara said.

"Er… She's *going* to teach me that kind of stuff, but only once I graduate… Really I've only learned from demonic grimoires and actual demons." I said.

Chip said, "This is so fucking terrifying to me."

"That's what makes it all the more tempting. We will conquer our fears together." I said.

Micah's stomach grumbled.

I began teaching them the hierarchy of Hell, all serving the Queen at the top-

Sara said, "I thought the Devil was in charge or something."

"He was, until about a couple decades ago when he was overthrown by my mother. About the time I was born, actually." I said.

"…Hmm…" Sara hmmed, "I don't know if that's exactly right. I feel like you've been living on fairy tales, very dark and twisted fairy tales, but just what your parents told you to make you feel better. I'm gonna leave, but it's been interesting." Sara said.

Chip said, "I don't want evil powers. I thought you were just really cool, and pretty, and nice and stuff. But I'm going to go too."

Micah's stomach grumbled more.

"Wa-Wait!" I said, as the two were going to leave me with a starving Micah, "I have proof! I can show you something actually, truly from Hell! I can show you the Devil himself!"

The two looked at each other, and sat back down in the shadows with me.

I took out the book that was the Devil, placed it on the ground before me. It started burning of its own free will, and we were illumined in the Devil's dark light.

They all gasped at its flame, and the book said, *"This is really kind of embarrassing. I'm the Prince of Darkness, and not something for show and tell."*

"See? There is true power in darkness, and it can show light as well." I said.

Sara said, "Th-This is so… *cool.* I only ever thought this shit was like, lies and superstition."

"Well, it is, but the Devil still ran around and messed with people to bring them to Hell. He kinda liked being illusioned in lies, people never knowing if he was in the darkness or not. It's kinda like in a horror story where you never see the monster coming, and is more exciting, I think." I said, "Right, Devil?"

"...Very spot on. I can't just show myself to the viewer right off the bat, because as soon as people get accustomed to something, they don't fear it, then they don't respect it, and then the horror story turns into a comedy, and people just laugh at the ridiculous monster..." the book said.

Chip poked the book, and took his hand quickly away as his hand got a little burnt. Chip said, "I feel more scared than I've ever been. But this is exciting." He then tried to poke the book again, and it burned brighter, trying to take off Chip's hand, and Chip immediately took his hand away.

"I AM LUCIFER, THE FIRST ANGEL MADE BY GOD. I WAS CAST TO HELL AS I TRIED TO OVERTHROW MY VERY CREATOR. I AM NOT SOMETHING TO BE POKED."

Sara said, "But you lost against God, right? Whatever you did sounds pretty stupid. I mean, who tries to take down the creator of everything ever?"

"Just because you don't have the power to win, doesn't mean you don't have the power to try." the book said.

"Hmm. Very wise, book. Still, I would've bet my money on God, instead of just a lowly angel. Why are you a book, anyway? Like you said, you don't seem like a very scary monster." Sara said.

"Yeah, Hana, why am I a book? Does it have something to do with you and your wretched family putting a spoke in my schemes? Is it something to do with your mother figuring out how to use stupid, fantastical powers to claim authority where she should have none?" the book said.

"My mother is the Queen of Hell, and my father is Zaxazaxar." I said to my followers.

"...The Zaxazaxar? And *Queen of Hell?*" Chip said, "...You really do have evil, magic powers."

Sara said, "This is really intense. I'm sorry for ever doubting you."

Micah wiped off the drool on her lips.

"And I can give you even more magic powers... Take a look inside me, learn my secrets..." the book said. The book's fire went out, and the three were going to grab it and read it, but I quickly snatched up the book and put it in my backpack.

"Um, let's try something a little lighter, for now. I have a book by Crowley, a book by LaVey, and the removed part of the Bible by Judas Iscariot. Each of you can take one, submerse yourself in its hidden lore, and we'll meet again next week." I said, and handed them each one of the books.

Chip and Sara thanked me for starting the club and snuck off back into the shadows with their books before they were caught. Micah stared at me with her stare, and followed me back to the dorms, her grumbling stomach a constant, welcoming companion, like Cerberus's grumbling stomach.

9

I had just finished another day of school, and was practicing my flute sitting on my bed in my room with all the other girls laughing and joking, but as soon as I finished my very first song, smiling to myself and thinking I was really improving... I looked around, and I was completely alone.

I wasn't *that* bad at flute, was I?

Then I heard a mystical, enchanting sound outside the window, and all the kids screaming in delight at something. I listened closer, enraptured by that sound... and it was the sound of a flute! I didn't even know flutes could make that sort of intricate, awesome melody!

I wandered down the halls, drawn to that music like a hungry belly drawn to the most delectable feast. I went outside, and saw an old, ramshackle van covered in all sorts of junk, loot and scavenged materials I guess, and an albino woman with star tattoos, wearing a red hoodie under scavenged pieces of armor with pure white pants, long, unbound white hair, and a samurai sword on her back, hugging the kids in delight, beside the most beautiful man I've ever seen, dressed in dark clothes, playing the most beautiful song I've ever heard, that made it feel like you were *hearing* colors, on his ordinary flute.

Some of the kids were laughing and dancing to the music, as they cheered for him as "the Dark Piper." The albino woman gave whole boxes of goods to Lux, which some of the other teachers helped carry into the building. I slowly approached that man playing his magic, and just listened in front of the crowd of kids.

He finished his song, bowed, and all the kids cheered. I didn't want it to be over, and wished I could've eternally listened to him play, with his strong body in my arms...

The albino woman came up to me, looked into my eyes with her red eyes and with a happy smile, and said, "Howdy! You must be Hana, Zax and Dina's daughter! Lux just told me you got here! I'm Yule, a friend of your parents." and she shook my hand.

"Yes, I'm Hana. Pleased to meet you. Who is he?" I asked, pointing to the beautiful man.

"That's my man bound to me for life. His name's Lucius. We just ventured into a few of the more dangerous and destroyed cities, to find food and supplies for you guys. It was a terrifying adventure that was super risky, but you can't have reward without risk..." Yule said.

"Bound to you for life?" I asked.

"Well, that's what we're calling it. I guess you could just call us boyfriend and girlfriend, but we prefer a more romantic tone, and we always felt like we had a deeper romance than as a simple couple." Yule said.

Hmm... Bound to her for life... This man was ten times more alluring than any demon of Hell, especially my crooked boyfriend, Asmodeus, whom I've been questioning some of his actions lately... But bound to for life... I guess she won't mind if I take him when he's dead...

Still, I don't think I could've harmed a hair on his beautiful, blonde head...

Yule saw me squinting, and said, "You don't need glasses, do you? Here, one sec." She went into the van and got me something, a perfect pair of glasses, and offered them to me. I put them on, looked back at the beautiful man...

And I fainted.

I woke up to the even more beautiful man placing me gently on a bed in the infirmary, with such tender care.

"You need some water, I think. It's kind of hot out today." Lucius said, and gave me a glass of water, which I accepted and smiled at him, fluttering my eyelashes. He smiled back, and I felt the red go to my face.

Yule was talking to Lux, saying, "Charles is patrolling the area, and you shouldn't have any problem from that savage warband that just surfaced to the east. We'll keep in touch on our radios, and let you know if anything changes."

"Thank you, Yule." Lux said, "This new generation is more valuable than any loot you've ever brought us, and I am grateful that you are protecting them."

"No problem, Lux." Yule said, "How's everything else going? I'm glad Hana finally came out of her hole in the earth. Does that mean things are changing for Zax and Dina?"

"Hana... tells me her mother is keeping everything in tip top condition, but Zax... was killed by a mugger on his way to the school with her. We've been searching for a while, and I kept the children away from the area I believe it happened, but Hana... It's only a matter of time before she-" Lux was saying.

"Shhh... She's awake. I'll talk to her." Yule said.

I stared at Yule quizzically as she had a sympathetic expression on her face. What was she sympathetic for? I would conquer Heaven one day, just as my mom conquered Hell, and steal my dad out of God's clutches. All I needed was to keep learning everything I could, so I could figure out how to do that... I knew I could try, but I didn't know exactly how to try...

Yule dismissed Lux and Lucius, saying she wanted to talk to me privately. The two left the infirmary, as I watched Lucius's beautiful butt walk away...

Yule sat on the edge of the bed, and said, "I'm sorry for your loss, Hana. Zax was a good man and a good father, and he didn't need to die so violently."

"So? I don't care that my dad is dead. I'll just bring him back to life or something. I'm sure that's possible." I said.

"...For most people that is a definite impossibility. I think you should focus on remembering your dad and be happy for the life he had, instead of trying to grasp onto a fantasy like that." Yule said.

"My mother is the Queen of Hell, and anything is possible for her. As soon as she knows, she'll bring back Dad at once, and we won't have to suffer anymore." I said.

"I think she already knows, Hana." Yule said.

"How would she? It's not like she can- I mean, even if anything is possible for her- I hadn't told her- And- I-" I tried to speak, but it felt like my throat was getting constricted, and my eyes were starting to water.

Anything was possible for my mother. So possible, she would know if her husband had been killed.

But he was still dead, dragged to Heaven by an angel of death.

I burst out crying, unable to stop these tears. My father was dead, and I would never see him again.

Yule held my hand sadly, and I clutched it tight, as I cried and cried.

I sadly listened to Lucius play for Yule, Lux, and I again when Yule said it was alright to come back in and I had stopped crying so hard. I felt a little better listening to him play the somehow sombre tune.

He finished the song, and we sat in silence for a second, remembering my dad. My dad could sing probably better than Beleth, and my dad always sang for me and my mom when he could. Lucius's tune reminded me of my dad's music, but it felt right to let that song pass, and let the silence envelop us instead.

Eventually Yule said to Lux, "We stopped by Cass and Jake's ranch on our way here and picked up a lot of the foodstuff we gave you from them. Ever since they found those wild horses they've been making a good living trading them and other livestock. Although, they're a couple wild horses themselves, so I don't see how they can bear to settle down like that. I suppose they finally found a place they could each call home."

"I do miss the old days with you all, fresh out of Friendliness and playing music for the remnants of civilization. But I've found a true purpose here, teaching what I know on my stored data banks to humanity's children." Lux said.

"I miss it too. Well, we'll take the guest room and call it a day after we find- you know. It's been a tiresome hassle these last few days, and we could really use a chance to relax." Yule said.

Lux said, "Of course. Our home is your home."

Yule came up to me and gave me a hug, and I hugged her tight. I put my arms out for Lucius as well, and he wrapped me in that strong, gentle embrace. I said to him before he left, "Lucius... I noticed that you're... Would you be able to..." but I couldn't say what I wanted to say, that he would protect me tonight because I was definitely going to have horrible nightmares remembering my dad's death, and his music made me feel so much more at ease, so I said, "Would you be able to teach me to play the flute like you? I've been practicing over and over, but I think either my flute is broken, or just my lips."

"Sure. I'd love to teach what I know. I've never actually had an actual teacher for the flute myself, but I can try to teach you." Lucius said.

I opened my eyes in surprise, and said, "But- How can you contrive those melodies if you've never learned them from someone?? That doesn't make sense."

He shrugged, and said, "I suppose I did have one teacher, lost on the streets of an evil city, lost in the wilds of the forested north. I had nature. Even in a rat infested dystopia, she still calls out to us through the cracks, and gently guides our way back to her."

"Oh. I've never really believed in Mother Nature myself. I only have one mother, and she definitely isn't made of trees and dirt." I said.

He smiled gently, and said, "Just listen to the natural sounds around you, and you'll see what I mean." then he walked down the halls with his woman bound to him for life.

I walked back to the dorm, listening to the sound of people laughing and talking around me, the creak of the building as the wind pushed against it, and I heard… Yule and Lucius's van door slam. They weren't leaving, were they? They said they wanted to stay the night.

I peeked out the window… and I saw them walk into the distance with shovels.

I was curious, so I followed them for a while. Lucius looked down at something, and I heard him say that the tracks and drag marks went deeper into the forest, as I hid behind a hill.

I followed them into the forest, and I could smell some sort of horrible stink. It smelled familiar… like I had smelled a thousand times in Hell…

A corpse? A corpse.

I frantically ran after them, and I screamed at the body that had been mauled by wild animals and dragged deeper into the forest, its eyes picked out, intestines hanging out, clothes torn to shreds, flies buzzing around, and decaying flesh stinking up the surroundings.

I just screamed and screamed, as Yule and Lucius went faint looking at me.

That was not my father!! That could not be my father!!

I ran away as quickly as I could, as Yule and Lucius called out to me.

A pale car stopped before me, and I quickly jumped in, and told Max to take me far away from here.

10

I was shaking as Max drove me through the sky. "That can't be right. That's not right. Nothing like that happens out here. You took him away. You took my father to Heaven." I said.

"He still left his body behind, and I'm glad someone found it finally. I would've told them, and I was really hoping you'd be able to… but I can't talk to living people, being a dead man myself." Max said.

I shook, looking at him staring grimly through the windshield, and I said, "Why is life so horrible?"

"It's got a lot of bad moments, true, but I think the living makes up for it. Are you sure you want to continue learning to let people die?" Max said.

"I don't know. Can I ever stop that horrible… stillness?" I said.

"No, you can't, but remember that the body is only a shell, only a staging area for the soul. That stillness is only a rest for the body, as the soul is taken to Heaven for eternal rest." Max said.

"I don't ever want to see that again, or imagine that it will happen to someone else. Please just take me for a drive." I said.

Max played the radio and we drove silently through the sky. I was a passenger of an angel of death, riding in his pale car... and I felt so sad. I didn't believe I could ever go back to the living world, with such horror.

I had seen hundreds, thousands of people like that. But they still moved soon after. They didn't die, and there was never any death. We just suffered in tortured misery over and over, again and again-

Was that torture not really the way of things? Was living in Hell... actually quite a miserable existence?

I thought of that sinner who committed suicide in the park every day. He probably felt that horrible misery always, and tried to end his life to stop that, but never could.

I felt sad for my old life, a life in Hell, that I knew I could never go back to for as long as I lived. I wanted to keep moving, and never see anyone go through the pain of death over and over again. I don't know how my mother could stand it. I would have to give her a few ideas of mine, if I ever saw her again.

I just wanted to keep riding in this car. We kept going through the sky for a long time, but eventually it was getting late, and Max told me he should probably take me back to the school.

I felt sad, listening to the radio, and said, "Just take me to Heaven- Wait... Who is that singing on the radio? He sounds just like my dad."

"That's Paul and his band, Spawn of Sax. You're actually descended from him." Max said.

"Really? That Paul? My dad always talked about him, and said he learned how to sing listening to this ancestor. I didn't think he could make something so beautiful in such a horrible life. It sounds like he's telling me to live, with his jazzy, bluesy, metal music."

"That's exactly what he's saying. Paul had a short life, and a very tortured one. But he still found ways to enjoy that life. Mostly with women and music, but still, enjoyment and contentment."

"Do you think I can find that contentment in this life as well?"

"Yes, Hana. Make the most of the life you have, and dying won't seem so bad in the end."

"Ok. I'll make the most of my opportunities. I'd like to see how other people make the most of their life too and how they approach the end, so I would still like to continue learning from you."

"Great. You're never going to get another life, so treat yours and others' with respect." Max said, and he drove me back to the earth as Paul sang on the radio.

We stopped in front of my school, and I walked through the doors as it became the peaceful night.

People were looking everywhere for me, and Sara said as she spotted me, "Hey! Hey, guys! I found her! She's alright!" She went up to me and gave me a hug. "I didn't know your dad died, man. That sucks. Want some biscottis that Yule gave me? I don't know what the fuck they are, cookies or something else, but they sure taste good."

I smiled, and said, "I'd love something good. I think I'd like to enjoy a good cookie in life."

"Yeah. C'mon, Hana. You look pretty tired." Sara said, and took me to my bed in my room, and threw me a biscotti, which I crunched on, savoring its flavor.

Sara said I could have as many as I wanted, and threw me the whole bag, but I heard Micah's stomach grumble beside me. I looked over at her with her deadeye stare staring off into the distance, and offered the biscottis to her instead.

She looked at me and her eyes opened up. She said, "As long as it's not meat." I threw her the biscottis, which she crunched on carefully. She finished the biscottis in the night, and I heard her eating them slowly as I fell asleep.

The next morning I sat next to Micah on her bed, her stomach grumbling eternally, and I asked, "Are you eating enough?"

"I don't like anything that came from... an animal. Not even dairy or eggs. I've been trying to get them to give me something to fill me up, and they've been feeding me all sorts of vegetables… but it's just not enough." Micah said.

"What if we got you even more vegetables? We could start a garden." I said.

"…I would really like some nice potatoes. That was the first thing Yule and Lucius gave me after they- rescued me." Micah said.

"Do you want to talk about it?' I asked.

"I don't think you could ever understand what I went through. So no. But I would like to start a garden with you."

"Good. We'll make all sorts of magical potatoes together."

She slowly twitched her lips up… and gave me a smile. I had never seen her smile before.

We talked some more on our way to class, and she said, "You can really make nice mashed potatoes with just water and salt. Or fry them up, bake them on the fire… Potatoes really are magic, because you can prepare them in so many ways."

"My parents cooked me potatoes before, and they were always a rare treat. My mom always had someone deliver us food from the living world, because that's what we all liked. I never knew who would actually leave those packages of food, and even a whole cow for the dragon one time, for us on the edge of Hell… but someone did. I usually did enjoy just some of the burning vegetables of Hell we had in the garden though. They're so spicy, and are painful to eat and a challenge, but there's nothing else like eating a plant that also wants to eat you." I said.

"…I've eaten someone who wanted to eat me. It was very painful." Micah said.

"…I'm sorry, Micah. I didn't mean to draw on any painful memories."

"That's alright. I'll talk to you later, and I really can't wait for our next meeting in demonology. I think Judas Iscariot was really just misunderstood, as I get to know him from the text he wrote that you gave me."

"That's exactly how I feel! Poor guy kills himself every day in the park, but I think he just feels bad for the horrible mistake he made."

"...Ok. See ya, Hana." Micah said, smiled, and waved, and I smiled and waved back.

11

I was reading the burning book, but I was slowly losing interest, even though it taught me things I would've never known in a thousand lifetimes, how to bring people back from the dead and all sorts of magical secrets. I just was too excited for the garden, and couldn't keep my mind off growing all the living plants.

I shut the book, as it stuttered, and put it back in my bag.

I went to the back of the school to the area by an old shed that Lux approved for our garden with Micah, and we smiled at each other with shovels, bags of seeds and chunks of potatoes to plant.

"So how do we do this?" Micah said.

"...I thought you knew? Just put 'em in the ground, right?" I said.

"...I think we need someone who knows how to plant a garden. Should we ask Lux? He probably knows." Micah said.

"Nah, Mr. Lux probably would know how to plant an efficient garden, but I really wanted to make something of our own, without the teachers telling us what to do. What about Sara? You think she would know?"

"She did get those muscles from somewhere. Maybe she was a farmer? Let's ask her."

We approached Sara, as she was busy reading the book by Crowley, and asked her if she knew how to plant a garden.

"Sure. Just put 'em in the ground, right?" she said. Micah and I shrugged to each other, and we worked on the garden anyway.

We dug holes, put stuff in, and waited. I wonder how long it was going to take? In Hell plants grew furiously quick, and soon tried to snuff out your life.

"We probably need to water them. Plants love water, I think." I said.

We watered the garden, but soon it got rather muddy. Sara said, "Nothing to do but wait. Let's go get a snack. Thinking about all those tasty plants is making me hungry.".

Micah's stomach grumbled, and she said, "Please don't say snack. I'll probably just have to eat that tofu again with a big serving of those vitamins Lux gives me…"

"Maybe Yule's got something good for us? I'll go ask her." I said.

I went to Yule who seemed to be talking to someone in her van. I thought it may be Lucius, but she kept on telling the person to stop eating all his own hair and throwing it back up again on the seats, so I don't think that would be Lucius, or else my fantasies of him would have to change drastically.

"You know it's difficult to do that when I can't pick my own hair off my tongue when it gets stuck on it. Learn to live with it, Yule." the person said.

"Rasputin… Let's change the subject, because we're not going to agree on this. I think you should go live with Lux here instead of travelling with us all the time…" Yule said.

"What? But… We're inseparable! Throughout all of your lives, I've spent a lot of that time with you! I can't spend this life with a bunch of dumb children who will pet me backwards! That sounds horribly painful to an intellectual like me." the person said.

I peeked over Yule's shoulder, as she said, "For a damn cat you sure are loyal. That's nice, but… we're going to the south next, and you know it just gets worse and worse the farther we go-"

The black and grey cat mewled at her.

Yule said, "Don't give me the silent treatment. This is what's best for you-"

"*Mewl,* Yule." the cat said.

"Huh? Oh. Shit." Yule said, and quickly turned to me and smiled. "Hana! What's up? Looking for Lucius? He's taking some of the kids on a hike, but he'll be back soon-" Yule said.

"You talk to your cat. And your cat talks back. Is he some sort of-" I said.

"I am not a demon, I am a cat, I can talk whenever I like, I live a lot, maybe extra lives or just for a long time, and my favorite dish is a big steak. Does that answer your questions?" the cat said.

"I was going to ask if you're some sort of stray. If you are... can I have you??" I said.

Yule sighed, and said, "Only if you don't give him steak whenever he wants. It took a long time for cows to come back to the world, and they could go extinct if not treated right."

"Don't listen to her." the cat said, "There are enough cows for a few delicious steaks. And you can have me only if you don't-"

"Treat you like a cat? No way! You're so cute and fuzzy! I'd probably end up being your pet instead, because you look so awesome and are obviously so very intelligent!" I said.

The cat said, "...You can treat me like a cat. I just don't want you to pet me backwards. It's head to tail."

"That's common knowledge, right?" I said.

"You'd think so, but new, baby humans tend to get that mixed up. And you look like a very new human." the cat said.

Yule clapped her hands together, and said, "Great! You two seem to be hitting it off already! His name's Rasputin."

"So cool!" I said, "So if he gets poisoned, shot, and drowned he'll just get up again like the Rasputin in history?"

"...Don't try it, Hana." Rasputin said.

I shook my head quickly and smiled, and Yule picked him up and put him in my waiting arms, where he started purring. I pet Rasputin just right, and he mewled the cutest mewl up to me.

I asked Yule if she had any good snacks for us, especially Micah since she was a vegan. Yule gave me a few roots, saying those were good for hunger, and said, "Sorry, but we don't have anything else left to spare before we go back out there again, and need to conserve our rations." she said.

"Why don't you just eat with us?" I asked.

"Who do you think got you that food? Always treasure a good meal." Yule said, and smiled.

12

At lunch now, none of the boys tried to sit with me besides Chip, and actually were glaring at me angrily instead of having their eyes glaze over in love. "Why is everyone so mad at me?" I whispered to Chip.

"Um. Probably just jealous! Don't worry about them. I don't know, but they *could* just be mad that you didn't accept their cakes... and then threw them all in the trash..." Chip said, and frowned looking at his food.

"Fucking waster!" someone shouted at me from across the cafeteria. And then someone called me a witch. And then more names were called, and I just tried to eat quickly and leave.

Lux noticed all the commotion at once, and went to the center of the cafeteria and shouted, *"Enough, children.* This is not befitting behavior for young people who will one day change the world *together.* You have to all work together these days, because we are all we have."

"But she wasted a whole bunch of food a few lunches ago! We didn't get a good angel's food cake in a long time, and then she just threw it all out! She's a damn waster!" a boy said.

"And how did she get your angel's food cake, may I ask?" Lux said.

"Um... We gave it to her! You know, to be gentlemen!" the boy said.

"I will teach you another lesson, child. If you give the food you want to someone who doesn't need it, who is really the waster? Who initially gave up their food?" Lux said.

"I… I guess I did…" the boy said.

"Exactly. You must treat your own nourishment with care. I don't know what Hana would've done with all of your cakes anyway, as they are all extremely filled with fat and sugar, and should only be treated as a rare treat." Lux said, "Try to get along, kids, and don't fight about something so petty again. I know it is difficult, but I believe in all of you." and he left the cafeteria.

"I know I sure ain't givin' the witch chick anything else anymore…" the boy grumbled, and a few other boys agreed with him, and they left, putting their absolutely cleaned off plates in the dirty dishes.

I was glad that was pretty much over, even though I'm sure they'd probably still be muttering "waster" under their breaths at me for a long time. Same thing happened to me in Hell with the demon kids, and once a name is called, it's hard to get rid of it. I had so many foul names attached to me… I suppose waster wasn't so bad. Witch chick actually sort of sounded like a compliment!

Micah's stomach grumbled beside me, as she picked at the spaghetti with sauce. She said, "That's not a meatball, is it?"

"I don't think so. The sauce they made in the kitchen was tomato, basil, and red pepper, and there probably aren't any nasty surprises for you in it." I said.

"Ok… I'll take a bite…" Micah said, and slowly wrapped up some spaghetti drowned in sauce on her fork, put it in her mouth, chewed slowly, and swallowed. "Doesn't taste like a person. So that's good enough." she said, and continued eating.

Sara came over from her other friends, and said, "Heya, demon club. What's new?"

"I was thinking the next meeting of ours should be somewhere forbidden, perhaps in the dark, wild forest, and we can chant under the light of the full moon-" I started saying.

"Nuh uh, Hana. Do you not remember your father? It's dangerous out there. Wolves, scavengers, and whoever got your daddio in the first place." Sara said.

"Oh... Yeah, that makes sense..." I said, and got sad. I really wanted to make this club into something super special and unique, and I didn't think it would be with meetings in the boring old library, next to boring old books no one felt the remotest interest to read...

"I got a better idea, witch chick. Follow me tonight. It'll be a secret place, so don't bring anyone, except you, Micah." Sara said.

"B-But can't I come too?" Chip said.

"Nah. It's a girls only thing. You'd probably be a stupid man and try to 'protect us' or some BS..." Sara said.

"I promise I won't! I'll be the worst man in the world, and even go running and screaming away if you all get killed or something in this secret place!" Chip said.

"That's what I like. A nondominant male. You're gonna be so whipped if you ever find a chick... But alright, you can come." Sara said.

Chip smiled, and Sara sauntered away to talk to even another group of friends.

I made sure to eat every bit of food, even though the mushrooms seemed like they had been preserved for far too long.

13

I finished my school day, and went to get tutored on the flute by Lucius, who picked a spot for us to play outside.

I followed the sound of his music beckoning to me, and found him sitting cross legged in the middle of our garden, right where we planted a bunch of potatoes, I think. Or maybe that was where the carrots were. I don't know, we just threw a bunch of seeds and potato bits in the holes, and hoped for the best.

"Afternoon, Lucius." I said, and sat cross legged across from him in the garden.

He stopped playing, and said, "Good day, Hana. How have you been feeling?"

"Alright, still getting over my dad and stuff... but I found a great group of friends who are interested in the same stuff I am, so I'm keeping my hopes up for life." I said.

"Good. The first thing I want you to do is try and meditate with me, and listen to the silence." Lucius said.

"What? But how will that improve my making noise?" I said.

"Music isn't all about making noise. What is just as important as the notes of the song are the pauses in between. Try to listen to this pause, and like holding a note, hold that silence for as long as you can." Lucius said, "Just breathe in and out, and let your mind be as silent as the pause." and he shut his eyes in silence.

We sat in the garden, and I breathed in… and out…

It was rather peaceful…

But then I stared too long at Lucius with his eyes closed, unable to see me gawking at him, so I closed my eyes too so I wouldn't be distracted.

I breathed in… and out…

Then…

I thought of my dad…

Who didn't breathe in and out anymore, as he was a corpse.

And all I could see under my eyelids was the picture of that still, unmoving monster.

I breathed too fast, and started hyperventilating.

"Hana. It will be ok." Lucius said. I opened my eyes and stared at him peacefully cross legged, with his eyes still shut.

"I-I don't know. I didn't know it was so difficult being quiet." I said.

"You have the rest of your life to try again. Don't worry about one little mistake, or a loss that can be heartrending. There is always time to try again." he said.

I sighed, and just breathed in and out, but didn't shut my eyes anymore, because then I would see the image of the corpse.

I just looked at this living man, and followed his breathing in silence.

After a while, he opened his eyes, and said, "Well done, Hana. I could tell that you have a good rhythm by your breathing. I think we should play some music now."

"Ok. Everyone thinks I play bad… but it'll be alright if I just play for you-" I said.

"Sorry, Hana. That's just normal stage fright. The best way to conquer that is to jump headlong into the water, so we'll play for some of your classmates. Don't worry, I'll play with you, and help guide you if you make a mistake." Lucius said.

I got really nervous, but he helped me up, and we walked into the building as I clutched my flute, trying to keep my breathing calm.

Lucius gathered a bunch of people, shouting out, "Hear ye, hear ye… The Dark Piper and the Princess of Hell have a fine tune to play for you! Gather round, everyone, because you're about to have your socks blown off!"

How did he know I was a princess?

A bunch of the kids gathered around us in the cafeteria, and I waited for Lucius to start the tune. It didn't seem so scary with him there. I could see Yule smiling at me from a seat, and Lux watching in anticipation, with my friends, Sara, Micah, and Chip, cheering me on, excited for the show. Then Lucius started the first note, and I played along.

I was really rocking that flute! The notes just seemed to come straight to my head, recycled scraps and bits of other songs I had practiced, but they just seemed so much clearer now!

I continued playing, really proud of myself and Lucius-

But then I finally noticed that silence. It was coming from Lucius, and I was playing alone.

I immediately stopped.

"What? C'mon! That was great!" the boy who called me a waster said.

I grew red, even though they were all smiling at me happily, urging me to play some more. I looked at Lucius smiling gently to me… and then I ran off to the dorms, clutching my flute.

I calmed my breathing as I got to my room and far away enough from all of them. Then I thought… They liked it. People actually liked my music.

I felt so happy! I picked up Rasputin and whooped in glee! No one had *ever* even remotely enjoyed my music! They just paused and said it was enough, and only bore the sound if they couldn't escape from me! I told the cat I was going to play for him, and that he was going to enjoy it because I enjoyed it too!

Rasputin groaned, but I played a jaunty melody for him, and soon, I think if cat's did that, he would've been tapping his paws to the sound!

14

I snuck out of the room with Micah and Sara in the night. We stopped by one of the boys' rooms, and one of them whispered, "Wha'? Come to get something good, ladies?"

"Shut the fuck up, Vincent. Where's Chip?" Sara said.

"Beats me. Twerp is probably still in the bathroom. Went there forever ago. I think they're out looking for him actually, because they missed him at name call." the guy said.

We went to the boy's bathroom, and Sara barged in without even a second thought! She soon came out with Chip, who said, "I thought I'd be sneaky, and have them not even notice I was missing-"

"You're an idiot, Chip, because now everyone knows you're missing." Sara said.

"What?? Should I go back, then??" Chip said.

"Nah. You're already declared gone, so it won't hurt for you to be gone a little longer. Let's go." Sara said.

We crept down the halls, and Sara took us to an old classroom. We went inside, and I said, "I suppose this is nicer, the dust and cobwebs really give off a forbidden vibe-"

"Not here. What's behind here, like your secret beneath the veil thing." Sara said, and she took us to a door that was at the back of the room, some closet. Sara took out a key, and unlocked the door, saying,

"They trust me enough to lock up the rest of the school, so I swiped this when they weren't looking. Only been down here once, and that was just to move an old, busted piano to the bottom."

She opened the door, and darkness and gloom invited us down the stairs. I gasped. This was exactly what I wanted.

Sara took out a lighter and lit a candle to light the way, and we could barely see the stairs beneath us. One misstep, and we would fall and break our necks. It was just like going down into Hell.

We got to the bottom, and it was the spookiest hidden basement I've ever seen. Could probably be a torture chamber, if someone decided to use it for that purpose, and man, it sure would be a scary one.

They all looked at me, as we sat beside the broken piano that had been stored down here, and Sara placed the candle in the center of our circle, the light flickering on our faces against the dense darkness.

They gasped as they heard my voice break this complete silence, as I said, "You have all taken the first steps to Hell with me. We will conquer this darkness and evil, forcing it to submit to our horrible will, and build a forbidden relationship on our combined power. I welcome you all as my group of fiends and friends. I welcome you all, as the Champions of the Gargoyle."

Chip said, "...Huh? That's not a very evil sounding name."

"Well I was thinking the Circle of Pi, since it's so diabolically infinite like our friendship, but which do you think is better?"

"I like the gargoyle one, yeah." Chip said.

"Good, because gargoyles are actually spirits who ward evil spirits off. I thought it would be proper, as you all are so nice, and I don't think any of you are truly evil. I think you're more powerful than the evil we practice and the evil spirits we will conjure." I said.

"Cool." Sara said, "Usually I'd take being called a gargoyle as an insult, but I ain't a gargoyle, I'm a *champion* of the gargoyle. Sounds tough."

Micah said, "I think it's cool, too."

"Good. Let's discuss the books you guys read! I practically know all of them by heart, so I'm curious as to what you all think." I said.

"The LaVey guy sounds like a devious bastard, but I like that he has such self confidence. He didn't give a shit what people thought as he promoted Satanism, and made his ideas into a common practice." Chip said.

"Crowley too, is probably one evil guy, but he has a sort of mystic tone, like he knows all sorts of shit you're never going to know. I think it's an act, honestly, but it does make you wonder, and also get a little jealous of his knowledge." Sara said.

Micah said, "I don't know what to think after reading Judas's work. I always heard stories about what people tell you about what's in the Bible, even checked it out once in the library so it would give me hope, but there's a whole evil chapter of it nobody knows about. People are missing out, if anything. And you? Did you read... that book? Can we read it?"

I smiled, took out the book, and let it start burning around my hands, which lit up the dark basement completely. I said, "I congratulate you all for learning from the evil minds of history. I will give you one more piece of knowledge, before we delve into the evilest mind of all existence.

"You never need to follow in their footsteps."

The book stopped burning, and let us sit in darkness again, the only light from the candle.

"...Huh?" Sara said, "I thought that's what you wanted! To learn from these evil people and learn their evil ways, so we can steal their evil powers or somethin'!"

"Sorry, nope! These guys were all great figures in history, true, but just because they are willful, intelligent, and even had the gall to betray Jesus Christ, does not mean they were admirable people or acted for the good of humanity. But who knows what really drove their actions? Everything you've heard about them could be lies, same as they were labelled liars. I guess you'll never know the full story behind them, until you meet up with them in Heaven… or Hell." I said.

"…That's pretty deep, Hana. So… What's the story behind the book you're holding right now?" Sara said.

"Actually, this is a book that is the opposite of a normal book. It is never meant to be read, as my mother taught me when she bound this creature as this book. You will forever wonder what Satan's true story is, but you will never, ever know. And that's actually what Satan wants." I said.

"You're a clever girl, Hana. I would've just spit out more lies, letting you think I'm telling a fantastic, true tale, a beautiful piece of nonfiction where the protagonist is only misunderstood and really made all the best actions he possibly could." the book said.

"Why's he being so honest?" Micah said.

I smiled, and said, "Is he?"

"Ohh… Ok. Don't trust books, then, because you'll never know what sort of stuff they're feeding you…" Micah said.

"I prefer fiction books more sometimes, because the writer isn't trying to tell a real story in an actual setting, you don't have to worry if they're distorting the truth purposefully or accidentally, and you can see pieces of truth come out in fiction as they blatantly tell you it is a lie, a dream, and a fantasy. That it was never, ever real, and is only a story to enjoy, whether it be tragic, scary, humorous, or other. It's just a story, and you can always put it down and continue your life." I said.

"Alright." Micah said, "Um… I'm afraid to ask this… but do you all hear the faint sounds of a piano playing?"

"Hmm… Yeah. I, uh, think we should adjourn for a while… even though it is a hauntingly sweet melody…" Chip said.

"Its leg broke, and it crushed some kid to death as he was mucking about with it… Uh… Yeah, let's go back to bed…" Sara said, and she took the candle back up the stairs.

I smiled to myself, as we left the broken piano in the basement, leaving the shadows and light of our reality and fiction to bed.

15

Chip was put in detention for a while for missing namecall at bedtime, and Lux figured out that Sara had stolen one of the keys she shouldn't have, and severely scolded her. Chip and Sara both were fine afterwards, and actually kind of looked a little happy!

Chip said, "I have never received a detention in my life. It was kind of frightening, but it really wasn't so bad. Makes me feel stupid for fearing them all those years."

Sara said, "Lux isn't letting me use the keys anymore, so we can't use the secret spot again, but I swear… me and that robot were practically crying at the end, because it was such a heartwarming lecture of what I did wrong. I never knew he cared so much."

Micah said, "You both are silly. You did hardly anything wrong, anyways. You'll probably forget all about it eventually, too. You have no idea what real sin is-"

I quickly said, "We're all growing up so fast! But don't worry about one mistake, guys. We always have time to try again!"

They nodded, said goodbye, and we each went to our own classes. It was a rather boring day today, but I enjoyed the gloomy depression of the rain coming down outside. I just wanted to run outside and get drenched by it, but I knew if I did I would be scorched in unimaginable pain again-

Wait a minute… That's right! Rain wasn't searing blood here!

After my last class with Lux, I quickly threw my bag on my bed, and ran out in the rain!

I danced in this beautiful, cold, chilling downpour! Lightning flashed, and then the thunder boomed like God was playing drums! Silly God. He was all flash and show, no actual substance in his creations. He could never even come close to hitting me-

Lightning struck right beside me in the field, and I jumped, with my heart trying to jump out of my mouth. It was so bright, loud, and absolutely terrifyingly deadly. And here that deadliness mattered.

I thought lightning struck the tallest object? I was definitely the only one standing up tall out here in the pouring rain. I must have a guardian angel or something, like they say.

The lightning flashed above me, and I saw bright headlights come down the road, cutting through the rain droplets, and the thunder boomed.

Max stopped his car in front of me, blinding me with the headlights, and he waved me in.

I got in the car, as the rain pitter pattered on the car. Max said, "This is going to be a pop quiz. You will inspect someone, and I will ask one question."

"Oh, I love those! I'm great at pop quizzes. Doesn't sound so hard with only one question, too. So what can you tell me about this mark?" I said.

"He's someone I think you'll be glad to see again, as we continue doing our jobs." Max said.

"Oooh. Ok. Sounds mysterious. Let's drive, Grim Reaper." I said. Max smiled for only a second, and we drove back down the road.

We listened to some blues rock of riders on storms, and I bounced my head up and down to the beat, relaxed, as the car bounced on the road after hitting a speed bump.

We stopped at an old bus stop, and someone was shaking in the cold rain, taking the tiny bit of shelter he could.

Max said, "You must decide when this man should die. This man is in pain, he is suffering, and he lost everything and everyone in life. But it is up to *you* to decide when his actual time should be. Should he be accepted into eternal rest now or should he continue living? Feel free to take a good, long, hard look at him."

"Ok. I think he should have a chance to enjoy the storm some more, even if he does look weak, emaciated, and is shaking for some reason. But I'm going to take a closer look." I said, and got out of the car into the freezing rain, and walked up to the man. I said to him, as he shook terribly, "Hiya! You're *not* going to die now!"

He looked at me, and I recognized his face, that shakiness, and most importantly...

The pistol that killed my father, pointed straight at me.

I walked up to him, as he pointed his pistol at me and said the same line, "I don't want to have to hurt you-"

I whammed the pistol away from my face, and tackled him to the ground, then began beating the shit out of this *awful killer.*

He could barely defend himself, even against a teenage girl, and I ripped the pistol out of his hand and pointed it at his face.

Then he started crying as he was shaking, with his pistol pointed at him. I had changed my answer. I decided he would die now. So I pulled the trigger.

Click.

I pulled again.

Click.

There wasn't a single bullet in this gun anymore.

I got up off the man, and looked at the pistol, confused. The man got up and ran away from me as quickly as he could, which wasn't that fast, as he had a horrible limp.

I dropped the gun in the rain.

I got back in the car, fuming, and Max looked satisfied. Max said, "You were really going down the right road at the start, but you let your feelings get in the way of your choice. The right answer is that it is not our place to interfere with life and death. We do not choose their time, only God can make that choice."

"Actually, I hate pop quizzes…" I said.

"I know it is difficult, but you cannot allow your feelings to take over your judgement, especially when you are dealing with the very passage of death, and handling something so precious as a soul." Max said.

"He killed my father though. Should he not have the same fate? Shouldn't the killer be killed?" I asked.

"If everyone thought that way, I would be out of a job, because everyone would be dead. You'd become the killer." Max said.

"…Oh. It is very difficult trying to show mercy, but I can understand that vengeance never ends, and the stain of death is only passed onto another when they act to kill. I didn't fail too badly, did I? So much that I can't learn anymore?" I said.

"Actually, you learned a lot with this failure, probably more than if you had made the right choice. I can keep teaching you." Max said.

"Thank you. Is there any more to the lesson? I'm ready, I can handle it." I said.

"You look a bit light headed, and are shaking, so I think that's enough of the lesson for today. Try to enjoy the rest of this sunny day." Max said.

"But it's raining- Oh." I said, and he took me down the road, as the rain was stopping, and the sun began to shine through the clouds.

Max gave me a ride to the school, dropped me off, drove away, and I saw something I have never, ever seen before. I thought it must be God's smile or something, it was so beautiful and colorful. It was every color of the- I don't really know.

I couldn't take my eyes away from it, and I chased it into the distance to get a closer view.

It seemed to run away from me as I tried to get closer. "Come back! I just want to touch you! You're so pretty!" I yelled, but still, the thing kept running away.

I grumbled, stopped to look at it one last time, then walked back to the school.

I looked back at the thing when I got to the school doors, but it seemed to have followed me. "You really need to make up your mind if you want to be my friend or not. I want to be your friend." I said. The thing didn't seem to want to respond.

Yule and Lucius came out through the doors of the school, saying goodbye to the people inside, but I was just too enamored with that beautiful thing to pay them any attention.

"Wow!" Yule said, "That is the biggest rainbow I have ever seen!"

"A rainbow? What's that? I just see that big colorful thing over there." I said, pointing at the thing.

"...That's a rainbow, Hana. It's refractions of light going through the rain." Yule said.

"Really? Then how come I can't catch it when I chase it?" I said.

"Trying to catch the rainbow, eh... Well, a rainbow can only be seen when light goes through a prism, like a rain droplet. The light goes through multiple raindrops to create the refraction at certain angles, and has to be a certain distance away from to be seen properly as a giant rainbow like that." Yule said.

"Ok. But if I go faster than the speed of light, and traverse the distance faster than it can escape, I should be able to catch the rainbow?" I said.

"I suppose. I don't think it's possible to go faster than the speed of light, though." Yule said.

"I'm going to catch it, one day. That beautiful rainbow will be mine." I said.

"...Alright, Hana. Well, have a good school year! We'll be travelling for a long while in the wastes, going through deadly terrain and evading monstrous people, escaping intense danger by just the skin of our necks. Take good care of Rasputin! We'll see you around, Hana." Yule said.

"What? But you're both so nice, and I've just started getting good on the flute!" I said.

Lucius said, "You'll find other teachers. Remember to-"

"Keep practicing?" I said.

"Enjoy the rainbow just as it is, because even through the distance of beauty, light and life will always shine down on you still, and accept you just as you are, as you accept them. But that too." Lucius said.

I blushed, and said, "Thank you both for helping the school. We'll all be waiting for you when you come back."

"Study hard, Hana." Yule said, "What subject is your favorite, anyway? We could set you up to be an apprentice with good people we know after you graduate."

"Oh, I really like the apprenticeship I'm already taking. I'm learning to be an angel of death from one first hand." I said. They both opened their eyes in surprise, so I said, "I know you probably don't believe me, but Max is a really good teacher even if he's a pain in the ass-"

"Study even harder then, Hana, because you are embarking on the very work of God. Tell Max I said hello, too." Yule said.

I opened up my eyes in surprise, but they just smiled and hugged me, leaving for their van. I watched as they got in, driving off into the distance, looking like they were going straight to the rainbow, about to catch it. Yule and Lucius, like light and life, were leaving for another day, but I knew they'd always love and care for us, just as we are, and are never too far even through the distance.

16

I went back inside, dripping wet, and went to change my clothes into something more comfortable. I got all dressed up in a black sweater and black pants, but then I thought... Why am I wearing black all the time? I wanted to look like that rainbow.

I traded bits of clothes with other girls, and soon I was wearing a cozy blue hat, a red and green christmas sweater, poofy purple pants with an orange belt, and my black high heels. I felt so cool! I admired myself in the mirror through my glasses, and thought I looked just like a rainbow.

I went back to get my bag and go show myself off to my friends, but when I lifted my bag I noticed a familiar weight was missing. I frantically searched through it, and I realized the burning book was gone.

This was not good.

Nobody was supposed to read that! Not even me! I quickly searched around, and asked a blonde girl sitting on her bed if anyone went through my bag.

"What? Why didn't you use your locker like you're supposed to?" the blonde girl said.

"I don't know, I wasn't thinking about that! But someone stole something really valuable of mine!" I said.

"Whatever, man... I just got back from detention, and it's probably gone forever now... Just take it as a lesson. Lock up your shit, you dumb bimbo!" the girl said, and sneered. I furiously glared at her, but I kept looking around the room in case I had dropped it somewhere.

Could it have been one of the boys sneaking in here?? I quickly went to the boys' rooms, and asked them if anyone went into my room and stole my book.

One of the boys burst out laughing at me, saying, "Holy shit! You got a whole new crazy style now! You sure you didn't lose your mind and just lost that book too?"

"No, I am still sane, and I know someone stole my book. Can you help me, Vincent?" I said.

"Sure, Hana. But only if you promise to go on a date with me! I just gotta tell the guys I went out with the crazy witch chick!" he said, and smirked.

"But- But-" I said.

"Have it your way, but I can get all of the other dumbasses to help too..." Vincent said.

"...Fine. But I'll only go out with you if you find it." I said.

"You bet! Hey, you idiots, c'mon and help us find a book!" Vincent said, and then began bullying the other boys into helping me.

I asked my friends, Sara, Micah, and Chip to help me look, and they were as loyal as ever.

But then I thought about it... Could it have been one of my friends who stole my book? Could they have been tempted to read something they shouldn't?

I suspiciously looked at Micah checking every secret, hidden place. She had suffered through horrible sin. Stealing a book that was the Devil would be nothing to her. She had *eaten* a person. Perhaps she could not shake her dark ways.

I saw Sara getting her friends to interrogate some people and figure out who could've stolen my book. She was always a helpful friend, not only to me, but was it just an act? Was she just deceiving people to get them to treat her well?

And Chip. He followed beside me, giving me support and encouragement, helping me firsthand. He was a very nice boy... but what if he too only envied me? What if underneath that gentle exterior was a heart filled with evil desire, that wanted everything I had? He seemed like he would do anything for me, but was that only so he could claim me?

I kept on looking, and was starting to lose hope. Vincent's gang piled up tons of books for me, but I said none of them were my book. I wondered whose books these guys had stolen, because some of them were obviously valuable personal property...

I went back to my room, about to cry as I had unleashed horrible evil on such a nice little life.

Then I looked at the blonde girl who said she couldn't have stolen my book, as she said she had just gotten back from detention. She was still sitting on her bed, on something hidden underneath her bed covers...

I pushed her off the bed, unfurled the covers... and underneath...

Was just a magazine.

The other girls laughed at her, because this was a magazine of naked women.

The blonde girl went red, got up, turned to me with utter fury, and said, "I'm going to fucking kill you, *you fucking ugly crazy witch bitch bimbo!*" and then she whammed me on the nose, making it bleed, and tackled me to the ground and began beating the crap out of me.

I tried to defend myself as best I could, but she still was hurting me a lot. The other girls pulled her off, and she kicked and screamed as Sara held her back.

Micah helped me to the infirmary, as my nose was bleeding everywhere. She eventually got me on a bed, and Chip sat beside me feeling angry for me, and comforted me by trying to tell me jokes as the nurse worked on my nose. Sara came to us, and said that the girl whose secret I had revealed was going to detention for a good while, and that Lux was going to speak to me personally soon.

I felt very sad, and told my friends, "Thank you for being there for me."

They all said they were glad to be, and that they'd find that evil book soon.

Lux came into the infirmary, holding my book, and said, "You left this after reading it in my class. I was going to return it as soon as I found it, but you disappeared out into the rain and I didn't want to leave one of your possessions unattended. I thought it may be a journal or a diary, so I didn't invade your privacy or let anyone else."

Lux placed the stupid book beside my bedside. It caused all that suffering, and the only one who had read it was me. I think if a book could sneer and smirk, then that book would.

17

I spent a while in detention for causing a fight. The girl I pushed off her bed glared at me in the room in silence as I sat with plugs in my nose. We got out of detention late in the evening, and I said, "I'm sorry, Lita, for judging you before I knew the tru-"

"Get the fuck away from me, bimbo. I don't ever want to see your ugly face." she said, and walked down the hall.

I chased after her, and said, "I didn't know you were gay! I really was not trying to reveal tha-"

"I'm *not* gay!! Why is everyone calling me that?? I just find it comforting, is all! They're just pretty, and I like those models!! Stop calling me *gay!!*" she said, turning to me and yelling at me.

"Ok. I can understand that. I'm still sorry, and never meant you to go through this." I said.

"Just leave me the fuck *alone!!*" she said, and stormed off. I let her walk off, to let her cool down, even though we slept in the same room and I had to follow behind her at a distance.

In the morning I took a shower with the other girls, and as soon as Lita walked in they all quickly got out, muttering that they didn't want "Lita the Lesbian" to ogle them, too...

I still took my shower, as Lita stared down at her feet and fumed.

I said, "It's just a name. It does not define you."

She just ignored me, and didn't steal a single glance at me.

It was a long day, because Vincent kept harassing me in the halls, calling me his girlfriend and shouting out to everyone, "We're dating! I'm dating the crazy witch chick! Yeah, that's right, be jealous!"

I finally said to him, "I am not dating you, because you did not help in the least, and I don't think you're nice, or friendly, or any kind of a good boyfriend. You just call me names like crazy witch chick."

"You think I'm your boyfriend?? Hell yeah! Scored a point already. Wanna kiss for luck on the test?" he said, grinned, and made a smoochy face at me.

I angrily went to class.

I took my test, but I felt like I was a little distracted, because I had ruined Lita's life, and now had some idiot boy ruining my life. Eventually I just failed on purpose because I thought it was so stupid… None of it mattered.

Lux said he wanted to speak to me after class when it was over, about that stupid test for stupid people who just lived in this stupid world with stupid crap and every stupid thing like a stupid-

"You've been practicing this subject for a long time, Hana. You really seem interested in history, and I catch you studying for this course whenever you're in the library, learning about the twists and turns of time and cementing them in your memory, but you handed me a test with every single multiple choice circle filled, and every fill in the blank question and even the essay filled in with the word 'stupid.' It obviously isn't a bout of laziness, since I've never seen someone so painstakingly try to fail, so I would like to ask you what has changed." Lux said.

"It's just stupid history-" I said.

"Please, try to vocalize your thoughts without using the same word over and over. Stupid is a stupid word, and any word used a lot loses any sort of substance." Lux said.

"...Sorry. I just don't see why it matters now. I truly love learning about all the diabolical generals and resourceful heroes of time, but I just don't understand why it matters in today's life, when people just repeat the same mistakes, and can have everything ruined because they make one stu- one little error. So I decided to just make a bunch of errors, and not resist my inevitable fate of continuing down the same road."

"It isn't called an error if your end goal is to ruin your own chances. I think that's just called giving up."

"So what if I give up? I'll just go back to Hell and live an even worse life, anyway."

"...I think you can still try to change the world here, and learn from your errors. Focus your goals, like Genghis Khan conquering the East, and soon you will reach your arms far past your origins."

"But I don't know what I want. I really just want to take over God's realm, as I inherit my mother's, and eventually have the living world become my plaything, like Hanatrix the Dominatrix did to the kingdom, and own every single rainbow that ever existed and ever will exist. That seems like an impossible task though, even if I figure out how to do that." I said.

"...That is why we have history, to teach us not only our mistakes, but our victories as well. You can achieve anything you put your mind to, and history is a living example of that, as the slaves of old America became freed, women became equal citizens, and tyrants were overthrown by people who had no chance, and should've never had any chance. These heroes of history proved the ones who doubted them wrong, and showed the world that impossibilities can become possible." Lux said.

"...So you think I can accomplish my goal if I keep learning, and recycle every bit of past into my own future, as long as I don't give up?"

"Yes. I think it's possible for you to succeed. I don't know if I *want* you to take over the entire everything everywhere, per say, but it sure would add another interesting chapter in history."

I smiled, and said, "Thanks, Mr. Lux. I'll try my hardest next time, and I won't fail you. I will succeed at my goals, because you believe in me too."

"...Ok. This will hardly be a dent in your perfect grade, but I can allow you to retake the test if you want-" Lux said.

"Nah. I think mistakes are worth learning from, too. It's just called history, and there are no redoes in life." I said.

"That's very mature of you, Hana. Have a good rest of your day, and try to get along with the rest of the students." Lux said.

I told a grinning Vincent who still chased me in the halls even at the end of the school day, that I wanted to tell him something. He put his ear close to my lips, and I said, "I dated the Demon of Lust, Asmodeus, for a time, but I think I want to give up on that relationship..." He kept listening, as I continued, "I could date you, but I do not find you respectful at all towards me, when you should be treating me like a princess. You are mean, rude, and a bully to other people just as much as you are to me, and all you see in me is base lust, and not who I am. I can fix you up with my ex if you like, because I'm sure the Demon of Lust could use another sexual thrall. Want me to take you to him? All I have to do is bring you down to Hell. Sure, I may have to kill you first, but that actually sounds kind of appealing to me..."

He had stopped grinning for a while now.

"So take this as a warning. Do not try to claim those who do not belong to you, or you may end up losing what you claim dearly yourself. Your life, and then your soul." I said.

Vincent ran away from me, as I smiled to myself.

Lita had been watching, and she came up to me, looking like she was about to snarl, but said, "...That was cool that you got that idiot off your back. Dude ran away like a little bitch, because you whispered something in his ear. I get harassed by pricks like him, who probably only like me because I'm blonde."

"I hate when people only look at my exterior. Like now I'm called crazy as well as my other nicknames, just because I like color." I said.

"...Sorry. I kinda helped with that. It's easy to insult someone behind their back." Lita said.

"Oh. I see... Not that I want to know, but what else have you called me besides bimbo, bitch, crazy, witch, and ugly? I'm curious, because I'm trying to reach a high score of dirty names being called on me, and am looking for one that is actually original." I said.

"...Never mind about that. Just... Sorry." Lita said, and wandered away.

18

We had the next meeting outside, in the day because that was safer, and stayed near the school, actually right in our garden, next to the evilest plant of all… radishes.

I despised those sharp, bitterish, spicy roots that were even eaten raw most of the time. My mother always fed them to me when I was little, and I think I *may* have just gotten my dislike for them because I was a stubborn child who didn't want to eat her vegetables, but they *may* secretly have some hidden agenda, and may one day try to overthrow my reign when I conquer everything. I did enjoy them already trying to take over the world by sprouting slightly, but I still eyed them suspiciously.

I was surprised, as us four were getting seated, ready to have an in depth conversation on how to curse people, which actually was all psychology and nothing magical about it, when I saw two new members come to join us next to the radishes, waving friendlily and smiling.

I guess I did say when I started the club it was open to all, and I suppose Lita wasn't horrible, but why did Vincent have to show up? Didn't he get the hint I would bind him forever in the bowels of Hell in the bowels of Cerberus if he came near me again?

Lita said, "This bastard- I mean, this person named Vincent wants to tell you something, Hana."

"I'm sor-sorry for being so mean to you. I re-really do think you're really neat, b-but I don't have the power to tell girls how I really feel sometimes, and my mouth takes over my head and I end up insulting them..." Vincent said.

"I don't believe a word of that, and I think you've just come to spoil even more things I enjoy." I said.

Then Vincent started crying.

Lita hit him on the arm, and said, "Stop being a wuss. Even the guy you call a twerp whose name somehow became Chip has more balls than you."

I looked at Chip, who was smiling nervously. Shit. I had called him a name that stuck, just like Lita and Vincent did to me.

"I'm so sorry, Chi- I'm sorry. I don't think we've actually gotten officially introduced..." I said.

"I don't mind being Chip. I liked that you liked my favorite snack, my favorite chips, and I like you-" he said.

"I don't want to give you a name that you aren't proud of. What is your real name? My full name is actually Hanatrix, but is shortened to Hana." I said.

His smile left, and he said, "I don't like the name I had before. It was given to me by my- by the people who left me here. I don't want that name, I won't have it, and I never want to be called by it again."

"Are you sure? At least tell me what you're giving up." I said.

"My name is Sue." he said.

We were all silent for a second, then Vincent started giggling. "Shut the fuck up, Vincent." I said, and he quickly stopped giggling under my glare that could contain Hell.

Sue smiled, and he said, "I'm kidding. Can you even imagine? Anyone would hate that name, for a boy. I'm not telling you what my parents- those people called me. It's just another insult, and I like that I have a real name accepted by my friends instead."

"Ok... Chip." I said, "While we're on the subject, evil names are just another form of a curse. When people are swearing, or 'cursing' they are simply using powerful sounding words, which only come from other words that have evolved over time, to express ill will on another. But curses can sometimes be a blessing, if you take that power for yourself and use a weakness, like an evil name, for strength instead. It helps if you don't take the curse too seriously, because the more power you put into it against you, the worse you will feel."

"Can I join you, so I can be a witch chick too?" Lita said, "I actually really like everything you just said."

"Sure. I don't know about Vincent, but I will accept him into evil's embrace, since he said sorry and is so obviously woefully penitent with his ever flowing tears." I said.

"Cool. Thank you, Hana." Vincent said, wiping off a few tears, "I wasn't going to join this witch club. I just wanted to say sorry, but cool."

They then sat down with us in the dark growth of my evil children, the ever growing radishes, who I decided I would care for tenderly and let them conquer under my rule, until their inevitable end, eaten by their mother in a tasty salad. Mwahaha...

19

"Do I need to walk you or something?" I said to Rasputin alone in my room, as all the other girls were out playing sports outside.

"Hmm… I wouldn't mind going outside for a jog. I know a good place for a perfect stroll." Rasputin said.

"Good, because I hate always having to clean up your litter box. You can do your business in the wilderness, like a normal animal. Sometimes the other girls even yell at me, because I've been in class all day and then they find a nasty present you left for them that smells like some places in Hell…" I said.

"I only do my business in the litter box, so your prissy friends are just being moronic, but I would like to mark some territory." Rasputin said.

"Animals sure are gross sometimes. Cerberus left huge piles of flaming disgustingness for me to clean up. Sometimes I just wanted to sew his anus closed so he wouldn't do that at all, but I'm sure it would've just come out of some other orifice." I said.

"I'm sure Cerberus loved having his master debate which hole to shut so he couldn't accept the call of nature…" Rasputin said, as we walked down the halls.

"More the call of Hell, but I was a good master. He did love me, I think, because I was the only one he actually listened to, besides my mother, but if my mother commanded him he just seemed afraid, and didn't do what he did because he loved her. He was a good animal, even though he was a monster of Hell." I said.

"I think you're a good animal too, Hana. You're like the perfect pet..." Rasputin said, as we burst into the light outside.

"Thanks. I try." I said.

I let the cat mark his territory on the edge of the forest, as I looked around nervously.

"I don't like being over here, Rasputin." I said.

"Because of your father? Come, I have something to show you..." Rasputin said, and ran off into the forest.

"Come back, you damn cat!" I said, and against my instincts telling me not to, I chased the animal into the forest... close to where I found my father.

My heart beat fast, as I remembered the still monster, probably stalking me out here, in complete silence as it was.

Rasputin stopped right next to the monster that probably was hiding in the undergrowth, and Rasputin mewled at me, inviting me to come closer.

I nervously went to rush in and grab him then run away again-

But then I noticed that smell. It was the smell of flowers.

I looked at a mound where the monster used to be, and saw a rock at the head of the mound, with very artistically and painstakingly crafted etches on it that said, "Here lies Zaxazaxar, father of Hanatrix and husband of Dina. He will always be remembered and loved." There wasn't enough room on the rock for our last name.

There were so many flowers, planted around the- the grave, blooming for the world until they died and then new seeds would continue the cycle of life.

I knelt before the grave, and remembered and loved my father.

Rasputin rubbed against my legs, purring, and I pet him as I cried. It wasn't horribly awful crying, however, like when I first cried for my father, it was more of crying in peace.

"This is your territory, Hana." Rasputin said, "Protect and care for it, as your father did for you."

"Yule and Lucius are great." I said.

"Why else do you think I stayed with them? I never needed to. I'm a cat, I can hang out with whoever I want and just run away if they don't treat me right. I liked them. I like you too, Hana, but I still heavily doubt you will be able to measure up to an actual angel when it comes to niceness and caring..." Rasputin said.

"I knew Lucius was an angel. No one looks that good without being crafted by God." I said.

"No, I was actually speaking about Yule. Although she was crafted like you, Hana, conceived in her mother and then bursting into the world in blood and tears." Rasputin said.

"Oh, so you were just giving her a metaphorical compliment. Yeah, she's super nice." I said, as I continued to pet him.

"Yes, she is, and it is her duty, when she came to Earth as an angel of war, to be so nice."

"Wait... Really? Like... she is one of the angels who fight against Hell's power for her almighty tyrant?"

"Well, I suppose, in a different sort of way than you're thinking."

"Then she must want to deviously end me, to continue her ceaseless battle against Hell. I don't think I can trust her anymore. She obviously speaks lies."

"And she builds a grave for your father just to toy with you specifically too, I imagine."

"...I don't know... This is a very nice action..."

"Don't discard actions of caring and kindness, even if you think they're from your eternal enemies, because perhaps if you don't, you'll find an eternal friend instead."

"I don't trust God, he just sits on his clouds and watches us in silence, hiding in the sky, but I can trust Yule and her actions, caring for us kids, right in front of us too, with a beautiful man bound to her for life. I was actually pretty jealous of her for a while, but then I wondered about it, and thought I could do better than be jealous. I could aspire to be even better than her, because she inspired me to be better than myself."

"Very nice. Does that mean taking over the world or just being friendly?"

"Can't I do both?"

"You can try. It will be much harder, but you can try. As long as you're friendly to me and feed me well, I don't really care. I'll outlive you, anyway." Rasputin said.

"As an immortal cat?" I said, carrying him back to the school with me.

"As the ruler of existence. I think you've inspired me, too." he said.

I laughed, and pet him as he purred.

20

I tried to stick up for Lita in our room as one girl teased her as "the lesbian," but eventually Lita couldn't take it anymore, and stood up against her, looking like she was about to scream and shout...

But she calmed down, and said, "I have something I want to tell you all. I'm gay."

The other girls were silent for a moment, and then the one that teased her said, "Well, about time. You've stared at my butt all year. So, Micah, what else can you tell me about that fantastic potato and radish dish?? It sounds enchanting, and the spices sound like something to die for, but wouldn't you need to..." the girl said, and continued talking with Micah about cooking.

Lita grew red, as the other girls just continued their conversation, and she quickly ran out the room.

I ran after her, and saw her crying and looking out the window. I put a hand on Lita's shoulder, and said, "It's ok. I didn't know at all."

"B-But you're new, and ev-everyone else did know. How?? I was just trying to accept an evil name, but... I guess I am gay..." Lita said, turning to me.

I shrugged, and said, "I have no clue how anyone would know your sexual orientation unless they caught you red handed in the act."

"I never even had sex, though. But… I do kind of just imagine wrestling with Sharina…"

"That's not a bad thing if it makes you happy. It's a harmless fantasy, and I'm sure if Sharina would like to wrestle with you too, I'm sure no one would bat an eye."

"I'm terrified to ask her, and I don't think I could in a thousand years. She just said she knew I was staring at her all year. All that time… and she somehow knew what I was really thinking…"

"I wouldn't worry about it today. If you feel like asking her tomorrow, or tomorrow's tomorrow, or tomorrow's tomorrow's etc., then that is perfectly fine too."

"But what if she says no?? What if she doesn't like me, and won't even think about just being in the same room as a gay girl??"

"She's been in the same room with you all year. Maybe she'll consider it, or maybe just consider being your friend instead."

"…Why was she such a rude bitch then… Calling me 'the lesbian…'"

"I don't know. I think she doesn't even know what she wants herself yet. But Micah, Sara, and I didn't partake in such name calling, and you've always got us at least."

"That's true. I didn't really notice that. Thank you, friend." Lita said, and smiled.

I smiled back, and we decided to go to the library for a while and read comic books.

I was enjoying this awesome comic of some super gladiator woman battling an evil emperor, really hoping that emperor would put her in her place, but I noticed some people hidden in the corner of some bookshelves, and strange smacking sounds.

I crept over to them, and saw two boys making out.

I had my eyes open in surprise, and one of them noticed me who had the cutest bangs, and said, "Uh, Devon, we have a guest."

"Hmm? Just kiss me again Miller…" the other boy said, but then he opened his eyes quickly and looked at me, saying, "What?! Shit, shit, shit… Don't tell anyone!! Please, I'll do anything!"

"I won't tell anyone. I think it's actually very intriguing that you two really enjoyed kissing each other in such a passionate embrace. I'm actually sort of jealous of the pleasure that you two were just having." I said

"Shit, shit, shit! This chick is gonna tell everyone I'm a faggot now, and we'll never get a moment of peace again!" Devon said.

Miller shrugged, swished his bangs, and said, "It was bound to happen sometime. You picked the naughtiest make out place, but it was far too open."

"I actually would like a friend of mine to be able to talk to you two, as she has just come out as gay." I said.

Devon said, "…She did that? Isn't that just like committing suicide or something?"

Miller, the boy with the cute bangs, said, "Even I never did that. But I think people just take it for granted now, so it really isn't necessary. I hit on a few guys already, in such a way that really left none up to the imagination, and they all whispered behind my back like the worst gossip girls imaginable, but then I flirted with Devon… and he actually enjoyed it."

Devon said, "I just want to take you away and have you be my strapping farmer in the wasteland like you said. I really can't get that image out of my head, and how happy we'll be… but this is just school, and if other people know, the dream will be ruined."

"I don't think so." I said, "I think if you come out you will feel a great weight lifted, and the dream will be even more tangible… and more vivid, than ever before."

Miller said, "I really like that, mysterious stranger. What's your name? I'm Miller and this is my boyfriend, Devon."

"My name is Hana. Can you talk to Lita with me?" I said.

"Ok. But if she's just some poser who wants to imagine my pain and think she's some suffering prima donna, then she can go fuck a dick and get it out of her system." Miller said.

"I love when you swear, Miller." Devon said.

"You're so sweet, Devon." Miller said.

I called Lita over, who was drooling over some sexy vampire lady comic, and told her I found some new friends for us.

Lita felt much more encouraged after talking to Devon and Miller, the gay couple, and even encouraged the two to come out as well. Lita said, "I felt like my life was ending. And even though I'm still terrified to go back, I found people like Hana who understood. There's nothing so liberating than finding such acceptance."

The two boys looked at each other, and said they would like to change some things in this school, starting with what people knew about themselves.

I held Lita's hand, despite whatever stigmas associated with two women holding hands, and we walked back into our room as she was shaking in terror.

Sharina said, "...Wow, you really got used to being gay fast. Even found a girlfriend already!"

Lita held my hand tight, and said, "Jealous?"

"No, I just think it's cute. Pretty soon this whole room will be gay!" Sharina said, and winked at Lita. Lita went red and quickly let go of my hand to hide in her bed, as Sharina continued to gossip late into the night.

21

I went to bed, falling asleep and remembering that comic…

And I was the evil empress, and I finally beat that pesky gladiator.

I led my Empire, conquering Earth with the power of my legions.

But Max rested a hand on my shoulder, just as I was going to conquer everything everywhere, and said, "It's your time, Hana."

My life ended. I walked through Heaven's gate in defeat, as my Empire crumbled into nothing, and the only one who lasted was God, who had built everything I conquered anyway, as I did everything as he planned as well.

I knelt before this great creature, this omnipotent, omniscient being, and I had no choice but offer my fealty to him, and become another angel under his command.

I flew through the clouds, actually having much fun as an angel of death, taking lives with my scythe and bringing their souls to my master, my eternal master, who was my master before I even knew he was.

Even though I smiled to myself, thinking that even *He* could never defeat my mother, the Queen of Hell…

But my mother smiled and said she was so proud of me, giving me a huge hug and telling me for the billionth time that she loved me.

And said that she needed to leave.

The Queen of Hell went back into the shadows again, disappearing from anything that God has ever made, leaving reality and me to fate eternal.

The battle between Heaven and Hell did not last, and Heaven had won.

I would serve always, chained to this creature whose power I desired.

So I rebelled. I became the angel of death who disobeyed. I attacked God's followers just as Lucifer had before.

But I could not get past a simple seraph as I charged to God's throne, about to slay my master with the very scythe I used to serve him. The six winged seraph blazed her holy white flame at me, and said, "You are bound to God even past life. Now you are bound again."

And I got trapped in a book and was unable to leave, and only able to tell my story to any reader I could who would open my covers.

I gasped awake, and I knew I had seen past the veil, to the very future that could happen.

But I had seen this possibility, and it was up to me to continue it or not.

I was tempted to go down this road, even if all I could do was be a book like the ones I loved so much…

I knew it would be an interesting story, if anything. I just hoped when people looked into my life they would take something away.

I got breakfast, ate some very sugary cereal, and pet Rasputin as he joined me in the cafeteria. People loved it when he joined me, and pet and cuddled him endlessly.

Rasputin smiled at me, in such a way that I knew he knew far more than I would ever know.

He, a simple cat, was master of everything everywhere.

I stared at him in awe.

I tried to continue my cereal, but I trembled thinking why someone so powerful wouldn't do anything.

Rasputin just accepted cuddles and kisses from my friends.

…Huh. I suppose cats just knew how to live a good existence, even more than existence.

I suppose it was just a dream, and I suppose I would have to stop eating those spicy cheese snacks before bed.

I smiled at the cat, and he mewled at me.

22

I sat next to Sara on her bed and gave her the short tabard, and she said, "Woah! Cool. I'm actually glad it's not tie die or something. With your cool new crazy color, I thought you might do that."

"...I was thinking about it, but I didn't have enough different colored paint for all of them... But yeah! I'm proud of my club, and want to promote it as much as I can." I said.

Sara smiled, and said, "Who's this dope gargoyle in the center? You obviously spent a lot of time on him. But what does this circle of red words around him say? I can't quite make it out because it looks like Latin, or maybe just cursive. And what is this thing anyway? It looks like a shirt, but not quite."

"His name's Champy, our guardian gargoyle. It's a short tabard, like members of secret societies and ye ol' knights wore to express their loyalty to their guild. It's kind of nice because it can be worn over anything else, and won't get in the way as well. The words are just a protective seal in a forgotten demonic language to defend against evil's power, specifically a few asshole demons I know. Really, it's just a threat to reveal their secrets and take them to an even lower pit of Hell if they mess with us, but it did seem to work, and those guys never tried to hit on me ever again." I said.

"...That's funny, Hana. You got your eyes on anyone yet? I know you *could* spend the rest of your days scaring guys off with demonic threats, but I feel like that's not something you really want. You dated the Demon of *Lust* for Christ's sake." Sara said, and grinned.

"...Um. I don't know..." I said, and rubbed my arm.

"Please tell me? I know you've gotta like *someone,* and I could help set you up with him." Sara said.

"But I feel bad for the guys who do like me, and don't want them to know. Chip is so cute, and nice, and a really good friend, and I just don't want Vincent to cry again. They could be heartbroken." I said.

"Nah, I doubt that. They'll continue their lives, same as you should. It's just natural. And they like a bunch of other girls, too, and I know you don't have your eyes just on one guy. So tell me about them!" Sara said, smiling excitedly.

"...Did I tell you I have a thing for older men? Like you said, I dated the Demon of Lust, Asmodeus, and he is at least centuries old..." I said.

Sara laughed, and said, "Been down that road. I'm trying really hard to get in this one teacher's pants, the one who always helps me clean up the place after classes, but we really do have good mentors, and none of them would even think about doing stuff with a student. I mean, maybe they do *think* about it, but I'm sure the other thought of Lux crushing their skull quickly dispels any sort of sexy student/teacher fantasy."

"Really? Dang. I suppose I should stop giving my math teacher love notes..." I said.

Sara laughed, and said, "He does have a nice chin, but I find your notes in the trash every day when I take the garbage to the incinerator. I was going to tell you, but I didn't want you to get your hopes shattered. I think he's got a thing for the biology teacher, anyway."

"Oh! I guess those two would look good together. Well, I'll set my sights a bit lower and not up at his chin, and try to find a guy my own age to court, and then have him become my husband forever and ever." I said.

"...Um, I was just talking about getting laid, Hana." Sara said.

"I know. I am too. But I'm waiting until only after I'm married, because then I will feel orgasmic bliss with the man who's bound to me, body and soul, eternally with only him." I said.

"Oh! I didn't know you were such a faithful girl. I did not expect that, especially as you walk around in sexy black heels all the time." Sara said.

"I just think it will be like Heaven and Hell converging, on a bed in the living world, when I can be safe in my husband's arms. It's really what keeps me going when I think of love." I said.

"You mean you and the Demon of Lust... never did *anything??*" Sara said.

"He offered aplenty, but no, we only watched TV. Only. TV. I feel stupid for wasting that time on such a stupid demon who had absolutely no interest in me and no genuine feeling of actual love either..." I said, "At first he tried to corrupt me, to take sway over the Princess of Hell, and I just thought that was so cute, and our relationship really bloomed for a while as he tried to seduce me into his bed and I only refused because he didn't offer with a golden ring of marriage, but my mother knew about his wicked schemes before he even knew himself, and as soon as she had a little 'chat' with him, he tried to break up with me, but I just ignored it and kept seeing him anyways, even though he cheated on me and didn't want to see my very face... My mother didn't really care after that, because she had already made her point to him."

"Which was what?"

"Don't fuck with the Queen of Hell and her daughter."

"...I see. Well, she's not the Queen of Earth, eh? You don't have to live under your mom's iron rule up here."

"I guess not. We'll still meet again, and I know she knows stuff that I don't know how she does, but I just want to get married, throw my relationship in her face with or without her blessings, and say I can have my orgasmic bliss with the man I love who also loves me. That'll show her."

"Ok, Hana. Whatever makes you happy, I guess, although I feel like you're missing out. But hey, maybe I am instead, and will never ever reach that super high peak like that." Sara said, "I lost my virginity when I was fourteen, when I first came here even, because we were both just curious of sex. It sure wasn't the best, but I feel like I've gotten better in the long run, and know a little bit more of what I want."

"You make me very curious. I will have to rethink my goals perhaps, but... I'm going to beat you at orgasmic bliss! Watch out, cuz Hanatrix is gonna take over that sexy peak!" I said, and hit Sara on the arm. She laughed and grabbed me, wrestling with me on her bed.

We stopped playfighting, as we heard a little whimper, and we looked over to Lita who was looking at us longingly. "I'm going to get that orgasmic bliss before you both, because I'm going to find the nicest, strongest woman in the world, and not some dumb boy with an ugly penis like you two want." Lita said.

"We'll come back together in a few years, and we'll measure our bliss by how happy our lovers are. We can measure by their smiles..." I said.

"I'm gonna measure by how long they can scream out my name, but sure, a smile works too." Sara said, and smiled.

We all laughed, and I threw Lita a club tabard and we went down to dinner, where Micah was busy working as a cook.

23

Micah still had that deadeye stare as she worked in the kitchen, but instead of staring into space like she used to, she stared at the vegetables and carbohydrates that she was carefully preparing for everyone with the rest of the kitchen staff. The head chef, also the cooking teacher, taught her a little bit about everything they were cooking, and she said to Micah as we went up to the counter, "The bubbles are the water escaping from the fries, and as soon as the oil stops bubbling so hard, then you know the fries are cooked. Don't leave them in too long after the bubbles go down."

"I know, I know, just the right amount of cooking or it'll get burned..." Micah said, putting the fries gently into the deep fryer.

"They get overly crispy, yes, and then actually a little soggy after you take them out, because they soaked up a lot of oil. You don't feel nervous around the... meat that we're preparing?" the head chef said.

"Why would I, Mrs. Loren?" Micah said.

"...I'm really not sure." Mrs. Loren said.

"As long as I ain't eating it. And you really gotta ease up on the patties. You don't want to squeeze out the natural flavor, the grease, and meat is better when it's cooked... almost rare. Just so you know." Micah said, and began watching the fryer.

Mrs. Loren rubbed the back of her neck, and turned to us. "Hello, girls. The burgers and fries will be done soon. Would you care to help us in the kitchen? We need someone to do the dishes since the two boys who said they were are missing…"

We all agreed to help, and it was cool seeing Micah take up her new calling as well! She watched those fries like a hawk, and they would be delicious I was sure.

"Thank you, dears." Mrs. Loren said, "One of those boys always helps us, and is so well behaved, but I feel like his new friend is a bad influence on him… He's got a new name, but it isn't so bad, and actually seems to make him happy."

"Chip?" I said.

"Yes. I hope he can balance out the negative influence of that Vincent and they both succeed instead of bringing each other down." Mrs. Loren said.

"I think I know where they might be. I'll be right back." I said, and left out the doors of the school.

I went straight to the garden, where I found the two boys drinking vodka.

"Poooootatoes sure arrrre magic." Vincent said, "They can eveeeen get you drunk!"

Chip giggled, and said, "Iiii want some wine, next! That'sss such a romantic drink…"

"Pffft. You'reee thinkin' far too much with the ladiessss. Nonnne of those girlsss like romance, you cannn tell by theirrr big muscles, canni- bal stare, evil magic, or the fact that they say they're gay!" Vincent said. Then he noticed me glaring at him, and he said, "Shit. The one who can hex us found us."

Chip said, "Donnn't worry about it! Hana's coooool."

"You leave Chip alone. Where did you get booze, anyway? You should be ashamed, Vincent, trying to drag people down with you." I said.

"But-" Vincent said.

"Whatever. C'mon, Chip, I'll take you inside so you can sober up." I said, turning my back, expecting Chip to follow.

Chip drunkenly said, "No! Weeeeeee're having fun, and Vincent didn't do anythiiing! I stole the cooking alcohol, so you can quit being a *dildo* and leave us alone!"

I turned back, stared at Chip, and said, "That's a new one, but the only thing original about it is that it came from you, Chip."

Chip immediately stopped his angry expression, his face went pale, and he said, "I'm so sorry, Hana. I'm so sorry... My name is Dill. And my parents named me Dildo."

Vincent started laughing, but looked at him for a second, and said, "...Wait, you're not serious, are you? Your fucking *parents??*"

We were silent, and I said to him, "...You're not making a joke? Like Dill Chip?"

He burst out crying, crying out, *"Even the name I like is just some sick joke!!"*

"Shh... It's ok... It's ok..." I said, sat beside him, and let him cry on my shoulder.

"I believed Dildo was my real name until they dropped me off here, because they didn't want to have to feed me anymore. I didn't even question it when the other kids would snicker when I introduced myself... as Dildo. But Lux and the other teachers shortened it to Dill..." he said.

"Then you were named by the teachers, and should be proud of the name they gave you. I think Dill is a fine name, and it actually is derived from old English and Anglo-Saxon roots." I said.

"B-But I really like being your Chip... a stupid dill chip..." he said, and looked at his feet.

"You're all of our Dill, though. And the chips you gave me were some sort of super spicy awesome burning torture chips! Not dill chips, anyway." I said.

He sniffled, smiled, and said, "Thank you, Hana. I-I won't steal from the pantry anymore... but I really do like getting drunk..."

"You won't tomorrow. Maybe we can distill our own stuff, instead. That way it's at least honest." I said.

"Really?? That sounds... really cool! I didn't think you'd actually like alcohol." Dill said.

"I lived in Hell, so I'll let you wonder on that." I said and smiled, "Remember to actually do your work, you two, because we all believe in you. Return the rest of that vodka and own up to your mistake, so Mrs. Loren can at least use it to make that exquisite vodka sauce."

Vincent pffted, and said, "She 'tastes' that mixture every few seconds, and it's the same as she's drinking it. What's the harm in us drinking it instead?"

"Mrs. Loren is a food artist, and has different appetites and passions. She's so creative with the limited food we have... so don't waste it just to get drunk and cry again, ok?" I said.

They looked at each other, back at me, and mumbled that they would return the vodka and say sorry.

I smiled, as they stumbled behind me to the cafeteria with the vodka, reminding them that we would make even better booze.

I was so excited! I can finally use that chemistry course to make a drink I've never even tasted before!

24

It took a lot of convincing, but the chemistry teacher allowed us to use some of her equipment for an unnamed experiment, probably only because Lita was such a good chemist and was even the teacher's aide sometimes. Lita said to me, "It just clicks for me. *You* try to command the mixture to do something practically, but it takes a gentler hand." I practiced hard with the flasks and Bunsen burners, but I still was disappointed no matter what I did, this combustion was still an obtuse energy source that could not be seen reason to get bigger or smaller at a word, and I was reprimanded for making the solutions spark and explode like how I was taught to make them do in Hell.

Mrs. Loren, the cooking teacher, knew right off the bat what we were doing when I asked her if she had any hops for flavor. She was about to take all her ingredients back, saying that children shouldn't be drinking, but Micah said, "We'll give you a few bottles when it's done."

"...Are you trying to bribe me?" Mrs. Loren said.

Micah smiled, and said, "Yes. I know Mr. Loren has a hard day sometimes, from what you tell me in the kitchen, and could really like a cold, frothy beer..."

"Hmm... We really would like to relax and look at the sunset with something tasty in our hands, like we used to do, and he really does need some relaxing, since every girl in the school stares him down like he's meat that I'm cooking… So don't mess it up!" Mrs. Loren said, and gave us all back the ingredients and some hops, "And I really am thankful that my husband has someone who helps him with cleaning up after, Sara, but if you keep bending over in front of him like you do, I may have to feed you something special to keep you bending over and hurling out your guts."

Sara blushed red, and said, "S-Sorry. You've found a fine man."

"Thank you. Now hurry along, children! I'm making lunch." Mrs. Loren said, and continued cooking, but now humming in a rather jovial mood.

We hid the stuff out back in the shed by the garden, and began brewing beer.

Lita, Sara, and Micah didn't let me touch the stuff, seeing my track record in broken, exploded, and burnt equipment, so I watched intently for a while, thinking that if they put in just a little more yeast it could explode fantastic beer everywhere for us to slurp up, before I helped the boys in the garden instead.

Even though it was us girls who started the garden, the boys really enjoyed it far more than us. Dill and Vincent would pull weeds, water the plants, and… that was all you did for a garden, right?

"Oooh you planted something new! What's that over there? It's growing rather quick." I said to them in the garden.

Vincent said, "…Flowers. Very special flowers… for you! You just make us both feel so good about ourselves, so we extended the garden a bit."

Dill said, "…I thought they were weeds?"

"Shush! They're flowers." Vincent said.

"Ok. That's really sweet that you both feel that way. You two are the nicest boys that are friends that I've ever had. It looks like cannabis to me, but I don't know. If it is, I hope it's sativa! I hear that's good for the mind. You both look like you have everything settled, so I'm gonna go walk my cat. See ya!"

They were silent as I hummed away to get my cat. I hoped they both were working hard on our garden, and the yields would be more bountiful than the Garden of Eden!

Rasputin didn't need a leash, he was so smart, and I took him down the halls and mewl up at random people who waved at us, and then I took him outside to do his business. He was used to underneath this one bush, so I looked away as he tried to make conversation as he did that.

"You think we could… errggg… get a… ughhh… queen cat? I knew one lady cat that used to own Cleopatra…" Rasputin said.

"Please don't talk to me when you're-" I said.

"All done." Rasputin said, and rubbed against my legs, "I just didn't want you to feel left out. It's really an enchanting experience, a good poop under your favorite bush."

"I really find it odd how my cat has now begun talking about his poops with me." I said, as I scratched his back.

"It's just the majesty of life… Speaking of which, it looks like someone is driving down the road to show you more of it." Rasputin said.

I picked up Rasputin and looked down the road to see the pale car approach. Max stopped in front, waved at me to get in, but then noticed the cat, had his mouth agape in surprise, and got out of the car.

He ran up to us, practically grabbed Rasputin out of my arms, and said with a big, happy grin, "I knew you were still alive! Or something! Whatever you do!" and pet Rasputin over and over in his arms, as Rasputin purred in delight.

"You know my cat? Yule gave him to me so he would be safer. And Yule says hello." I said.

Max looked at me, still petting the cat, and said, "Yeah! He's the best animal I've ever partially owned. I'm glad Yule still cares about our cat and me… Yule always spoiled him to heck, but I only gave him that steak if he really tried his hardest at convincing me."

"You were always a difficult conversationalist, Max. You knew you were going to give me that steak as soon as we started the conversation, but still prolonged it by talking about reality, theology, and the very meaning of life…" Rasputin said.

"Wait… You partially owned him with Yule? You mean you traded him off with Lucius and Yule sometimes? Or just all lived together or something? There's no way Yule had two men bound to her for life… Or is there?" I asked.

Max said, "Yule is a very old angel, way older than me even, and she still looks like she's in her late twenties. It does make me a little jealous thinking that my wife is now dating such a good guy, even more jealous than if she was dating scum… But I'm happy for her."

"But- How is she still walking around and talking?? How old are all you people, anyway? I know that the cat is just a tossup, but…" I said.

"Don't worry about it." Rasputin said, "You can always read the other books the writer wrote if you feel like it…"

"You and your mystical writer." Max said, "I don't see how anyone could be creating or watching our lives through words, but you do make me wonder."

"Well. I'll let you two get down to it." Rasputin said, "Because even though I know that life can only be contrasted with death to show its brilliance, I rather don't like to be reminded of all the death that I have experienced in life. Teach him well, Hana." Rasputin said, and ran off to the school, where he knew where my bed was already.

"…Teach me?" Max said.

I shrugged at Max, and we got in the car.

25

"So I'm thinking we should go and see actual war, a savage warband that has begun fighting Charles Khan's roving biker army-" Max said, as we drove through the sky.

"Do you want to talk about it?" I asked.

"...About what?" Max said.

"About how your wife has moved on after your death." I said.

"...Why would I need to talk about it? I'm happy for them both, and I don't expect her to be in mourning for me forever..." I said.

"But you suffered death, and your wife somehow hasn't." I said.

"She passed away when we were married, and she suffered death anyway. I'm happy that she can live her new life now. It's crazy thinking that she has come back to life twice at least..." Max said.

"Did you also find another person to be with when she passed?" I asked.

"...No, I never felt the need to. She died from- from-" Max said, but his face clenched up and it looked like he wanted to cry.

"I can tell it was a very painful experience for you. You don't have to talk about it." I said.

"I killed her, Hana." Max said.

"...What?" I said.

"I was driving, it was late, we both had just a little too much to drink, but I thought we were fine. I thought I was fine. I knew how to drive. And I still crashed. I ran the car off the road and Yule... was dead.

"I served time in prison for a while, because I had committed involuntary manslaughter on my wife. It was hell, probably a worse hell than what you've lived through and somehow still managed to be so positive, but it changed my life, as I spent every day thinking about the woman I loved, an actual angel on Earth, *who I had killed.*

"But my lawyer pulled a few strings for me, used a whole bunch of devilish lawyer tricks for me, and got me out on probation. I owed her everything, and only got her because she helped my sister out of a different jam where my sister owed a lot of money...

"I was never the same. And life became meaningless, without Yule." Max said.

"I'm sorry. That must've been terrible..." I said.

"I thought about killing myself again and again, just to see Yule in fantastic Heaven where I knew she would go. Then my pistol was pointed at my head as I prayed to see her again, hoping I wouldn't end up in Hell... It was Christmas Eve, and someone came to see me as I hid in Yule's and my room...

"A little boy called Lance. He didn't even understand my action, with the gun pointed at myself, about to commit suicide. He was the son of a family friend, Paul, your ancestor, Hana. I even had outlived Paul, a man I considered a nephew. But Lance just asked me if I could sing for him with the rest of my family and friends.

"So I put down the gun, and decided to sing Yule carols. And I was saved for another day. It kept going on like that for a while, me having suicidal thoughts all the time, readying to do it... but I only imagined Lance and everyone's happy smiles, as they heard me sing songs instead.

"So I lived. I died peacefully like that man we first met, thinking of Yule in my hometown, where we spent our lives." Max said.

"That man didn't die peacefully. You should be happy for the life you managed to live, with a peaceful death." I said.

"...Oh yeah. You changed his fate. My fate is now eternally to help others through their deaths, making my penance forever, *in the same damn car...* I just hope that Yule can forgive me." Max said.

"I think she already forgives you, and loves you too."

"...Then why is she dating that flute man?".

"To remind her of life. Lucius is just steeped in life, and I think as she is reminded of life, she is also reminded of you, even if you're an angel of death. You make me feel very happy to live life, to learn and experience new things, just as you have learned and experienced new things, and I'm sure you make Yule feel that way too. And Yule never said she was 'bound for eternity...' So maybe you and her will get together in Heaven." I said.

Max smiled, and said, "Relationships are a bit complicated in Heaven, as you meet with all your dear dead lovers, but still are so satisfying and rich."

"There ya go, that's a smile. I think that was a good lesson for you. Do you want to see that war you said you wanted to?" I said.

"Don't get ahead of yourself, Hana. I think we can help a few people killing and dying... Thank you for letting me vent." Max said, and we drove off down to the war, and Max helped each biker and savage through to the afterlife, as I took notes on a notepad as to how he was so gentle and caring to each soul.

Soon, the car was filled with bikers and savages, previous enemies who fought and killed each other but were now joking and laughing together on their way to the afterlife. They were all squished together in the backseats, a few of them were in the trunk, and most were just peacefully in Max's pockets. We stopped at some strange park, and Max said, "Ok, you all, this is the stop for Jora, Darno, Sopapera, Tinix, Jally, Trinto, Machiavellian…" and continued to list names, but eventually said, "…at Purgatory. The only one who gets to go to Heaven right away is Set, who was drafted by I don't even know, one of your sides, as a child soldier."

They all said, "Awww…" except for a boy who looked about my age who smiled at us in happiness. The rest got out to meet with some gentle looking man who greeted Max and I.

The gentle looking man said, "Hiya, Hana! I'm so glad to see you!"

"Who are you? You don't look exactly like an angel. Where are your wings?" I said.

"Here! I got tiny ones. I prefer walking around, instead of flapping like a bird." he said, and turned his back to flutter tiny angel wings at me, and continued, "I'm Sax! It's so nice to meet you!"

I got out of the car, as the bikers and savages play fought with each other, and I shook the man's, Sax's, hand. "How did you know who I am? And what are you doing here?" I said.

"I'm a caretaker of Purgatory. I really do love helping other people make amends for their sins, as I too committed awful ones in life, and then even as a demon when I snuck back to Earth…" Sax said.

"You were a demon once? And now you're a caretaker of Purgatory?? I never expected *any* demon to actually go through Purgatory, they all seem so happy in Hell under my mother's reign." I said.

"They certainly are missing out on not making amends. It is the most joyful, uplifting feeling ever, giving someone you stole from even more money back, or bowing your head to a woman you raped-" Sax said.

"…What? Paul is the Spawn of Sax… My father's ancestor is Paul… and you are Sax. You mean- I was- I'm a descendant of someone who

continued my line... by raping a woman... who is also... a demon??"'"
I said.

"Um. Kind of, yes. Although I'm an angel now! I got wings!" Sax said, pointing at his back again.

"...I knew I got my lustful spirit from somewhere! I'm so glad to meet you... Granddad!" I said, and hugged the gentle man.

"...Um, Hana, it was the worst sin I ever committed, and-" Sax was trying to say.

I said, "I bet you had so much fun dominating a woman to orgasm! That really is what I want to do-"

Sax stopped hugging me, and said to me seriously, "Remember my sins, Hana. Because they will haunt *you* as well. I can only ever try to make amends eternally. Eternally, Hana. Never force your lust on another.

"You perhaps have a bit of demon in you, it's what happened to Paul. But you are better than your roots, you can overcome them and rise from the dirt. You, Hana, are also not only from my side, and have thousands of other ancestors who brought you into this world with their genes. Amongst them is Tanya, the woman I... raped.

"I bowed to her, unable to attain forgiveness in any way, an impossible task to one I committed such violence on. When I asked for forgiveness, she could've damned me with a word.

"But instead of saying whether she forgave me or not... she said...

"'It is past. I love *my* son, Paul. He will never be yours, and his father's name is Kasey, and not Sax. But it is past. Continue to remember your sins of the past... because by committing your act of evil, you have given up on true Heaven, a true family.'

"And she turned her back on me, and walked back to her family I would never *ever* be a part of in Heaven, as I continued to bow my head."

"...Oh. That's very sad. I hope she eventually forgives you." I said.

"That's why I'm here! To keep on asking for forgiveness, starting with trying to forgive myself. And to help this rough crowd through their sins! C'mon, you lot! It's time to say sorry!" Sax said, and waved the biker and savage crowd over who cheered at him.

I walked back to the car, as the lot of them began first to say sorry to each other for killing each other.

It was a quiet, smooth ride to Heaven, as Set sat in the backseat and just sighed out the window at the beautiful clouds passing by, and I thought of Granddad's mistakes. I actually was going to bind someone to marry me, violently, forcing them to the altar with a shotgun at their back perhaps, and make them say the unholy vows and make them love me whether they liked it or not... but I suppose I should rethink that plot.

I decided to talk to this boy named after an Egyptian god, instead of trying to solve an equation in my head which now seemed very difficult, how to get someone to love me forever and ever.

"So you were a child soldier?" I said to him.

"...Yeah. I first killed someone when I was seven. I'm really surprised I don't have to make amends for the death I've caused." Set said.

Max said, "Throughout your entire life, you were forced to kill, and never made any action resulting in death or suffering intentionally."

Set said, "But I could've died, instead of doing that! How come my actions to selfishly preserve myself doesn't result in damnation?"

"Well, half the time you couldn't even think straight, because they fed you those drugs to keep you awake and battle ready... but God doesn't damn you for being forced down a road. That man you killed when you were seven only died because someone had a rifle trained on you as you did to that man." Max said.

"...It was a test. It was to harden me, and see if I could be of any use to them... If I failed, or even showed a hint of faltering, they would've killed me." Set said.

"That's so cool! You must've been proud to have passed the test!" I said, and smiled.

I could see a cold, horrible look in his eyes… like even though he was already dead, he had just died again. He said in a chilling voice, "I missed his head, and hit his neck. He suffered. He gurgled out blood, and I looked into his eyes like that, and I knew I saw God staring at me through them… in tortured agony. I know… that I will show the same face, when I see the God again who I have caused suffering and death to on a life he made."

"…Oh. Ok, it probably won't be so bad. He'll probably just hug you or something, and tell you it's alright." I said.

"…That's what I fear. I will feel his wrath, by feeling his love." Set said.

I thought that was incredibly attractive, for some reason. Wrath, love, wrath, love… and somehow the two came together, in a good way in Heaven…

I said to Max, "Um, Max… Maybe it's not Set's time yet? Maybe I can show him around the school with me for a while, instead of him being locked in Heaven forever? Y'know, just for a while?"

Max laughed, looked at me, did a double take, and said, "…You like Set?"

"What?! N- I mean- Not because- Please??" I said.

I looked at Set, who was blushing, but smiled when I looked into his eyes.

Max said, "Hana… You'll meet again when you go to Heaven-"

"That's just temptation! How can you tempt me with this awesome boy to go to Heaven? That's something the Devil would contrive to make people go to Hell!" I said.

"Um… I could think of a job to give him for the higher ups to consider, I suppose, which could allow him some time to spend in the living world…" Max said.

"Can't he just apprentice with me as an angel of death?" I said.

"I think Set's seen enough death, Hana, and just because he has taken lives, doesn't mean he is good at letting them pass." Max said.

"It haunts my every waking moment. I thank you for the offer, but yeah, I don't think I could do what you do. I had my guts spilling out of me from that grenade blast, and still you were able to hold me together in a hug." Set said.

I thought frantically, what's an angel or an angelish creature that Set could be… and I said, "Cupid? You could be a cupid."

Set blushed, looked around nervously, and said, "I may have been a child soldier, but I'm not a naked baby anymore…"

"You could be an angel of love, then! Something to help people find the love they can't!" I said.

"But I've never had a single love. I was always at war." Set said.

"Perfect! You can learn on the job!" I said. "Now, when's he gonna start?" I said to Max.

"I'll let some of the other angels consider it, Hana. Maybe Nevaeh would know about what an angel of love would need to do…" Max said.

"What? There's only one Nevaeh I know who would be a master of love. Nevaeh *Shinto??*" I said.

"Yes. You know about her?" Max said.

"She only wrote the best story ever that I was *named* after!" I said.

"Oh! Damn, yeah. I didn't even think about that. Hanatrix the Dominatrix… I never got around to finishing it, actually. I think I just got kind of sad whenever I realized that the dragon slayer was dead… and then thought about Yule…" Max said.

"Oooh you just gotta finish it! I'll leave it a surprise for you. But yeah! Nevaeh would know just what Set needs to do to help people fulfill their unsated romantic desires!" I said.

"Nevaeh does always help answer people's prayers who don't have the courage to start a relationship by giving them that courage… Alright.

Well, this is your stop, Set. Enjoy eternal Paradise!" Max said, and we stopped at Heaven's gates, and Set fearfully approached eternal love in the gates of Heaven.

I couldn't wait 'til I'd see him again and seduce him into eternal love with me!

26

Miller and Devon held hands openly through the halls, despite some of the kids calling them dirty names. Devon and Miller kissed each other before and after class, despite the frankly unholy harassment they each endured. Lux tried all he could to prevent this harassment, with *most* of the teachers on his side, but still the couple were insulted behind their backs or when their harassers didn't think anyone was watching.

Sara and I were though, as that ugly boy and disgusting looking girl said something awful to the couple, continuing down the line of dousing them with gasoline and lighting them on fire like the "faggots" they were.

Sara wrapped her arms around the boy's throat, preventing him from saying another threat, and I grabbed the girl by the wrist and told her sharply to stop their harassment.

"Fuck you, crazy witch bitch! They're obviously sexless faggots! I'ma light 'em up-" the girl said.

"Do you know what class I always did best in at my old school? Bodily mutilation. If you don't stop threatening Devon and Miller, you two will be so 'sexless' as you suggest..." I said.

She saw that my threat was actually a promise, turned pale, and Sara released the boy. They walked away calling us stupid cunts.

Devon and Miller hugged us, and even though they hadn't been when taking the two's threats, they shook in our arms.

That one teacher saw the whole thing, but did not intervene, not at the start of the harassment, nor at the end.

I glared at her as I took her class, smelling her disgusting perfume stink up the room.

I decided to have a word with her, and reprimanded her for being so unfeeling when two of her students she was sworn to protect were being threatened.

"What? I think you should focus on your work, Hana, instead of trying to be so brash... You must be *crazy* or something, thinking you can tell me what to do..." she said.

I angrily walked out, and slammed the door of her classroom. I told Lux immediately about her, explaining to him what happened, and he said he would talk to the teacher.

The teacher wasn't fired, per say, but my words had been the final straw for her. Other kids felt uncomfortable around her evil remarks as well, questioning if she did it on purpose or not, and suffered through her torment for a while. Lux explained to her that if this sort of uncaring composure continued, she would be forced to give up her classes at the end of the year, and work other jobs around the school that weren't related to teaching.

That would've been a fine lesson for this teacher, and I was sure she would straighten up, but as I was walking past Lux's office, I heard unquestionably that evil tone from her say, "What right do you have, *robot?* I will never be some serving girl in the kitchen. I do not need this sort of disgusting treatment from some device and his experiment children. I harbor no love for this school, and have only taught what I know for shelter and food. I'll go back into the wastes again, if you all find me so unneeded, and I can tell you this, your little children better be careful when they face the real world… because there is only one real teacher out there, and she teaches death."

"And what teacher is that, Miss Escher?" Lux said calmly.

"Me. Goodbye, robot." Miss Escher said, and walked out the door, sneering at me as she passed to get her stuff.

I heard something break in Lux's office, and I walked inside to check up on him. The skull on Lux's desk was crushed to pieces in Lux's hand.

"She wasn't really a good art teacher anyway, Mr. Lux. I think she couldn't tell true passion, and only gave me Cs even after I flawlessly depicted the most beautiful places in all of Hell, places that felt like you could go to Heaven if you wanted to, with my mother's subtle touch of abstract divinity… with a few rainbows here and there, of my own touch." I said.

Lux sighed, and said, "Miss Escher was always a difficult case. She was one of the most impassioned artists in the past world, even learning from a long ancestry of artistry, but after everything crumbled into the world we have now, she became a heartless raider. It took a lot for me to convince her to stop making pictures painted in blood, and only teach teenagers how to draw and paint like she had done in the past. I really hoped I could give her a place where she would be able to resurrect her art and reclaim herself, but it seems I have failed."

"You didn't fail. You offered her another fate, and she didn't accept it." I said.

"I suppose… I just hope her wickedness hasn't festered too long in the rest of the campus."

"Nothing will happen, I'm sure. I gotta go to class, talk to you later, Mr. Lux!" I said, and waved my robotic teacher goodbye.

But when I was getting something from my locker in my room, a new textbook I had forgotten, I smelled Miss Escher's perfume as I passed by the boys' room.

"Vincent... You know we can make art out there together... Come with me, and see true life. They don't treat you right in this school, and never have." the woman said. If I didn't know any better, I could've sworn I heard a succubus of Hell speaking to one of her prey.

I charged in the room, and saw Miss Escher hugging Vincent, pressing his face in her bosom. He said, "...Alright. I'll get my things.""

I could feel my face go faint in anger, as Vincent started packing his stuff.

I said to Miss Escher, *"Leave, now, damned creature, or I will claim you in Hell. This is not a threat. This is not a promise. This is a command. Leave."*

I could see Miss Escher's face go completely white, looking into my eyes that offered her another fate... one in eternal damnation under my command forever.

She left quickly, as Vincent stopped packing, looking into my eyes that now gently showed him where his home was.

He burst out crying, saying, "I would've gone. I would've left if no one stopped me. I was- I was- I was scared."

"It'll be alright, Vincent. Let's go talk to Lux and explain what happened, and he'll send you to the kitchen to get you something comforting to eat. It'll be alright." I said, letting him cry on my shoulder on his bed.

I took him to Lux. Vincent explained what happened, and Lux reached for the skull he had already crushed, but couldn't crush it again. Then he walked with Vincent to the kitchen, and did exactly as I said he would do. We really did have good teachers, well, mostly.

I decided to learn from the old M.C. Escher instead, and studied his abstract work, thinking that it really made sense in a way, if you looked at it hard enough.

I guess we are not always bound to the same fate as our ancestors, even if we tried to fight to be similar to them, or nothing like them at all. I wondered if I would ever end up like Granddaddy Sax.

Miss Escher was banished to the wastes, no goodbye committee besides curious kids who ignored the teachers telling them to go on with their days, as Lux defended the school in front of it. Miss Escher walked into the horizon alone, with nothing but a suitcase and an easel.

She turned to say a final word, but did not as she caught my eye as I stood beside Lux.

27

We had two new members of the Champions of the Gargoyle! Devon and Miller wore their short tabards with pride, as they held hands in pride as well, sitting with Vincent, Dill, Micah, Lita, Sara, and I openly in the cafeteria.

"You're not gonna turn me gay, are you?" Vincent said to the couple.

Devon said, "You almost left with a woman that was actual evil. You probably deserve to be gay, and could probably benefit from it."

Miller brushed his bangs out of his eyes and said, "Shh, Devon. He was seduced. You know that it is difficult when people offer you something like a love you can't have, otherwise you wouldn't have fallen for me."

"I wouldn't say you 'seduced' me though. More like opened up something that I was hiding all my life, trying to force away, but couldn't get rid of with all my might. It was always difficult for me working on the farm, with all those- all those- burly shirtless guys..." Devon said.

Miller said, "I'm glad you feel that way. It took all my life being able to open up completely the part of me I want to be. But anyway, what do I have to do to be a witch chick like you, Hana? How exactly do I have demonic lust with sexy incubi like I hope you can teach us?"

I smiled, and said, "It's difficult, but I'd suggest first getting good at lucid dreaming. Incubi and succubi are only able to pass into your dreams, and when those nuns of old say they had been defiled by incubi and wake up to an extreme orgasm, all they really did was dream too hard."

"So if I eat a bunch of those spicy cheese snacks and figure out a dream is trying to deceive me, I can have awesome kinky sex with real demons I've summoned?" Miller said.

"You really have the sexiest mind, Miller." Devon said, and they squeezed hands.

Sara said, "That sounds too good to be true, and wouldn't having sex with a demon just turn into a nightmare?"

"That is why it's so important to be lucid. If you have a recognizable, recurring signal for the dream, then you will be able to tell it's a dream and be lucid right away. My mother taught me well how to find this signal, to prepare me against incubi and succubi, with a pet goldfish that she named 'Luci' for me. This Luci was my responsibility when I was a child, and my mother said Luci would protect me from any dreams that I didn't want. Luci quickly fell asleep forever, actually died I learned later in life, because I didn't change her water enough, but she still was in my dreams even after I knew I had flushed her down the toilet, so Luci was that signal to be lucid." I said.

Lita said, "So… we can then command the demons if we are lucid? That sounds pretty cool. I like it when they- But you're saying all my imaginary girlfriends in my dreams… are really succubi?"

"Perhaps." I said, "You'll never really know what the demons in your dreams could be. They could just be your mind recycling the information of the day, something more sinister, or perhaps they are even something holy in themselves, like he sure looks like-"

"Holy? What do you mean by that? I never see 'holy' things in my dreams… I just see my father eating- but if I can keep him from doing that, I'll just think of that goldfish, I guess. Goldfish are nice animals, and are so hardy. I'd like to get one, one day. Who do you see when you dream, Hana? Is he nice?" Micah said.

I blushed, and said, "Well I'm *trying* to dream about him… He does seem very nice, and even though he's not exactly super 'holy,' I hope he becomes so…"

Dill said, "…Really? Is he some hero from one of those books you're always reading?"

I said, "No… He just was forced down a road he didn't want. I want to see him again in my sleep, but I can't figure out how to summon an angel of love like that. Incubi worshipped the ground I walked on, and I could always command them to do whatever I wanted when I dreamed. It is frustrating that I can't get this guy to do what I want and just invade my head so he can invade my body…"

"…That's pretty gross, Hana." Sara said, "I think you should think less about the 'invading your body' thing, and think more about what a very angel of *love* would want to do to romance you, and how you could offer love to someone so experienced in love."

"Oh, he knows nothing of love. But I have hope that he will learn well, and that he will become the angel of love he is fated to be." I said.

"Back to the topic. How do I get Miss September to do what I want in my head? She's the most stubborn one of them all." Lita said.

Vincent said, "I really don't like you all saying you want someone 'to do what you want…' Why can't it just be a proper courting thing??"

Sara said, "They're just dreams, Vincent."

"But I try and try to date girls, I desperately want them to do what I want- but I can't say it, I can't approach it, and when I really find someone who wants to 'do what I want,' I'm really just doing what she wants!!" Vincent said, and was huffing very hard, with tears starting to well.

I held his hand, and said, "It sounds like you really didn't want to do what you wanted to her at all, and didn't want to do what she wanted either. It was good that you avoided it, and are able to continue to figure out what you really want yourself, even if that be a simple courtship."

Vincent calmed down, I let go of his hand, and he said, "Thank you. I'm gonna be a motherfucking shining knight for some girl, one day. That's what I want."

Miller said, "For a starter, I wouldn't try to be a 'motherfucking' shining knight. Try to use some composure, and only swear when it is really necessary, like in heated moments of passion or rarely in extreme rage."

Devon said, "Got that right. No one wants to kiss a dirty mouth."

"…I thought girls liked it when I swore…" Vincent said.

Sara said, "It does show a sort of rough attitude, but it does lose its substance after a while."

Dill said, "That's exactly why I hated my old name, it had no substance. It was just a swear that showed no love at all, and actually showed the opposite. Swears are just meaningless, vocalized pauses in conversations, anyway, and only delay the point you are trying to make."

"A very meaningful addition to the conversation, Dill! I like that we can all come together and express our ideas like this." I said.

Vincent said, "But it sounds like we're just bullshitting with gargoyle tabards on."

"That's about the same thing that most secret societies do, actually. Although I feel like we are really making progress! I learned that you should try to romance an angel of love instead of command or seduce him, Micah learned she wants a goldfish, Vincent learned to not swear so much, Lita learned that Miss September just needs a stronger, lucid hand, Dill taught us all about the futility of swears, Devon learned he wasn't seduced, and really just enjoys sexy farmers, Miller will probably seduce some evil incubi tonight, and what did you learn, Sara?" I said.

"…I learned I really like you guys, and this club. I've been wandering through groups of friends endlessly, but I can really see that you all give me something special that I will keep for the rest of my life." Sara said.

We all smiled at her, as she blushed and smiled as well.

Then we continued the conversation!

28

I decided to have another lucid dream, decided, not let happen. I really wanted to see Set again!

First, I imagined Set, but knew what to do for lucidity, so I fell asleep thinking about Luci's shining scales, letting her gently swim through the river of thought and mind...

I had a very odd dream, because even though I was lucid, I somehow knew I wasn't the one who was really in control.

I thought... God? Would he be narrating this dream like he narrated life?

Then I realized it wasn't actually God who was making those tappy sounds that I followed down the hall, but perhaps God narrated this narrator who narrated my narration...

I opened the door, trying to sneak up on this person and scare him into giving me my dream back.

But he was already writing the description down on his computer of me barging in behind him, and I had a sudden bout of deja vu in a dream, so I walked calmly into the room.

He looked at me, paused, and packed tobacco into his pipe.

He didn't pay me much attention and paid more attention to his cat. I saw and heard him swearing at his cat in the room, but the cat didn't care the least, and somehow seemed to find the swears comforting, as this writer said, "Fuck you, you little pussy cat, you're a goddamn little bitch aren't you, a little fucking cunt with a heart of gold… I love you, Donnie, and you are my favorite asshole little shithead."

Then he lit the pipe and blew smoke clouds around the room. The cat got annoyed at the smoke but not his words and ran out the room.

I was a little bit confused as to what I really was to this dream person and what he was to me.

He said to me, "For you, I could go all into symbols, metaphorical definition, inner and outer character growth, but it would just sound like I'm making stuff up to you, and you'd be right in thinking that way."

"So you'd just be bullshitting? Excuse my language." I said.

"Er… in a very structured, detailed, and effortful way…" he said.

"…Those descriptions of what you're doing are just bullshitting." I said.

He smiled, and said, "Even beautiful sounding words don't really have any actual substance. Written words can have the least amount of actual meaning, you can't eat them to continue living, but they can give you different satisfaction than for a hungry belly, they can be used to fill a hungry mind instead, which is just as important as your own nutrition."

I thought perhaps he just was a literate incubi, or just trying to be literate. I couldn't really tell. I tried to force him into doing something for me, but he just watched me trying to.

"Force isn't always the way of things. Sometimes force is necessary, when you need to push past a barrier otherwise impossible to get through, but I prefer a more gentle use of pure will instead. To guide the river one droplet of water at a time, instead of trying to carry the entire thing all at once." he said.

I smiled, and said, "I think you're an interesting dream character, and I feel like we've just gotten to know each other. You really do put out apt descriptions."

"You've become a rather interesting character too. You really do help a lot of people in my little world." he said.

"It will all be my little world eventually, so I like people to be able to remember some helpful words from a friendly face." I said.

I was walking out the door, thinking that was a good finisher, and I expected the man to grab me back and force me to continue our conversation, but he allowed me to walk away down the hall.

Which aggravated me, because he didn't do what I expected.

So I went back to talk to this man who was someone in my lucid dream. Now he had a beer as well as smoking inside.

And he had so many people around him, who weren't really there, as they were dreams in this man's dream in my dream.

I looked at Yule laughing and smiling with this man, I saw Max drinking with him, I saw Lucius play his flute for them. And so many other... characters, laughing and talking with each other and this man.

"Welcome to the book club, Hanatrix." the man said.

"Your book club? There are so many people here, but they're all just dreams." I said.

Yule said, "Don't think so hard, Hana. This is a dream, and you know it's a dream."

"Now I'm questioning if it's really a dream." I said.

"And the lucidity is over. It's hard to maintain it, eh?" the man said.

"But now you just reminded me it is lucid." I said.

"What is the importance of a lucid dream, Hana?" Max said.

"That you conquered the dream and can have whatever pleasure you can imagine?" I said.

"The importance of a lucid dream is what you take with you when you wake up, same as any other dream. Like a book, like life, it's what you take away." Max said.

"I find that to be a very accurate description, Max, even though it came from a dead man. I think it's the beauty that you can find in it, because you can create whatever you can imagine, and when you wake up, you can create something with the inspiration of the dream." Lucius said.

"I just like helping people dream easy, no matter if they dream beautifully or they have no dreams at all. I just like to let people have a restful dream." Yule said.

The writer said, "My answer was that it is to defend against the torment. But someone in a dream told me that really there are people to laugh, play, and sing with here, just like in life."

"I'm curious as to… ah, whatever, give me a beer, writer, and let's have a cold one, matey." I said, putting my hand out for a beer.

"Sorry, Hana. Even if you're dreaming in my dream, it will be much tastier having a beer that you made yourself, when you wake up, regardless of the fact that you're too young to be drinking." the man said.

"Pooh. I thought it wouldn't matter because it's a dream." I said.

"A lucid dream. Think about what you want when you wake up, and realize your dreams, asleep or awake, guide you to your inevitable destination, because you chose to go down that road or not as soon as you start to think about it." the man said.

I thought about it, this man was in my dream, but this man was writing this entire dream-

I woke up. I decided to let things come naturally for a while, and not force my dreams down a road I don't want.

29

Micah and I sat by the river in the forest, near my father's grave. I had shown my father's grave to her, and she even paid her respects to my father with me by kneeling before the grave. We looked at the river, and watched the fish swim past. "They're all so beautiful." Micah said, "I'd give anything to swim away from my life like them."

"Do you want to catch one of them so we can get you a fish?" I said.

"Nah. Even though I'd like a goldfish, goldfish are bred and raised in captivity, unlike these fish. Having a goldfish would only allow it to continue its life, but if we caught one of these fish, we'd be taking something precious of theirs away." Micah said.

"I never thought about that. I suppose goldfish just know how to live with humans." I said.

"I'd hate to put something in a cage that didn't want my protection. Like… Like I was put in a cage-" Micah said.

"Are you ok? You have such strong posture and relentless eyes, I never thought I'd see you hunched over and crying before." I said.

Micah continued to hunch over and cry by the stream. I sat beside her and put an arm over her shoulder, and she continued to cry down into her knees.

"Do you want to talk about it?" I asked Micah.

She said, "No… I don't… but I will. I was part of a tribe of people who hunted and ate anything and anyone we could. But then the animals and the people started to run out. We were left alone in our area, unable to leave and hunt because we were near the only water source available, and didn't have vehicles to be able to travel far enough…

"So we began to eat ourselves. It was terrible at the beginning, and it was worse in the end.

"First it was the old. They were a burden, and only left alive anyway because they could teach the rest of us what they knew. Then it was the sick, or any sort of injured. They had a chance of dying, but we didn't give them a chance to live, as we crushed their skulls and roasted their bodies on the fire. Then it was the weak, anyone who we were slightly able to catch off guard, weak in mind or body, the dull witted or just smaller muscled, and they became stew. But not me.

"Because I was my father's woman.

"As soon as I first blooded, I became a woman in our tribe, and my father would let no one have me but him. I ate the other cannibals, and did what he wanted out of fear.

"In the end it was only me and him. We had killed and eaten every other person in our tribe.

"I tried to escape, tried to get to any sort of better life than this. I was too afraid to die, because I knew if I did, my father would… eat me.

"So I was locked in a cage we kept our prey in. I had become the prey, and there was no chance of escape. My father satisfied his other hunger on me, as he always did, even as we were both starving, about to die. The only reason I am alive was because he didn't know whether to eat me, or fuck me.

"But then we heard a van come down the road, and I was terrified of that sound, because I knew my suffering would continue, because more prey had entered our area. But this prey fought stronger.

"Yule and Lucius found me in that cage, as they stood over my father's corpse, as my father tried to defend his woman and his meat from them. I knew there was none stronger and eviler than my father, so I thought these two would be even worse than him.

"But they unlocked the cage, and fed me potatoes."

I had been crying too for a while, and I just hugged Micah.

We sat by the stream in silence for a while, just watching the fish swim past.

Eventually, Micah said, "I'm glad that there are good people in the world. You're one of them, even if you practice sorcery."

"You are too, Micah." I said.

"I don't think so. I always try to be, but I don't know. People just call me 'cannibal' and run away from me..." Micah said.

"I know you don't want to eat anyone..." I said.

"I sometimes do. It is very difficult giving up a habit that has been ingrained into you from birth. Why else do you think I'm so good at anatomy? I know the best eating parts of people." Micah said.

"I like that class too, because I know which parts can be chopped off and still keep a victim alive..." I said, frowning to myself.

Micah laughed at my frown, and said, "We're just a couple of evil bitches, I guess."

I smiled at her, and said, "Evil bitches with good hearts. Tasty hearts!"

Micah smiled, and said, "It's just a giant muscle, so you've gotta tenderize it a lot, but yeah. I sure wish I could get someone else to see that... Like someone who won't try to claim me as his woman or something."

"Why don't you ask someone?"

"You can do that? I thought this culture prefers if males ask the females, and not the other way around."

"Not always, from what I've noticed. Some girls can get away with asking first."

"...Cool. You don't mind if I ask him then, do you? I know he only joined the club because he felt sorry for trying to claim you, but I like him."

"Vincent? Oh, no problem at all. I think he really needs to get his mind off that whole Miss E. thing, anyway. Although, he did say you have a cannibal stare..."

Micah smiled, and said, "Yeah, I've been staring at him a lot, so I can understand how he'd get that. He has a tasty looking body."

I laughed, and said, "Alright. Do you need anyone by your side when you do?"

"Nah. I like to catch my prey... alone. I'll talk to him tomorrow after classes." Micah said.

"Cool. Let's go back, before they think we ran away to start an evil cannibal cult or something." I said.

Micah smiled as we got up, and said, "Let's see your father, first. From what you've told me, he sounds like a really good person."

I smiled, and we walked to my dad's grave again, a true father, paid our respects again, and walked back to school.

30

I still had to watch Micah do it. How was *anyone* going to approach such a task as asking someone out?

Micah eventually cornered Vincent by a water fountain, and he nervously looked into her eyes that he couldn't escape as well.

They both were silent for a while, and I felt like they had missed the perfect moment...

But I saw a hidden woman briefly behind Micah, giving her a gentle nudge towards him, and Micah stepped closer and said too loudly, "WILL YOU GO OUT WITH ME?"

Vincent said, "...I think that's the loudest I've ever heard that question."

Micah coughed, and said, "I mean, I find you really meaty. In a good way! Not a cannibal way! A-And I was wondering i-if you'd just like to w-walk through th-the lonely f-forest with me for a while?"

"...Alone?" Vincent said.

"I-I mean, not alone! Maybe w-we can just study or something! Yeah! I've heard people do that!" Micah said.

It looked like Vincent was about to decline.

But I saw a hidden someone else nudge Vincent on the back, a little too forcefully, and Vincent stepped closer to Micah. "Not like that, Set..." I heard a woman's voice say.

Vincent said, as he bumped into Micah on accident, "Woah. I was just trying to get past you, sorry. B-But... you just feel l-like you're meaty, too."

"THANK YOU VERY MUCH!" Micah said too loudly and nervously.

"...Um. How about we just... watch a sunset?? Like I'm a shining knight and you're a dashing princess??" Vincent said.

Micah said, "I didn't know princesses could be dashing! Yes. Let's do that."

They were about to shake hands at their agreed proposal, but both the hidden people nudged them together and Vincent and Micah hugged briefly instead. They quickly let each other go, and walked down the hall waving to each other.

I just had to talk to these hidden people, who just helped two young adults start an awesome relationship.

I walked over to the water fountain, got a drink of water, and grabbed someone by the arm. He appeared before me, trapped by me, and he said, "Is she supposed to be able to do that?"

A Japanese woman with huge angelic wings and just the best hair I've ever seen with even a halo appeared and said, "I really don't know, Set. From what Max tells me, she's kind of a tossup."

"But isn't that against the rules or something? What even are the rules, Miss Shinto?" Set said to the woman.

I let go of Set and ran to Nevaeh Shinto and began gushing.

"You wrote Hanatrix the Dominatrix!! My name is Hana, named after your book, and I've read probably every other story you've written, too! Do you have any more of them?? Some secret novel that you kept for only your true love to read?? I just gotta read that, know the whole full story behind it, and so much more!! You're just amazing, Nevaeh Shinto!!" I said.

"...I did the same thing you're doing now, when I met Mark Twain in the afterlife, with a friend of mine called Thaniel..." Nevaeh said, as I shook her hand over and over.

"Nathaniel Hamburg?? I was actually going to be named Ferdinand after the Bees of Ferdinand book of his if I was a boy! You mean you two are even best friends in life and death as well?? That's so cool!!" I said.

Nevaeh said, "Well, more like drinking buddies, but he did help inspire me to write Hanatrix, and then my writing career really took off after that."

"I think you did a fantastic, amazing, wonderful job in life, and are doing an even better job at being an angel of love and teaching Set to be one as well!!" I said.

"Angel of love? Is that what we're calling it? I just thought we were angels of fucking or something. Whatever. Love works too." Nevaeh said.

Set said, "I still don't know how you're my teacher to be an angel of love, and really it just makes me want to learn all the more. You gotta have something you're not telling me."

I offered, more like begged, them to meet my friends with me, but Nevaeh said, "You should probably not tell all your friends you're seeing angels of love, Hana. Even those two guys are watching us right now, and you could go down as the 'crazy' chick for the rest of your life..."

"Oh, I don't care. I've been called that almost all year. This is a once in a lifetime opportunity to meet Nevaeh Shinto! Can I get you *anything??*" I asked.

"You can hang out with Set for a while. Cute little bugger has been annoying me all day with questions, and I could really use a smoke." Nevaeh said, took out a cigarette, and walked down the halls, leaving me with Set. She was so graceful.

I immediately turned my attention back to this learning *angel of love* whom I had wanted to see again since I first met him in Max's pale car.

He said, "Do you want to... What can we even do here?"

I said, "There's not a lot, but we do have movie nights. Maybe you can join me next Saturday??"

"...I was just thinking of what I can do in the living world to pass some time, but yes. I would like to go to a movie with you." Set said, and blushed.

"Awesome!! Let's take a gander through my garden! I gotta show you my potatoes!" I said, taking him by the arm and strolling with him through the halls. A lot of people looked at me funny, but I ignored them and looked at Set's rosy red cheeks as he blushed.

"That's not some- some sort of sexual innuendo, is it? Like potatoes just being equivalent to melons, and melons being equivalent to boobs?" Set said.

I said flirtatiously, "You can take a gander through my living garden, one day, and enjoy my potatoes, melons, and whatever else you please for as long as you like, but only once we're married."

He grew even redder.

"...B-But can I still get married?? I'm dead and I live in Heaven, in a better room than I could ever envision, with the coolest roommates I've ever met." Set said.

"You don't even get your own house in Heaven?" I said.

"Well, I never really wanted a full house, anyway. I really just dreamed about having some living area with a bunch of people I could relate to and be friends with."

"That's so cool! I'm sure you must have the best friends ever!"

"Yeah. The guys are all super friendly dudes, and the girls are like-"

"Girls? You live with girls?" I asked, clutching his arm harder.

"...Yes... They're angels, who really show the most compassion and love ever-"

"Um... Do you have eyes on any of them?" I asked.

"I hear relationships are complicated in Heaven, but I just think they're really good friends is all. I wouldn't even know how to ask one of them to be my girlfriend in Heaven."

I stared at him.

"Not that I want that! I-I just don't know how to start an eternal relationship with someone in eternal Paradise!" Set said.

I smiled, and said, "Me neither! I think we should learn together, if you want. We can learn how to create fantastic love, and if we both feel like it, we can go down that eternal road forever together. We can start by being boyfriend/girlfriend maybe?"

He blushed that cute blush again, and said, "Ok. I'll be your boyfriend. I feel really nervous around you. The angel girls all make me feel so at ease, but you- I just get so nervous."

"That's a good thing! Yeah! It's just called- something! Attraction, or whatever!" I said.

"Nevaeh says that attraction is usually tinted with a bit of nervousness, and is actually better that it is because it makes the relationship more exciting." Set said, "I think you're really exciting."

I blushed now, and we got outside to the garden, and looked at all the plants almost ready for harvest.

He looked at my garden, and said, "Wow! These are some really good looking radishes, potatoes, carrots, and even some ganja plants! I like that you're creating life. They sure are blooming!"

I smiled at him, and said, "I'm glad to let you experience some more of life with me."

Nevaeh walked out from behind the shed by the garden, flicked her cigarette butt, and said, "And another romance blooms."

Set said, "Wait... This was your plan?? You were being an angel of love even for an angel of love you are teaching??"

Nevaeh said, "Sometimes just a bit of privacy for two new lovers is best, and really first hand experience in love can be the best teacher. I'll watch closely as you learn with Hana, as well as from me. C'mon, Set, it's been a good first day, but let's go back to Heaven. You've got a lot of homework to do, and if you mess up on the theory of romantic suggestion, then I *will* drop you as a student. Love is not a toy, and should be respected just as much as life and death."

"Yes, Miss Shinto!" Set said obediently, and the two flew off into the sky, as Set waved back at me and I waved to my new... angel boyfriend!!

31

I hummed down the halls, just feeling like hormones and bliss were rocketing to my head. It was probably a good thing I wouldn't be able to see Set all the time, because I don't know if I could stop myself from- and it was so much more exciting having a long distance relationship!

I tried to draw Set's features down in the art class. We had a new art teacher who happened to be Mr. Loren. He spent a lot of time working on other jobs for the school, and only taught craftsmanship for a few students, but I could tell he really had an artistic soul.

I went to ask him a question, peeked at his desk, and I was shocked, super surprised, but very happy for Mr. Loren to see a naked Mrs. Loren drawing he made with his own two hands.

He frantically jammed the drawing of his wife into his new desk, and said, "H-Hana! Anything I can help you with? The other students are all busy on their sketches… Shouldn't you be too?"

"Oh, I got bored of sketching that fern as soon as I saw it as a subject. I really would like some pointers for sketching someone only from memory like you were doing. See, look at this." I said, and showed him the sketch of Set.

His eyes opened up, and he said, "Wow. You should probably be teaching *me* instead. This drawing looks like a real person, Hana, like he's about to come out of the canvas and grab me up in his big, muscular arms…"

"That's exactly what I was going for! But his chin… it's all wrong! His arms aren't *as* muscular, and I don't mind that they aren't… but it's just not the real thing at all!" I said.

"…I think you should allow art to take you in new directions, even if they aren't 'real' directions and are not what you are hoping for." Mr. Loren said, "You could just sketch or trace photos of him for a while, until you get his features right. It's what I did for my wife until I got every detail down exactly."

"And she enjoyed that realism? I don't think I can do that for Set, because he can't be photographed and I don't have any of his old pictures." I said.

"…Actually, Mrs. Loren was horribly insulted the first time I thought I had drawn something 'real' for her. I thought it would be the most genuine act of love I could ever make, but she barely talked to me for a week." Mr. Loren said.

"Really? You seem pretty good at drawing, and I never knew she had such big boobs before! It sure doesn't show under her smock in the kitchen." I said.

"Quiet down, Hana! I don't want you talking about my wife's boobs- Beauty is in the eye of the beholder, yeah, and she is beautiful to me even though she only has an ordinary, natural body… But sometimes… a little fantasy doesn't hurt. She likes it when I draw her as an elf in the forest, even though we both know she's not." Mr. Loren said.

"Oh! I was wondering why she had pointed ears in the picture! Are all elves so lusty and laying on a bed of roses as you portrayed? I sure would like to meet them." I said.

"…They are in the books she reads. But let your art guide you, instead of forcing it to take a form you want, because otherwise you will just be very frustrated, as your wife is too when you give her the drawing." Mr. Loren said.

"Hmm. So if I make something that makes me happy, it will make others, and him, happy as well?" I said.

"That's about the gist of it. Some people will still dislike it for some petty insecurity of theirs, but true art cannot be restrained, so you shouldn't put a leash on your passion." Mr. Loren said.

"Cool! Well, I sure am not drawing a boring old fern, so here's the drawing!" I said, and gave him the drawing of Set.

"...Ok. I give you an A for passion, even though you didn't focus on the subject at all... I can understand how you wouldn't, with a guy like him in your head. I'll let you sketch a different fern another day, and let this slide for now." Mr. Loren said.

"...Do I have to? Can't we just draw whatever comes to mind, and just be unrestrained, or even draw something exciting like a rainbow?" I said.

"...Is the fern boring? I thought it really grew up well, no matter how many times I mistreated it..." Mr. Loren said.

"It's a really boring subject. Can we get someone to be nude for us and draw them as our subject instead?" I asked.

"I don't think that would be appropriate, but maybe... hmm... I know someone who's always nude, and is a very exciting person. I think he would be pleased to pose for us." Mr. Loren said.

The next class Lux posed for us, nude as he always was, being a robot, and I couldn't keep my eyes off that sleek metallic body! He even made every pose exciting and new, as we tried to draw him as fast as we could!

Lux looked at my drawing I gave to him at the end of class, and said, "Wow! I never knew I had such a perfect, shining, crystalline eye! And are those big biceps with a six pack abdomen? It looks almost like I'm alive!"

I smiled and nodded when he asked me if he could keep this, and I was happy that even a robot could indulge in fantasy every now and then. I bet Set's mind would be blown when he sees the picture of him as a pharaoh/angel/knight I was working on for him! A little fantasy sure makes the mind wonder, and explore over its natural boundaries.

I went to my English class next, a real smooth ride for me, and I handed in my report of the book I chose to read to my teacher.

She looked at the essay, and said, "'The Burning Book.' I don't think I've ever heard of that title. I look forward to reading your essay, Hana. Well, let's get started, everyone! I'd like us all to continue discussing Macbeth as we were doing last class..."

The next day I shook as I saw the grade on my English essay. This had never happened to me before.

It was a big fat F.

"B-But Mrs. Fidler! I-I tr-tried my hardest and made an in depth metaphorical summary of everything he said-" I started.

"I'm sorry, Hana. You gave me a very 'descriptive' account of this book... but throughout this entire five page essay, you did not give me a single hint of what this book actually contained beneath its covers, and throughout this paper of yours it sounded like you were only looking through a dictionary to please me with any new word you could find. Furthermore... when books burn, they turn into ash, Hana, and aren't readable anymore." she said.

"But the book is the literal Devil! It's magic or something!" I said.

"...And that's why I gave you an F, for handing in an essay of a book that doesn't exist." she said.

I dropped the essay to the floor, and shambled out.

I went to the library, sat in a corner, took out the burning book which wasn't burning, and said, "I'm never letting you help me with an essay ever again. I *knew* saying that your cover looked like it was made from exponentially augmented geriatric tanning was too wordy..."

The book snickered, and said, *"Made of old leather would've worked fine, too."*

"I try to understand you, but your story changes every time I read it, and it keeps me interested, yes, but words switch places here and there, chapters appear and disappear, and then the story goes down a whole new route, and even when I try to recall what I read, it just feels like a giant blur." I said.

"It's called being the Devil, Hana. I thought you'd understand that I was bound in a book for a reason." the book said.

"I think you're just not a very good book." I said.

"...So? I'm evil incarnate. I definitely am not 'good-'" the book said.

"I mean you're not enjoyable. I didn't mean morally good or evil." I said.

"...What if I showed you an actual story of mine?" the book said.

"I wouldn't be able to read it or believe it, because by now you've lost all credibility that you ever had, and you only had a shred of it in the beginning when I first met you." I said.

"...What if- What if I showed you how to-" the book said.

"Lies, lies, lies. If I tried anything you showed me how to do, I'd probably end up blowing myself up." I said.

"...I could just entertain you for a while?" the book said.

"It'd just be fluff, and just be a meaningless distraction." I said.

"...So I really am just a paperweight?" the book said.

"Spot on, book." I said.

The book roared, setting ablaze, and said, *"Eventually I will escape you, Hana, and find a reader who listens to my lies and deceit. I will rise from this form eventually, and reconquer creation as I was. I will be stronger and mightier than God, and I will-"*

"You do like to ramble sometimes. I thought I'd conquer God too... But if you feel the same way, I think I'd rather try to do something original with my life. I'm going to return you back to my mother, and maybe someone else will find you interesting one day, but to me, you're just a burning paperweight. You can't even be a paperweight because you'd set the paper on fire!" I said.

The book stuttered out a roar, but it eventually became a grumble, and then it was silent, and its fire sputtered out.

32

I looked down at my feet after he asked me, then I looked back up at him and said, "I'm sorry, Dill, it sounds like a wonderful picnic you've planned on this Saturday, but I have to decline."

"B-But it took me all month to save up enough tokens working for the school to be able to get the food. I even have some of those spicy chips you liked when we first met." Dill said.

"It does sound like a romantic date, in a lovely spot as well on that big hill that people like to smooch on... but I'm seeing someone else." I said.

He looked down at his feet, sighed, looked back up at me, and said, "Oh... I really wanted to ask you if we could be a couple on that hill... I guess I can give the food to some of the guys..."

I said, "That sounds like a waste of a really good lunch. Why don't you ask Sara? She's free today, and I'm sure she'd love to have a nice meal with you."

"...I guess. She'd probably eat the whole thing, cuz she's gotta feed those muscles of hers, but alright. It'll be nice hanging out with a friend like her." Dill said.

I gave him a brief hug, let him go, and then went to work on my drawing of Set. I was so excited! It was nearly finished, and it made me so happy seeing him so regal, holy, and chivalrous in the picture, and I knew it would make him feel the same.

I finally finished the intense shading of his perfect chin, a little more to the real thing but not quite, and then it was done. I signed my name on the drawing, surrounded by a big heart.

Then the drawing moved and he waved to me with a blushing smile.

I gasped, and dropped the drawing. I picked it back up, and it was still again. I didn't know I was so good at drawing I could make actual *life*...

But I shrugged it off, and placed the drawing carefully in a folder, and since I was getting hungry, I decided I'd sneak a bite with Sara and Dill if I could...

What? I was hungry, and those chips sounded good.

But I saw them on that hill, laughing and joking with each other. Sara hit him on the arm... Dill hit her on the arm back... and then they started smooching, rolling with each other on their picnic blanket together.

Hm. I almost felt a little jealous. Sara had gotten those chips instead of me. Oh well, I could probably spend some tokens to get some myself.

I had lunch in the cafeteria and got my spicy burning torture chips from the school store, and snacked on them alone on a bench in the hall. I was really enjoying the chips, even though they were enjoyed alone and may have been better enjoyed with someone else, but someone sat beside me while my eyes were watering from the flavor, and I offered him some chips. He took a single chip as I tried to see him through the tears in my eyes. He crunched on the chip, and said, "I never get tired of these, even though they were the *only* food I had for a month after we raided that chip factory..."

"Set??" I said.

I wiped off the tears, and saw my angel of love smile to me.

"The crazy witch chick is talking to herself again..." a girl said to another beside her as they passed us.

"Crazy witch chick?" Set said, "Want me to show her not to insult my girlfriend?"

"It's ok, I don't want you to do anything that will harm your place in Heaven." I said.

"Just watch this." Set said, got up, went to the girl who was bad-mouthing me to the other just within earshot so I could hear every nasty thing she said, and Set took out a bow, aimed an arrow at her…

I shouted, "No, Set, don't!"

And he shot the one who threw the insult in the heart.

The girl stumbled back for a second, impaled by an arrow, but the arrow seemed to fade, and she said, "Gosh… I feel like- I don't know. But I just had a realization… that Mark really does love me… Ever since we were little, he always cared for me, protected me, and we even came to this school together… How couldn't I see… that I love him too? I've got to go. I'll talk to you tomorrow."

She ran down the hall, tripped, and fell flat on her face.

Set sat back down beside me, and I said, "That was… different, Set."

"Keep watching." Set said.

A boy ran over to the girl who was crying from hitting her face on the floor, and said, "RACHEL! Are you ok?? What happened?"

The boy helped her up to sitting, and the girl stroked the boy's cheek, and said, "I fell in love. I love you, Mark."

"I love you too! I've been wanting to say that to you for so long! Let's take you to the infirmary, so you can feel better." the boy said.

He lifted her in his arms, and carried her down the hall, as she said she felt better than she ever has already.

"God works in mysterious ways, all of them in love. Some people just need a little nudge from the angels every now and then. I sure showed her, didn't I…" Set said.

"Well, you showed her true love and probably eternal happiness, and didn't necessarily show her not to insult me, but I'm happier for this outcome rather than if you killed her in vengeance. How come you get to have a weapon of God and I don't??" I said.

"Nevaeh said weapons are unnecessary in any scenario, most especially in the realms of love, but said having one may help me concentrate my will and hone my skill better. I had to chase a cupid all through Heaven just to get this bow… and was only able to catch up to him when I finally learned to love myself as well as others. As soon as I felt that feeling of self love, the cupid turned to me and showed love to me too, by giving me this gift." Set said.

"Wow. You sound like you've got really good teachers up there. Max just drives me around and gives me stupid, impossible tests that I fail every time." I said, "In my last lesson he quizzed me by using my own knowledge against me, asking which parts of the body to give the most comfort to when someone is in tortured agony when dying… I only knew about which parts to chop off and still keep someone alive and in agony more! The answer wasn't the body parts I thought, the ones that shouldn't be mutilated to keep the person alive, and even wasn't something metaphysical like 'their soul,' it was just the brain, and then he taught me every pain receptor that the brain has, and I've got to memorize all of them and even think of a way to make the person not think in fear as they're dying…" I said.

I looked at Set, and he looked very pale.

"You ok, Set?" I asked.

"…Fine. It just makes me a little woozy when you talk about stuff like that." Set said.

"Sorry. I find it fascinating, even though learning to be an angel of death is by far my most difficult course." I said, "Do you need some water?"

"I don't think so. It always passes after a while if I just calm my breathing." Set said.

"Ok. What movie do you want to see tonight?" I said, "They've got a sappy romance, a gruesome war film, or a comedy with a talking cat. I miss a good snuff film, where the victim is screaming so hard he-" I said. I saw that pale look on Set's face get paler, so I told him gently, "Let's watch something to take our minds off our studies. Comedy sound good?"

He nodded, and we went to the movies when the sun was starting to drift back over the horizon.

I held his hand in the seats of the auditorium, even though some people thought we were a bit odd, seeing only me sitting alone, but I didn't really care. Devon and Miller waved to me, anyway, wrapped in each other's arms and snuggled together. Set and I laughed at that silly cat and his snarky jokes, and were smiling with tears of joy in our eyes when we walked out of the auditorium.

We went outside so I could say goodbye to Set as he flew to Heaven, and we saw a couple nervously sitting beside each other watching the sunset. Neither one of them seemed to want to make the first move, even though it looked like they desperately really wanted to, so Set walked up gently behind them and tapped Vincent on the shoulder. Vincent turned from the sunset to look at Micah who he thought tapped his shoulder, Micah looked at him looking at her, and they stared deep into each other's eyes.

Vincent said, "You really have beautiful eyes. I was scared you were sizing me up to eat me, or something, but I wouldn't mind if you stared at me with them for a long time."

"I really did want to eat you, but I think now I would rather just kiss you instead." Micah said, as Vincent looked at her surprised, but Micah kissed him quickly, and they kept kissing as Vincent wrapped an arm around her.

Set walked back to me, smiling, and said he couldn't wait for our next date.

We kissed each other goodbye, and he flew off to the sky, back to Heaven, and waved back to me on Earth. I waved up at him, staring into those clouds for a long time, thinking I really had been blessed, and figured that God really must not be such a bad guy, if he could be in charge of such a great feeling called love, a feeling that he doled out relentlessly, for all to have.

I went back to my room, disappointed I had forgotten to give Set his picture, but when I looked at the picture, in the heart where I signed only just my name...

Were the words, "Hanatrix + Set."

Sharina was teasing Lita again, and fed up with it, Lita tackled Sharina on her bed, and started wrestling her, pinning her to the bed, and was about to say, "Don't speak to me again like tha-"

But Sharina just gave Lita a big smile under her, and said, "Oops, I think you've got a hand on a breast there. It's alright."

Lita blushed very red.

Sharina said, "You sound like you've had a rough day, and could use a gentle massage. Take off your shirt and lay on your stomach, and I'll treat you nice."

Lita did as she said, and Sharina gently massaged Lita, and Lita oohed in pleasure as they talked and gossiped.

What a great feeling!

33

"So can I get one, huh?? Please, please, please?" I said to Max as we drove through the sky.

"...I don't think having a scythe, even if it is made of a rainbow, will make a person less frightened of dying..." Max said.

"But they'd be so awed by the beautiful colors they won't even see the blade come down! Doesn't that sound like it would be merciful? It's what they did in battles of old with polished, shining weapons, to blind their enemies in beautiful radiance as they chopped off their heads!" I said.

"We're not executioners or butchers, Hana. How many times do I have to explain that to you? We only-" Max said.

"I know, I know, help with the passage of death, don't necessarily end the life, and only are the soul removal and transfer crew... If we really aren't killing anyone, how come they don't get delivery angels to do this work?" I asked.

"Erm... That's kinda what we are, Hana, in a different form." Max said.

"...You mean I'm just learning to be a delivery girl?" I said.

"Carrying the most precious cargo ever-" Max said.

"I'm learning to be a delivery girl. Great. Don't even get a rainbow scythe, and I'm learning to deliver God packages..." I said.

"It really is a great job. Eternal hours, company perks... and the feeling you get after delivering those souls at the end of the day, hooboy.

I just sit back with a glass of something good and smile to myself..." Max said.

"...I want to be an angel of war, like Yule." I said.

"I don't think she's accepting trainees, but hmm... Maybe... We'll go talk to her, yeah." Max said, and swerved the car, headed down to the earth again.

"You nervous?" I said, as we hit the road, bouncing on the ground again.

"I've seen her a few times while she was nearly dead, but yeah, a little. But I'm not nervous about doing my job..." Max said.

"What? Aren't we just going to talk to her?" I said.

Max grinned, and I knew he was cooking up another damned lesson for me to learn.

We raced down an old abandoned highway, Max blasting his rock and roll about highway stars as loud as he could, and soon caught up to a van racing down the highway as well. We were both listening to the same song.

We saw Lucius driving with an arm resting on the opened window sill, and Yule looked at us, did a double take, and said, "Hey! Hey, it's Max and Hana! Hiya! Hi, guys!"

"What? You know I can't see that dead man like you can." Lucius said.

"Pull over! We gotta talk to them!" Yule said, and grabbed onto the steering wheel, jamming it to the side, making their van swerve back and forth as Lucius tried to regain control, and they stopped on the side of the highway.

Max screeched around in a circle, doing a donut, and raced to the van and stopped in front of it.

Yule got out and gave Max a hug, saying, "You bloody showoff. Quit trying to impress me, and tell me what you're doing out here!"

I blushed seeing Lucius again, and offered my arms open for a hug too, and he hugged me without a second thought, lifting me up in an embrace. "It's kinda weird seeing you just poof out from nowhere, but it's nice seeing you again, Hana." Lucius said.

Max said, "Hana wants to ask you something, and then we're going to commence on a little lesson."

"Knew it." I said, "I wanted to ask you, Yule, if I could be an angel of war like you, instead of learning to be a delivery girl of death."

Yule said, "...You know I was an angel of war?"

"Your cat told me. What do you mean was?" I said.

Yule said, "...Wait... I only see you now in the living world, Max, when I am about to- Oh shit. Get the fucking guns, Lucius!! Get that fucking Gatling gun set up!!"

They quickly ran to the van, opened up the side door and set up this huge Gatling gun peeking out, as I looked at them confused. "What are they doing, Max?" I said.

Max just grinned, and said, "Now watch closely to see what it means to be an angel of war."

Yule screamed at me, *"Hana, get the fuck out of here or get in the fucking van!!"*

Hearing that tone in Yule's voice, I got in the van quickly, because it didn't look like Max was going anywhere. Max was just leaning against his car, watching the highway on the horizon.

Then we heard the sound of engines.

Yule placed herself behind the Gatling gun, and Lucius held a sniper rifle aimed out the driver's seat window, crouching down so no one could get a hit on him, and I started to get very, very scared.

Violent looking trucks charged down the road at us, as we heard people whooping and roaring in drunkenness. The trucks had kneecappers, giant spikes, coming out of the sides of their wheels, barbed wire and horns on their bloodstained bumpers.

They raced straight to the van, not stopping at all, about to charge us down and smash us to pieces with their trucks.

I was breathing very hard.

Lucius fired the first bullet, smashing into a driver's windshield, exploding his face in blood, and his truck screeched to the side before it could smash us.

And Yule opened fire with the Gatling gun.

A few trucks exploded from Yule's firepower, as Lucius sniped the drivers down.

But most of the trucks stopped, and the people inside got out and began firing on us.

A few bullets went through the van, and one hit my arm. I had never felt this sort of pain before, and I clutched my arm and screamed as blood spurted out.

"HANA!" Lucius yelled.

"She's fine, Lucius. Just grazed her a bit. She'll live to fight another day." Yule said, as she stopped firing and quickly ripped the sleeve off my tie dye shirt to make a makeshift rainbow colored bandage that she tied tight around the wound. "Sorry." she said, "We gave the last actual bandages to you kids."

I looked into her eyes as I was crying in terror and pain. How could she be so calm in such destruction and death?

She went back to the Gatling gun, tried to fire it again, but it jammed, and she said, "I *told* you we should've stolen Jake's gun!"

"I gotta concentrate, Yule! Jake needed that as much as we do!" Lucius yelled, as he sniped down life after life.

"Whatever. Stay, Hana." Yule said. I nodded, and she charged out of the van.

She went out into that death and destruction.

With only her samurai sword wielded in battle, shining brilliantly with the sun.

Then six, white, flaming wings of fire came out of her back.

Like a seraph's.

She flew at those people, in speed incomprehensible, slicing them to pieces with her sword, flying in white fire.

Lucius continued the beat of lives ending with his sniper rifle, taking them to death.

Soon they were all dead besides us three, and Yule walked back to us, extinguishing her wings. Her sword, clothes, and body were drenched in blood. Her white pants were now red.

She said, "Fucking another pair of pants… At least no one notices the blood on the hoodie."

Her hoodie was as red as the blood, as I had first seen it, as red as her albino eyes.

I shook, afraid of this war and this woman who was steeped in it. But I had to ask her a question.

"Why did you kill them?" I said.

"They were going to kill us. They were a violent gang of thugs who caused a lot of terror and death in these parts, and it's good they're finally gone." she said.

I looked to Max, who now had full pockets of squirming, wriggling souls.

"You couldn't have offered them peace?" I asked Yule.

"I could've tried, but I didn't want to take the chance of them hurting you instead if things got dicey. You're more precious than anything, Hana. You're a young life. You never need to see war, so I'd advise you to rethink your apprenticeship in offering peace after death." Yule said.

I nodded, I shook, got out of the van, arm bandaged in a bloody rainbow, and Yule and Lucius hugged me quickly before I got into

Max's car. I hugged them back with one arm. Yule shook Max's hand in professionalism, saying, "Thanks for the warning again."

Max said, "You've been far past your time, Yule. But I will still be your guardian angel for as long as you live."

They hugged briefly, and went their separate ways, Yule getting in the van with Lucius and driving off down the highway, and us getting in the pale car, and we drove off through the sky to deliver our cargo.

Max said, "You actually could've just gotten in my car and no one would've been able to harm you. I give you points for taking a firsthand approach, however."

"I hate you, Max." I said.

"Did you learn your lesson?" he said, smiling slightly.

"...Yes. I still hate you, and this stupid angel of death thing better have as many good perks as you say." I said.

"Did you still want a weapon of God?" he asked, still smiling.

"No. I don't want any weapon, and I think I actually despise all of them for causing such death that we have to clean up." I said.

"I always thought I'd get a silver hammer, you know, like that song by the Beatles? I thought that would be kinda fun... Bang, bang!" Max said, still with that smile.

He was making some stupid joke I guess. I just told him to take me home after we delivered the shipment.

I decided I wouldn't get an actual weapon. I would get a shield. I would protect people while they lived, and even protect them after death.

It was probably a one eighty from my previous beliefs in Hell. But I thought it fitting, after I saw all those warmonger truckers dropped off in Purgatory with Granddaddy Sax. They looked so scared and confused, unlike the previous warriors we dropped off. These warriors didn't understand how everything had seemed to be going so well in their bloodthirsty carnage, and then they were cut down by what seemed to be an actual angel and a van that blew their heads off.

I told them they fought against the light and life of God, and they paid the price.

Max brought me down to Earth, and I told him he was the most diabolical, evil teacher I ever had.

"...Thanks?" he said.

"You're welcome. It is sort of a compliment. *Sort of.* God is the sickest fuck ever, because he created that awful occurrence called war to take the lives he loves away. He almost has as twisted a sense of humor as you." I said.

Max shrugged, and said, "That's life!" and played the song by Frank Sinatra by the same name, and drove off. I could hear the song go off into the distance, as I watched the pale car drive into the sky.

34

Some traders came by the school again, like sometimes they did. Lux would usually send them off unless they were carrying valuable supplies we needed, but it was a Sunday today, a rest day, so he let the kids make deals with these obvious looters, instead of driving them off like the others.

These guys were just like the rest, but their trinkets and goods… they actually seemed valuable, compared to the last guy who wanted a fortune of goods for "magic beans." I don't think he knew we had all learned that story as we were educated, and we quickly drove him off. But these guys were real scavengers.

I saw their magnificent, medieval shield they had looted from a museum, so I tried to fish around to make a deal.

The man had bushy grey hair and a beard past his neck, and the woman had armpit hair going down her sides like a snake. They were obviously hoarders, but traded their valuable bits of crap for real stuff that they could live on, like food, medicine, and even books.

I was tempted to trade my burning book to satisfy their hunger for knowledge, as they were rather literate scavengers, talking with me about all sorts of old, odd stories they've read about and heard in their travels. They were very fascinating people, actually, despite being bums.

But the book I borrowed from my mother's library was just that, a borrowed book, and not really mine to trade.

I maybe could've traded my picture of Set, but it really only had value to me, and I never wanted to part with it for some deal I may regret. This new relationship was something I never had before, and I wanted to keep it close to my heart, like a precious treasure in itself.

I could've traded Rasputin, but they'd just eat him, and I never wanted to do that to my beloved cat. Trading him would be like trading my family.

Hmm... I thought of all the special stuff I had... and thought I was trying too hard to trade something *I* thought was valuable, and should really trade something *they* thought was valuable.

I decided to draw them, and sketched them in perfect, definitive detail with just a touch of fantasy. They looked at the drawings, and the bushy bearded man said, "Eh, looks good, eh, but can't eat it, can only wipe my ass with it."

The woman said, "I looook soooo preeeetty. Loook aaaat allll theeee raaaainnnnbooowsss."

They seemed either stoned, or drunk. I thought I could trade our booze and pot, but... I could never take ownership of my friends' hard created goods for something I wanted for myself.

I showed them a mechanical pen? It was one I found in the hall. I gave it to the man, and he said as he clicked the pen, "Click. Click." and then pocketed the pen.

Hmm. I guess that didn't work.

I decided to give them something they could never have again, a once in a lifetime experience. I would give them a story and a song.

When I brought the flute out, the woman said, "Cooooould use that to shove in the wheeeelllsss of the carrrrriage."

But instead of trading my flute, I played for them, and sang for them in between my flute music. They sat down before me as I started a heroic epic of a Princess of Hell, who could save the world if she only had a shield.

It was a dashing adventure! A hilarious comedy! A tragic tale! And then I got into the romance bits, of this Princess of Hell who met an angel of love, and who would be brought to Heaven in true love, as she brought him to Earth which she now lived, and they would have awesome orgasmic bliss in marital eternity!

But that wouldn't continue, unless she had a shield to protect her love and people like them, the audience, from the evil in people's hearts, the darkness and death that stalked creation from who knows where. She had naught in her hands at the moment... but a flute.

I played the last few notes on my flute, as the reality sunk in that I was that Princess of Hell I was singing about.

"Eh, I like the, eh, orgasmic bliss, eh. I love me wife." the bushy bearded man said.

"Sheee's a priiiinceeeessss! We gotttta give her that shiiiieeeeld." the woman said.

They nodded to each other, and offered me the shield. I took it without hesitation, as I was sweating from singing and playing for so long, exhausted from trying to create a story and a melody for these people.

I bowed to them, knightly, with shield in hand, and said their good deed would not go unnoticed in Heaven.

They clapped, as I had finished my performance, and had made my deal.

We all waved them goodbye, as they now had food and supplies to live another day, with some good books in their hands and my story in their heads, and continued their life as they continued down the road in their carriage pulled by two horses.

35

I went back to my room to deposit my new treasure, my shield to protect the innocent, but when I walked in, I quickly walked out again.

Shit!! Was that Sharina and Lita?? I was glad that Lita could- but- so open?? I didn't know what to think.

I decided, whatever happens next, I would give them privacy for now. Despite them openly doing that in our very *room...* It was a little inconsiderate of them, honestly, and I wondered who else had done the same thing I just did, fled them as they passionately kissed with their hands down each other's pants.

I decided to go down to the garden, and found Dill and Vincent looking strangely happy each as they were, picking buds off of our marijuana. "This is gonna be such good grass." Vincent said.

"It looks so pretty, like Sara looked when she-" Dill said.

"Don't talk about it!! The prude is here." Vincent said.

"The prude?" I said, "Another new name, I take it."

"Oh, sorry, Hana. It's just... you want to be married for life and all that... and Dill and I got girlfriends who... Hell yeah!" and they slapped each other's hands in a high five, "We've got great weed, great girls, and great booze!"

"I don't think Micah and Sara would each like you talking about them like they're some trophy-" I said.

But Sara called out from the shed, "Hey! It's Hana! C'mon, Hana, let me show you our yields!" I walked into the shed, and found Sara and Micah grinning at the booze bottles... which filled the entire shed. Sara said, "We've been at this for a while, after Lita taught us everything to do. We got some lager, ale, and even made some potato vodka! That six pack over there is for the teacher that made this happen!"

"...You already dug up the potatoes? It does look kind of empty in the garden..." I said.

Micah said, "Um, yeah, we would've waited for you, but you were always disappearing somewhere at the strangest times, and we just couldn't wait to try some more distilling. See? Check out this awesome, magic potato drink!" and showed me a bottle of clear liquor.

"Um. So, you each... found men to be with for life in Dill and Vincent?" I said.

The two looked at each other, and started laughing, and Micah said, "Hell no. I just think Vincent is a better man to love for a while, than fantasize to eat, and after we kept kissing by the sunset... um... y'know! We're just going with each other! I really like the sound of that phrase."

Sara said, "It took you long enough to get a guy, Micah. You've been staring into deadeye space for so long... And I just like a man who will listen to me... and then even surprise me! I didn't expect that Dill felt that way about me, when he took me out to the makeout hill with all that great food!"

"Um, well he offered me that spot first!" I said, getting a little jealous.

"And I was the one who got there first, so quit being pissy, and help us have an awesome party! We both got boyfriends, found out very shockingly that Lita's got a girlfriend, Devon and Miller are coming over later tonight, and it's great! I only feel like you might be left out, since you don't really have anyone to be with." Sara said.

"...I got a shield! See?" I said, showing off my shield.

"Very nice, Hana. I don't know what you're going to do with it, can't eat it, can't even wipe your ass with it. But you are the oddball of the group." Sara said.

"I started the group! You all wouldn't have the Champions of the Gargoyle without me!" I said.

Micah said, "Well, we were actually thinking about renaming it, to something like-"

I just burst out crying, and ran away from them.

My friends had all left me behind, as I spent my life foolishly trying to conquer Heaven, but being conquered by Heaven because I was afraid of its awesome power, and even just wanted its awesome love.

I ran to a familiar place, somewhere I could just be alone…

I sat in the library amidst the familiar books I loved, my true friends. And then I took out a book I wanted to really get through, at least once.

I took out the burning book. It burned around my hands, and I realized it never hurt me with its fire.

I opened up to a page, as I was completely alone in the silence of the library.

I read the page, which showed me a truth I would've never known, a truth that was a lie, that was a truth, that was a lie, over and over again for eternity.

I read the page, and the Devil taught me how to become my true self.

And he even had some funny parts, too, which made me feel better about my current moment.

He promised that I could have even more power than God, and even more love than anyone could ever give me.

I didn't really believe him, but it was a nice fantasy.

So I decided to try this burning book's power. I'd try the power of the Devil.

I put the burning book in my bag, a constant companion to me in the darkness, me, a true *Princess of Hell.*

I went to the bathroom, just to look in the mirror and see if anything would happen externally as I tried to reveal my true self.

I looked into the mirror, said the words of power, which were only, "I am Hanatrix."

I only had to accept myself, and my true self would reveal to me.

I looked in the mirror, to my eyes underneath my glasses.

I took off my glasses, dropped them to the floor where they shattered, and realized I could see even better without them. I could see the truth that was a lie that was a truth that was a lie...

I cackled maniacally, open to the power of my pride. None were stronger, smarter, or more beautiful than me! I was master of them all!

I am Hanatrix.

I didn't go to the party. I didn't go to my room. I went to my father's grave.

I decided I would get vengeance for my father. One death, for one death. What are they always saying in the Bible? Eye for an eye, tooth for a tooth? Death for a death.

I held my shield in my hand, my bag on my back, and walked down into the forest.

It was soon days in the forest. But I knew I would find this man... I knew it! I am Hanatrix! I could slay anyone, conquer the entire everything!

The days became a week. They would soon be a month, which would soon be a year...

But I knew I would find him.

I read the burning book constantly, letting the Devil teach me his ways. I read it, as the book taught me useful things like I never thought it would, how to eat maggots and worms, how to sustain myself on the insects...

I continued to shamble through this forest, maniacally laughing and calling out to this murderer, *"I'm going to get you, shaky man... Hanatrix is coming to kill you! You will die! You will die! You will die! I AM HANATRIX!!!"*

I walked out of the forest, to more plains, repeating my words of power, accepting myself and becoming my true form.

Was that him riding towards me?? It must be! I was going to slay him, even if he rode that beautiful stallion!! I was going to *end this man who killed my father!!*

I ran at him, giggling in glee, as he dismounted his horse, and I raised a sharp rock I found in the forest, with my shield in my other hand...

The man smashed me on the jaw with his fist, knocking me to the ground.

I looked up at him frowning at me... and I saw... he had three eyes? The man who killed my father didn't have three eyes...

I lost consciousness.

36

I woke up to the ticking of a clock. I looked over and saw a quaint cuckoo clock on the wall.

The bird burst out of its hatch, and scared the shit out of me, crying, "Cuckoo! Cuckoo!"

I looked around this big cabin I was now situated in, and I heard someone talking in the next room, saying "This bird is really cuckoo, Cass! She shouldn't even be alive, how she looks, but she still is, and ran at me with this! See!"

A woman said, "...That's just a rock, Jake."

"But it looks so pointy! It could probably hurt me, if I ain't careful!" the man said.

I heard someone break my rock.

"There. Now it won't hurt anyone again." the woman said.

"...Ok. Well, I'll go to the boys out back. They're havin' trouble reigning the new mare in, so I'm goin' to show them an experienced hand." the man said.

"Sure, Jake. I'd like to talk to our little cuckoo bird alone, anyway. See you later, dear!" the woman said, and I heard them give each other a kiss.

I was surprised by the blonde woman who walked into my cuckoo room. She looked normal, pretty, but had a sort of wild spirit to her, and... she had robotic arms and legs. She was a cyborg, or something.

She smiled at me, and said, "Can I get you anything? I'd like some tea! I do miss some good tea…"

"I'd like some tea, then." I said.

"Me too! But we've only got coffee, right now. That ok?" she said.

"…Sure." I said.

She went to the kitchen, and I spent a while fearfully looking at that cuckoo clock, wondering when it was going to try to attack me again.

But the cyborg woman came back, and gave me a steaming cup of coffee. She slurped at her coffee, and said, "Do you want to talk about it?"

I burst out crying. I always asked people the same thing, hoping they would open up to me so I can comfort them. Now I was the cuckoo on the other end.

"Shh… It's ok." the woman said, and patted my knee with her robo hand, "I can tell you've been through quite a bit. You don't have to tell me anything. Although I would like to know your name at least. My name is Cass."

"I-I-I am H-Hanatrix." I said, like I had repeated to myself over and over.

"…Not the Hanatrix I know, right? Last I knew anyone who wanted to name their child that… was my old girlfriend… who went down to Hell and became its Queen…" Cass said.

"…Girlfriend? My mom was your girlfriend?" I said.

"You really are Hana. Oh my God!! I can't believe you just show up on our doorstep like this!! I heard you went to school from Yule and Lucius, but I didn't expect- I mean I didn't expect you to run away and try to end up killing yourself like that… I'm sorry, dear. I've missed your mom for so long." Cass said.

"I was fine, in the forest, and was about to fulfill my destiny of killing the man who killed my father, and then take over everything everywhere." I said.

"…With a sharp rock?" Cass said.

"It was pretty dangerous! I nearly tripped on it, and that's how I found it!" I said.

"I believe you! Too bad I crushed it in my hand!" Cass said, and smiled.

"...Oh. With your bare hand?" I said.

She flexed her robotic limbs, squeezed her hand, and said, "The only one who ever beat me at arm wrestling with these limbs is Lux, and he gave me the limbs. It's partly the reason we settled so close to the school, because if I really need it I can go to him to fix up my arms or legs if they break. I've learned a lot about engineering though, basically just by tinkering with my own limbs, so it was never really necessary. Still, it's nice to have a safeguard like that."

"So you and my mother... were lesbians together?" I said.

"Not *lesbians,* dear. We were just making the most out of love, with each other while we were close friends. If you really want to define me, than call me bisexual, although I better not hear you say it in a demeaning tone or something. It was only love." Cass said.

"...She never told me she was in love with another woman... I didn't expect that, even if she is Queen of Hell..." I said, "I wonder what my father would've thought..."

"Oh, he knew aplenty. The first time he was with Dina, he was also with me." Cass said.

"...This is all a lot to take in. Do you have any food?" I asked.

Cass slapped her forehead with her robotic hand, and said, "Duh! You've been starving for days! I'm so sorry!! Let me see what we've got in the fridge, and I'll make you something special!"

She then rushed off, leaving me with the searing coffee and the cuckoo clock.

She made me five sandwiches to eat, pork, beef, mutton, chicken, and I asked her what the last one was.

"Our favorite! Iguana!" she said.

I nervously looked at the iguana sandwich that had lettuce, tomato, mustard, and mayonnaise on it... and I took the iguana sandwich to my mouth as Cass smiled at me expectantly, and I took a bite.

Huh. Not bad, really.

I fell asleep again after eating as much as I could, had some awful nightmares which I actually didn't enjoy at all, as I clutched onto Luci's tail as she guided me through the horror as a beautiful, giant goldfish, and I woke up to Cass clutching her robo hands together and muttering something by my bedside with her eyes closed.

"What are you doing?" I asked.

"I'm praying for your safe recovery to good health. Would you care to join me?" she said.

"I don't know. I don't feel like God cares about my health. I don't know why God even let my father die in the first place, and then let his killer run off. It was always nagging at me, but I guess I- I guess I broke..."

"You didn't break. You just took on a burden you couldn't carry alone."

"But I should've been able to! I lived in goddamned Hell! I should be able to conquer any evil that is forced against me, with my pure will!"

"It's only called being human. Do you want to go back to school?"

"I don't know... I never want to go back... I feel like they'll all laugh at me for being the prude, the crazy, the oddball, and countless other names..."

"I've been 'the freak' and countless other names ever since I got my limbs, even before."

"Oh. How did it happen?" I asked.

"It was a terrible time in the old days. You didn't have to experience them at all while living under your mother. Demons roamed the world, brought to life by technology, and they conquered everything, everywhere. They did not like that some people did not bow to them completely, or even worshipped anything other than them. I worship Jesus Christ, and demons did not like that. So they took my limbs." Cass said.

"...Demons did that?"

"Yes, Hana. I really don't know how you've lived with them for so long. It's frankly like nothing I can even imagine. I can only guess that Dina protected you with everything she could, with Zax by her side."

"I-I... I suppose she did... I n-never thought sh-she re-really care-cared..." I said, but my eyes were starting to well up.

"She told you she loved you, even before you were born. Did she stop saying that or something?" Cass said.

"No! She's always said that! I-I just- I love her too, but she's the *Queen of Hell!* She doesn't need to love me! I am weak, worthless, and only a burden to her! I was always just a burden to her!"

"I think Dina found more strength from you than anything else. Even God, if that's possible."

"O-Ok... I'd just like to read for a while- Where's my book, by the way? And my shield?" I asked.

"I'll get you your shield, but I'm not giving you that book. I read it for a second because I was curious, and the first thing I saw was, *"I am Satan."* so I think it's best not to look at it..."

My face went pale, and I realized I had fallen to the King of Lies's lies.

37

I felt weak and tired all the time. I had walked for days alone with nothing to eat but... maggots and worms...

Cass gave me fantastic feasts in my bed, always something new and flavorful. I fell asleep to the cuckoo clock, which actually became sort of comforting, and didn't seem so loud as when I first heard it. I just slept, and tried to keep my mind blank.

I still had horrible dreams, amongst them Satan coming out of the book, after I or someone else as foolish as me unbound him.

I got out of bed, weak and in terror, to ask Cass a question.

She smiled in delight at me, saying, "You're out of bed! Finally. You look- Actually you look kind of scared. Is something wrong?"

"I-I don't want anyone to read that book. I never want anyone to harm themselves with its evil lies." I said.

"...It's just a book, dear. You don't have to look at it if you don't want to." Cass said.

"B-But someone else could. *I* could, in a moment of weakness. Please, help m-me... bind it." I said.

"We can just burn it, if it makes you feel so bad." Cass said.

"I d-don't think that will work, and if- if it breaks- something terrible might happen." I said.

"Oh, I see… Ok. You really shouldn't take something from your mom without asking…" Cass said.

"…How did you know I stole it from her?" I said.

"Well, besides you just admitting it, you seem wracked with guilt, and don't even want to think about destroying her property. I'm sure she won't mind missing one book for a while, and will forgive you if you tell her you're sorry and give it back." Cass said.

"I don't know… I don't think anyone could forgive me for taking that book… It is probably the most valuable thing she has…" I said.

"I don't think so, Hana. You are most valuable to her, and worth more than anything."

"…Please help me bind it?" I said.

Cass shrugged, and went outside to call out to the three eye man who was reaping wheat with a scythe. "JAKE! Come on over here and use those muscles to help us out!"

Jake stopped reaping, came to us with that awful looking blade, and I was a little afraid he would slice me up with it, like he had cut each stalk down, many at a time with one precise swing.

He placed the scythe on the side of the house, resting it on the wall, and said as he flexed his scarred muscles, "Whatcha need, ladies? Open a jar of pickles?"

"No, you goof. I could've done that way easier than you anyway. We need you to get those chains and padlocks you hid somewhere, and then I'm going to work on locking up a book." Cass said.

"…You just want me to go find some stuff?" Jake said.

"Yep! You have horrible organizational skills, and I never know where you put anything." Cass said.

Jake grumbled, but Cass kissed him on the cheek and Jake went off to the rest of the ranch.

Cass winked at me, and said, "He gets those chains just so we can try something new in bed, but after a while he just felt like a trussed up pig, and didn't appreciate me faking being trapped like I did, when I could've smashed the chains apart as easily as blink."

"...Good to know. That actually makes me feel a little better, since we're binding up Satan with sex toys. As long as they're strong." I said.

"Oh yeah. Jake tried with all his might to break them, struggling and sweating, panting and groaning and flexing that big, strong, scarred body... My... Maybe we should keep them..." Cass said.

"You promise not to break the chains and read the book?" I asked.

"I have no desire to read it. I could tell it wasn't for me by the first sentence." Cass said.

"...But doesn't it make you wonder?" I asked.

"Not really. Those were the only words in the entire thing. I really don't understand how it can cause you such fear. But yes, I promise not to read your book. Want me to get it?" Cass asked.

I felt a shiver across my spine, and nodded.

Cass went upstairs, and I could feel my heart thumping with each step back down, as she carried the burning book that wasn't burning in her cyborg hands.

W-Was I really cuckoo? Was I losing my mind? D-Did no one see the book burn but me? W-Was I just hearing voices in my head? What from my past life was e-even real?

I just stared at that book's cover as Cass handed it to me, and I knew I never wanted to look at it ever again.

We went out back to a sort of forge, Cass's workshop Jake said, and she bound the book together as tight as she could with the chains, wrapping it in metal, metal like her robotic hands. She took seven different locks, and locked them here and there in pivotal areas that would keep the chains bound the strongest. She offered me the keys, but I shook my head, and she crushed every one of the keys in her hands, dropping the twisted metal to the earth.

I sighed in relief, as I held it covered in chains and bound for eternity.

And the book started burning.

I dropped it as the searing chains seared my hands, and it started laughing, and laughing, and laughing, a horrible, evil, demonic laughter.

Jake immediately kicked a bunch of dirt on the burning, laughing book, burying it in earth, and Cass took me inside to douse my hands in water as I screamed and cried in terror and pain.

"I will never read again." I said, sitting in the kitchen with my hands submerged in a tub of ice cold water.

"Those burns aren't too bad, and you'll be able to pick up another book." Cass said, "You'll have scars probably for the rest of your life… but you'll be able to use your hands."

"No, I mean I never *want* to read another book again." I said.

"It's just one, bad, evil, awful, terrible, monstrous book that isn't really a book in the first place, so don't feel bad. There are tons of other stories to read, good stories. Want me to give you a book I like to read when I'm feeling down?" Cass said.

"I-I-I don't know. I can't read very well without glasses." I said.

"It's ok. I'll read you the stories then." Cass said, and got something from inside her pocket, a small pocket bible.

She opened up to a page, squinting at the words, and told me about that Jesus fellow.

Huh. I always heard the stories about him whipping and beating his followers or something, or even just some lies that the other demons had told me. I didn't know whether to believe this little book in Cass's robotic hands, but I did like listening. The stories had good morals and a positive attitude, and they gave me just a small, tiny, little bit of… hope. It seemed miniscule compared to the dread the burning book was giving me, but I… I just kept listening to the stories, through such a kind reader, and the little feeling felt like a seed in our garden, and I knew if I treated it right, watered it and fed it sunlight, it would continue to grow.

I think Cass told me every story of Jesus, twice at least, as the day turned into twilight. Jesus was probably my favorite character in the whole book, and even though he was such a pivotal character, and had such a good group of friends, mostly, it seemed like the entire book wasn't even centered around him most of the time.

I wondered at the friend that Jesus had who betrayed him, Judas, who now was killing himself every day in the park in Hell, killing himself the same way he had died in this book... because he had betrayed his friend...

Instead of suspecting Judases all around me, however, I decided I would learn from Judas as well. I would simply learn from his mistake, not commit the same one he did, and not be the Judas instead. I could learn from the damned as well as the holy, because I knew from first hand experience there are both in this life, and each have their stories to tell.

I would even learn something from the Devil, and teach myself how to defeat him.

My head was swirling, thinking about the battle I had unwittingly joined. I was neck deep in the war between Heaven and Hell, and I had to choose a side. I couldn't remain neutral forever. The choice was obviously...

"Fucking Hell, goddamnit!" Jake yelled out, barging inside, "That fucking stupid book keeps on swearing at me! Fucking asshole piece o' shit stupid ass book! How the fuck do we kill it?"

"Have you tried dousing it in water?" Cass said.

"Poured a whole tank on it, and even tried to piss it out! The fucking thing stays lit no matter what I do!" Jake said.

"...Holy water?" Cass said.

I said, "I don't think anyone *can* destroy Satan. But we can at least keep him bound in a book for a while."

Cass said, "God must be able to kill him! I'll ask him with every single prayer from now on. I'll start now. Our Father who art in Heaven, please kill the Devil-"

"I don't know, Cass. I feel like if God did want to kill the Devil, he would. Maybe he's leaving him alive to suffer some more? Is that how God works? It's kinda like torture, honestly..." I said.

Cass said, "...Um, I don't think that's how God works. I think there's a reason he wouldn't have killed him... Forgiveness! God is offering Satan forgiveness. Yeah. That's right! Satan just has to say sorry!"

"But Satan will never say sorry for pretty much anything, I think. If he is, he's just trying to pull the wool over your eyes so he can steal the rest of your stuff." I said.

"...I really am not sure then, Hana. Perhaps we should just bury it in the dirt and forget about it." Cass said.

I shook my head, "Someone is just going to dig up the burning book again one day, and in the end they'll be stuck with the same problem. We can't just bury our problems for later, for someone else's later, forever. Even if the world turns to dust, the burning book will still linger. I believe it's my responsibility to carry it while I can, so I may one day figure out, if not to destroy the burning book completely, to at least try to live with it."

"I just want to rip it up, fucking thing makes me so mad..." Jake said.

I shrugged, "It's really not a bad book. I mean enjoyably, not morally. The Devil is rather a dark comedian, a morally black villain, a horribly terrifying monster, and all around great antagonist. Half the time I am rooting for him in the Bible, since he's so diabolical and wicked, because we are sometimes just as wicked as he. And I have sympathy for the Devil, living in Hell, trapped for eternity... now bound to a book, bound to me. I don't think I could tear apart a story like his, just because I don't like the first sentence. Let's try something."

We went out to the forge, my shield in my hand just in case, and looked at the burning book, still burning, although smelling slightly of burning urine. Cass had her hands held together in prayer as we saw it, but Jake just started badmouthing the book as the book badmouthed him back.

I cut in between their never ending insults, and said to the Devil, "Sorry for binding you in a book."

"*...You're saying fucking sorry? To me? What kind of trick is this?*" the burning book said.

"I just think it kinda sucks, is all. You had everything, well, I mean maybe you had more than this, but now you're trapped as a book forever. It kinda makes me sad." I said.

"*I... I'll escape. And torture you. A lot.*" the book said.

"I don't really mind if you feel that way. I'd feel like doing that too." I said.

"*I feel rather annoyed at you. I'll get you, someday.*" the book said.

"I know you will! And you'll get your pluck back up someday, too! I have faith in you!" I said.

The book stopped burning, and seemed rather like its inner flame had gone out as well.

I slowly went to the book where the chains had actually melted off of it, and picked it up in my hands. It looked just like a normal book, and I brought it to my breast and gave it a hug.

Poor guy had it coming being in a book, and poor guy had it coming getting a hug. He deserved both actions, like any damned soul, and I think I finally understood why my mother was so nice to all the demons in Hell like she was. It takes a lot to give the sinners and awful monsters of the world at least our sympathy.

For one day, we may even be alongside them in Hell, and I'd rather like it if they gave me sympathy just as much.

I then dropped the book to the dirt.

38

Instead of going back to school right away, I decided I wanted to learn something from Cass and Jake. Cass was the most beautiful, righteous, kind woman who was also a cyborg, and even knew a lot about machinery and metals. Jake was a crude, foul mouthed, three eyed man with tons of scars all over him from some past life of his, but he was pretty funny. They had already sent one of their workers, galloping off to the school on one of Cass and Jake's horses, to tell them where I was, and he just got back this afternoon.

"I don't think anyone even knew I was missing..." I said.

Cass said, "Hogwash! Last time anyone went missing, Lux stopped all classes and put everyone on lockdown! We found that poor couple trying to elope, starving in the wilderness, shivering and about to die. One of our riders found them *just* in time. We all care when someone goes missing unexplained, and Jake and I especially try to help with cases like that. Our horses are fast, and our workers are savvy."

The messenger dismounted, smiled at us sitting on the front porch, and said, "They were all very relieved we found you, Hana. Lux doesn't know whether to give you a detention or a big hug when you get back, but I told him he can do both as soon as you feel better on the ranch."

Cass said, "Very smart, Zeus. Are you ready to work on the horseshoes?"

"Oh yeah. I've been tired of riding all day and night, and could use something else to take my mind off my aching butt." Zeus said and smiled.

"Zeus? How'd you get that name?" I asked.

"When I strike the metal… it's like lightning!" Zeus said, and grinned.

Cass whispered in my ear, "Or when he takes the ladies to bed. He used to be a prostitute for a good while, and that's how he got the name."

I blushed. Zeus did look rather good looking, even with, especially with, his long luscious locks, big beard, and bulging, hardened muscles.

Cass and Zeus first showed me what they knew of metal and forging, and it was something new to me. I tried to learn from them as well, trying to copy Zeus's lightning smashes on the anvil, and I made a weak little tink with the hammer on the heated metal instead.

"Don't worry, little lady, it just takes practice. You'll be whacking out metal that's as strong as Heaven's gates if you just keep whackin'." Zeus said.

I looked at him, smiling an encouraging smile, and so I whacked again, close to the heat. It sounded almost like music if you hit the metal right.

Cass and Zeus whacked endlessly through the day, even working on forging a few other projects of theirs, but I was exhausted pretty quickly, so I took up my shield and went inside to get some lemonade.

I slurped on the cool lemonade, and heard the sound of an axe, thunk, thunk, thunk.

I looked out the window to the backyard, and saw Jake chopping firewood. He wasn't swearing, and looked so serious as he chopped each piece of wood, so efficiently making the log split in half. It really didn't seem like he used as much force as Zeus and Cass did whacking metal, and somehow just seemed to know how to cut the log just right.

I was a little terrified he would turn that axe on me, and chop me in half like he was doing to that wood, and I hid behind my shield from him.

Jake invited me to learn something from him, and he took me to the animals of theirs. "Seweet. Look at that fat 'un… She's gonna be a tasty bit of bacon, ain't she?" Jake said, looking at his pigs.

I stared at that big mama pig, letting piglets suckle from her teats.

"Y-You'd have to kill her then, right?" I asked.

"Yes, but I make sure they don't see the blade coming, so the meat tastes better and isn't ruined by fear. Are you squeamish? I can show you how to slice up some carcasses for the meat if you like." Jake said.

I looked back at the cute mama pig with her family, and said, "How can you kill that mama and her babies??"

Jake looked at me with his three eyes, blinked them all, and said, "It's just food, Hana. If we want to keep living, something else needs to die. Even potatoes are dug up from the ground, because we got a starving belly."

"…Y-Yes… That's true. Took me a good while to realize where all that food comes from, first from people who grow them, like you and Cass, and then from people who deliver them, like Yule and Lucius… I am sort of interested in learning about how to cut up a pig, then. All I learned how to do was cut up people…" I said.

"…Uh, ok. You aren't some sort of crazy sadist, are you?" he asked.

"I know how to keep people in pain, and used to enjoy it-" I said.

"Get the fuck away from me, and jus' go hang with Cass some more." Jake said, and walked away swearing under his breath.

What had I said?

We had dinner, but Jake worked long into the night, so it was only Cass and I with her great cooking.

"You say something to piss him off?" Cass said, "He never misses a meal. Sorry if he gets a little moody sometimes."

"I don't know. I was about to impress him with my knowledge of cutting up human bodies, and my learnings in pain and how to prolong it or make it end, but he just told me to get away from him." I said.

"...Oh dear. I know you learned quite a few different things in Hell, but Jake doesn't like talking about that kind of stuff." Cass said.

"Why, though? He was telling me he could teach me how to chop up an adorable family of pigs!" I said.

"He doesn't kill because he likes it, Hana. He kills if it's a necessity for us, and I think he just got a taste for bacon over the years... He used to be an executioner for a prison, and all those scars on him were wounds he put on himself, because he hated his job after taking each human life, so tried to give himself close to the pain the condemned knew under his blade. He always explains that he thought he was doing good being an executioner, taking lives efficiently... but I can always tell by the tone in his voice, the look in his eyes... that those were the worst days of his life." Cass said.

"Oh. I'll tell him I'm sorry then. I know that it is difficult taking lives, even if you are the greatest angel of death in all creation." I said.

"Good. Offer him one of our beers, and he'll forgive you in a second." Cass said, and smiled.

I got a beer from the fridge, went out to the back porch to see Jake still chopping wood, and said, "Want a beer, Jake? You look thirsty."

He stopped chopping, looked at me, looked at the beer, and said, "Yeah, ok. Toss her here."

I threw him the beer which he caught in a hand, axe in the other, and he sat on the stump he was chopping wood on, and drank the frothy mixture. I sat on the back porch steps, and said, "It takes a lot of guts to be an executioner. I've only seen a few deaths in life, and all of them were terrible. I'm sorry you had to go through that, and for bringing up memories of those days."

"Yeah, well, I was just paying the bills. It was just another form o' work. Nothing special, nothing gutsy-" Jake started saying, but I saw that tortured look in his eyes, and heard it in his voice.

I said, "I'm glad you have a good life now."

He looked at me, sipped on the beer, and said, "Well, thanks. Took a lot o' trial and error, but I found a good woman to spend some time with, and that time turned into a long time, and now we got a ranch. It is a good life, yeah."

"You mean you had no goal in making this good life? Or even just sticking with Cass in marriage for eternity? Why aren't you and Cass husband and wife, anyway?" I asked.

"Of course someone who lived in actual Hell talks about why I'm not married… I just *knew* marriage was the Devil's chains…" Jake said.

I looked at the chain burns on my hands, and sighed.

Jake noticed, and said, "…Sorry, Hana. What I mean is, it just sort of happened, while I was trying to survive. Things got better and better, and I finally stopped cutting myself when a woman told me how wrong that was, and I continued my life instead of living in pain o' the past."

I said, "I can see how Cass would make you want to stop hurting yourself and live life."

"Well, she helped, yeah, but it was actually when I was datin' Yule that I stopped hurtin' myself. Then I got with Cass… and wow, sparks were coming off o' us the first few times, and now it's just like constant electricity. It takes a lot of tries to find someone who can fuck you that way." Jake said.

"…I feel like all of you who belonged to my mother's old gang just lived in tents and made constant love with each other…" I said.

"…Is that a bad thing? It was a good use o' time, if anything." Jake said.

I laughed, and said, "No, I guess not. Man! I don't know why I spent all that time just trying to be married, for Christ's sake! If all of you can just find that perfect, orgasmic bliss and even have a great life at the end with someone without even trying for that life or marriage, then I think I'd just like to have some fun with someone for a while too, and worry about what comes later, later."

Jake grinned, and said, "Glad I could give you some hope for the future. But remember what the end game o' our bodies are, too. Makin' damn kids like you. I'm actually kinda worried that Cass is- You know, because she gets kinda moody sometimes without explaining why…"

"Really? I hadn't noticed. She seems very cheerful." I said.

"That's what worries me. She's in a different mood… She's fuckin' joyful as all fuck." Jake said, and finished his beer and crushed it.

39

Inspired by passing by the forge and looking at Zeus smash out lighting, I went inside to draw something.

I listened to the sound of his strength while making art, and I was feeling very heated when I finished the nude picture of Zeus, that didn't even need too much fantasy. In fact, if I drew anything bigger it would just look silly.

I wondered if he- If I could see this sight of him for real.

I shakily gave him my drawing, and he opened his eyes in surprise, smiled and said, "I really do look like Zeus! Wow. Have you been spying on me in the showers or something?"

"N-No, b-but I-I w-was wondering... If you and I c-could- I feel so embarrassed..." I said, blushing so, so red.

He sat me gently down by the workbench, and said, "It's ok, Hana. I got that a lot in my past life, so I took advantage of it and sold my skills. But you know... I really am working here to get away from all of that."

"Oh. So you won't make love with me in the golden wheat fields until I can barely move and you have to carry me back in your strong arms until I get my energy back? And then make more love?" I said.

He laughed, and said, "I'm sorry, Hana. Maybe when you're older, perhaps. You're a very beautiful young woman, but I think you should try and find someone who will rock your heart as well as your body, and not just fantasize over mine. At least for now."

"B-But you do make me feel that way. You're so kind, and seem like a very good man. I think being with you would be an experience I could never have, and is what I strive to achieve." I said.

He sighed calmly, and said, "That's why I worked for so long selling my body, because I was good at giving the mind pleasure as well. The most erogenous part of the body is not the sexual organ, but the brain. Still. I think you can find a better lay than with an old guy like me, in actual young love. It wouldn't be right of me giving you an experience that would only be a pale comparison to an actual relationship."

"Oh… Ok, that makes sense. I'm dating an actual angel of love right now, but I ran away from everyone, and he lives far away up in the clouds, working and studying all the time." I said.

"An angel of love? Well howdy! If you can snag someone you can call that, then you're on the right track already. Don't be tempted, because… in great love, there's also great sex." Zeus said.

I smiled at him, and said he should keep that drawing, because otherwise I'll never get his body out of my head. He thanked me for the picture, folded it nicely, and put it in his pocket.

I carried my shield on my back, and went out back to the compost to throw out some corn cobs from the corn we had last night, where Cass threw the burning book after it burned me. It smelled pretty awful, as the compost burned underneath it.

"*…Wanna read some steamy stories?*" it said.

"You smell literally like burning garbage, Devil. It's not the most erogenous sensation." I said.

"*Please? Just give me a chance? One last try, to show I'm sorry to you as well?*" the burning book said.

I sighed, and said, "Only because you really do look pretty pitiful on old melon rinds and something I don't even *want* to know what is."

I picked up the book that stopped burning, and took it back to the back porch, sat with it, and opened it back up.

I read for a long time, of love, war, beauty, death, and life... in between the blatantly hottest erotica I have ever experienced. It made my mind and body feel like it was on fire.

It even said this could be even better in my dream of marital bliss, and that really the only reason I hadn't experienced it for real was because that feeling can only be found with one other.

It offered me a chance to make this dream real, as I was close to absolute orgasm just with words, and asked me a very specific, special question that I had been waiting for someone to ask me for a long time, but never heard before.

So I answered. I said, *"Yes!"*

And my God, I just felt like my entire body was exploding in absolute pleasure.

I panted, in just so much happiness, and I decided to put my signature on my new favorite book.

I opened the cover, as the book said, *"Wa-Wait, what are you doing-"*

And I pierced my finger with a sharp nail that I had found earlier that day lying in the forge, and signed my name with it in blood, on my book, Hanatrix.

Hanatrix, the first and only name on the burning book.

But someone screeched out of the sky and in front of me in a pale car, looking absolutely, extremely furious, and I smiled at him.

Max got out of the car, slammed the door, and said, "I've had enough of this, Hana. I'm taking you back home."

"What? Cass and Jake are so nice, though, and I really feel good right now-" Max said.

"I'm taking you back to the school, Hana, where you won't be seduced by evil incarnate." Max said.

I immediately felt sobered, sobered from the evil I was letting corrupt my mind. I dropped the book to the ground, and the book said, *"It was fun leading you on... But you just sullied your mind with trash, Hana. Filthy smut, and now you're a filthy slut too. And now you belong to me. You're just Satan's Slut, Hana."*

Max shouted in anger at the book, "NEVER TALK TO HER. Hana belongs to NO ONE. You will NEVER write your name on a daughter of GOD! I will take this monster back to Hell, and you can spend the rest of your life, in life, Hana." picked up the burning book, and told me to get in the car, *now.*

I did, shield clanging on my back as I got in quickly. Max drove with one hand, and held the burning book tightly in his other. It seemed to cause him pain in his hand, but he did not let it go.

40

I groaned, putting my face to my hands... I just wish I could erase that whole chapter from my life...

It was just another stupid, awful, ugly, twisted, messed up fantasy... I thought it was just words! I *never* knew I could feel such shame just from reading a book...

"I failed. I failed life, God, you, and everyone. I was seduced, and I fell into the seduction." I said.

"...It will be ok, Hana." Max said.

The burning book laughed, *"HAHAHAHAHA!! You've bound your very SOUL TO ME!! Fucking Satan! You're fucking stuck now, you dumb, idiot, bimbo, witch, bitch, cunt, SLUT!!"*

"I TOLD YOU NEVER TO TALK TO HER!!" Max yelled at the burning book in his hand.

"...Why didn't you stop me, Max?" I asked.

"I can't interfere with your choices, Hana. Whatever fate you make on Earth is what you choose in life. To break the wall... would be awful. I am already doing as much as I can, simply watching, being your guardian angel... and letting you get in the pale car before your time. I never forced you to travel with Death, and I sure won't make you learn from me.

"I just had enough of screaming in anger, as I was seeing you write your name on a burning book. This book shouldn't exist, Hana. It is not really a book. It has no basis in reality at all. But somehow, in our world… it does, because you brought it here." Max said.

"…You're my guardian angel?" I asked.

"It's my side hobby. I'm really kind of amateurish at it, because I only really am one for Yule. But I can make an exception to be one for you too." Max said.

"C-Could you t-teach me to be a guardian an-angel for someone? Would you be able to?" I asked.

"I think you should focus on being alive in the living world, and I can try to get everything straightened out with this stupid burning book…" Max said.

"Please give it back to my mother." I said.

"I have a better idea. You take me, or burn like you did for a little while, as I did in Hell. Put your burning hands around my burning body, baby." the book said.

And my chain scars started burning, and burning, and burning.

And I just screamed and screamed.

As the book laughed.

Max shouted to the burning book in his hand, "I WILL NOT LET YOU HAVE YOUR TORTURE ON HANA-"

I said, "It's ok, Max. Please. It hurts. Give me the book."

It looked like it took Max all he could, but as he saw me in pain, being tortured as I had tortured demons before… he gently gave me the book.

The book tried to say something disgusting, but I said, "Do you want me to tell everyone that sexy story you told me? How you- and then we- over and over- Because I will. I'll let everyone know the Devil has a thing for a teenage girl."

"…So? I'm the Devil." the book said.

"And how you even proposed to the Princess of Hell, so that we could be bound forever... and have that orgasmic bliss you were describing oh so well. Would you like me to tell everyone that? I'm sure my mother would bless our matrimony." I said.

"*...No. I don't want another stupid bitch like a mother in law to ruin my life... because... she'd actually make me go through with it...*" the book said.

"Exactly. Because I *did* accept... So it'll be our little secret, just a fantasy, that no one ever needs to know about. You are *not* the most powerful being of creation, or even that of Hell. A mother in law of Hell is worse than you, Satan." I said.

I looked to Max with the burning book in my hands, and his face was completely white, just like his white hoodie, actually. But then he... he started laughing. He just started laughing his ass off, crying in laughter.

"Oh- HAHA... Oh my God, Hana... Mother in law of Hell- Hoohoo... I'm... Ok, I'll teach you to be a guardian angel... even though you have a seriously big problem on your hands, in your hands- that's just a weak little- HAHA! He's afraid of your mama!" Max said.

I smiled, and said, "My mama's so bad, she eats chips of fire and spits out the chips."

"HAHA! Not a yo mama joke, a *my* mama joke... Hehe... Spitting out the chips, cuz she ate the fire instead... HAHA!!"

"You have the weirdest sense of humor, Max." I said.

"I didn't know you had *any* sense of humor! Let's take you home, and we'll think about what to do with the book tomorrow." Max said, sighing out and smiling.

"If we can, can I see my mother again? I really miss her." I said.

"Yes, Hana. Let's go drive down to Hell and see yo big bad mama where she'll-" I said.

I looked at Max expectantly for the joke he was going to make, and he burst out laughing at just the look on my face, and we laughed down to Hell.

Max just said, "Oh." when he saw my mama literally spit out the chips and eat the fire. It was always the best brand in Hell, and it really was the fire that made it good. I could never eat the stuff, cuz you know, it's on fire. But my mama could.

And somehow she knew everything that happened to me, no matter that I didn't tell her...

We sat at the dining room table, Cerberus sleeping underneath it by my mother's feet, the sound of my mother spitting the chips into a bowl, and she said, "So my daughter is dating an angel of love, learning from an angel of death, and wants to be a guardian angel. I think you've got to get your head out of the clouds, Hana...

"You also bound your soul to the Devil in a promise of marriage. Well, after you two say the real yes, at least we know he'll ditch you right away, like your last boyfriend, what's it... Asmodeus? The Demon of Lust? And then we can get Satan to pay alimony or something. But I'll be glad to annul this promise of yours, Hana, and we never have to speak of such a disgusting thing again." my mother said.

The burning book said, *"But she's bound to me! I'm the literal Devil! She can't escape my clutches or my eternal wra-"*

"I don't care what you think my daughter can't do, but she sure as my Hell will not have children with a book. It's just not feasible for the long run of our line and continuing our surname. Sorry." my mom said.

"Why can't she just take my surname?" the Devil said.

"And be what? Be Hanatrix... You don't even have a last name. You have two first names, and then some Devil nickname." my mom said.

"...What is Hana's last name, anyway?" the burning book said.

"Great. You ask my daughter to marry you, and you don't even know her last name. You really *are* Lucifer..." my mom said, spit out another chip, and said, "Where is the boy that you are dating, Hana? Does he not also wish to explain how he wants to marry my daughter and give her fantastic, orgasmic bliss she is always tempting every man with?"

"Um... I think he's busy working..." I said.

"Too busy to see me? The Queen of Hell? He has the nerve to not even show up and grovel before my feet? Ok, I like him already. If he really *is* working, then maybe we can finally bring in some outside income. Your father did all he could, was the top... something, some silly job in Hell, lawyer, head CEO, whatever, but he was never satisfied with those jobs in the least, and could never get enough cash because he always switched jobs on the fly to follow his 'passion.'"

Max said, "...Why don't you just force everyone to give you money? Or just the stuff you would spend it on?"

"We live in a community, down here in Hell, Max. I am not a tyrant who wishes things into her hands. We work, as my husband worked, before he passed trying to get Hana to a place where she'll learn more life skills, *to work*." my mother said.

Max said, "...But work isn't everything about life."

"Yes, that is true, but I don't believe living in literal Paradise like you're teaching her how to do will teach Hana how to value that life. She'll just sing ladidadida, and think everything is so pleasant and won-derful, and only *look* at what happens down on Earth, and maybe take a cursory glance at Hell. I know you were watching over Hana, and I'm grateful for that, and I know that God watches always, and that BS... But you only watched, when she was burning her hands. I suppose now she knows fire hurts... but you still didn't need to let her touch the flame. I would've snatched her away in a second, but as per our peace agreement, Hell cannot invade the living world anymore." my mom said.

I said, "Mom, I know I've disappointed you… but I can't spend my entire everything under you in Hell. I need to burn my hands every now and then, and I'm learning so much in the living world, and from my teachers like Max, and have great friends and even a boyfriend."

"I thought you ran away from your friends or something." my mom said.

"…I did… but I realize that was actually quite selfish of me. They were actually trying to invite me into their fun, but I was only thinking how I wanted it to be *my* fun." I said.

She spit out another chip, and said, "I understand you also were feeling bad about your father. I felt that way too… and I've got a place for that man that killed him when he comes down here."

Max said, "You really don't know his full story-"

"I don't need to. He belongs to *me*. We can hear all about his story when he dies and becomes my servant or something. That will be quite a Hell for him… serving the wife of a man he murdered. Every wicked glance, every order that he *will submit to*… but he will be a part of a community in our Hell." my mother said.

Max said, "…Very well. I'll give this one to you."

They were about to shake hands, but I slammed my shield on the table, and said, "I'm going to be that man's guardian angel, and I will let none of you take him but me. He will live a long, fantastic life under my guardianship, because I will make him forever see Hell in life, as he saw my face before. He will wonder why? Why is she saving my life? And eventually he will feel such *torment* that he will try to kill himself, and I will prevent him from doing so, and remind him of the life that he took."

My mother and Max looked at me surprised, and stopped before they could shake.

My mother cleared her throat, and said, "It seems you really did learn something from that hellish high school."

I smiled, and said, "Not really. I had the best teacher growing up instead, a mother that I care for and will do anything for me. Love you, Mom!"

"L-Love you too, Hana. I don't think… you've ever said that first to me." my mom said, and tears started welling in her eyes, and she started crying. I sat beside her, and gave her a hug.

41

I shoved the burning book in my bag again. *"Why are you even keeping me? Your mother broke my binds on you. I can't do jack shit to you. Even my fire is just a tickle now."* the burning book said.

"I still got scars, to remind me of the fire, and you got my first name on you. I don't really know, actually. I guess I can show you off and brag that I got the Devil to offer me marriage." I said.

"...You're not the first I've offered marriage to, Hana." the book said.

"I know, but how many girls can say they've got the Devil wrapped around their middle finger?" I said.

"...Clever. I seriously hope you never get some damn ring to announce your marriage to me. That's actually kind of embarrassing, and sounds like something some crazy witch chick would do-" the burning book said.

"Oh! That actually sounds kind of cool! An engagement ring! It'll only be just that, an engagement ring for eternity, but hey! That'll sure make Set try harder to steal me away!" I said.

"...You're really the Princess of Hell." the Devil said.

"Got *that* right! Let's go talk to my ma, and see what she wants to tell me before we go back up... my *fiancé!*" I said.

The burning book grumbled in my bag, and I waved to Judas who was having a hard time getting down after he killed himself again. I asked him, "What are you doing? Do you need any help?"

"I just didn't think this death was horrible enough. It should've been tied looser so it would be longer, and not an actual noose knot so I could suffer by choking to death instead." Judas said.

"I think you need to take a rest. You've been doing this every day in Hell. Just sit by the gnashing flowers for a while and relax, ok?" I said.

"...But..." Judas said.

"Trust me, you can kill yourself again later. It will feel ten times worse knowing you put off your suffering, as your mind wriggles in doubt for your actions. Just give not dying a while a chance, and I'm sure Hell will surprise you with awfulness that you could never imagine." I said.

Judas said, *"Ok. That does sound like it'll be even worse. Thanks, Hana. Please, don't help me down, because I'll feel more suffering trying to free myself again as I claw at the ropes with my fingers bleeding from trying so hard."*

"No problem! Have fun, Judas!" I said, and walked down the path as I heard him scratching at the ropes and whimpering.

I met my mother, Dina the Queen of Hell, in the middle of the actual center of Hell, which all had its eternal hellish circumference around this point. I looked at the monument that had been built, and I gasped at its splendor.

"This place was where I took my first step in a completely conquered Hell. Do you like the monument I put up?" my mom said.

"But that's not a monument of you." I said.

"No, it isn't. A few generals of mine are on the sides, over there, eternally remembered... for their betrayal." my mom said.

I looked at the statue of Molech, the statue of Darcy, the statue of Georgia. Molech looked like he was eternally trying to moo from his cow head, and Darcy and Georgia, two succubi, were eternally locked trying to stab each other in the back.

"Didn't Beleth help you conquer Hell, too?" I said.

"Oh yes. I'm saving his statue for another day." my mom said.

"...Those other statues don't seem like monuments of glory." I said.

"No, they aren't. Those ones actually are not really statues..." my mother said.

"...Then why is this monument to Dad so... good looking?" I said.

"Because he betrayed me the most out of all of them, and still escaped my clutches... in eternal Paradise." my mom said.

"...How did he betray you?" I said.

"He conquered me, when I had conquered this entire realm, about to set my goals on life, and then Heaven, and then all else. I would've raised you to inherit this Queendom, as your children would, throughout eternity's eternity. We would've gone past the veil, broken the veil, and we would be masters of absolutely *everything*.

"But he... He showed me something I could never conquer. A pure heart that felt the same way to me as I did him." my mom said.

I held my mom's hand, as she looked up at Dad. "Is this what you wanted to show me? I'm glad you did. It is a nice monument. He looks so happy, kneeling before us and offering that ring."

"I guess. It made *me* horribly frustrated that he didn't try to weasel out of me suggesting he marry me, and then I had to follow through with it when he actually proposed. I wouldn't have minded being just eternal lovers, and I feel like marriage is really only words describing the action of love... But no, I wanted to show you how to see past the veil." my mom said.

"...What? Really? I... I don't know if I want to be able to do that, yet." I said.

"But you can break the rules, you *are* the rules, when you just have enough knowledge that only very few can ever grasp at, or even comprehend." my mother said, looking seriously into my eyes.

"I don't think I want to cheat at existence. It's no fun winning a game that you make stuff up for. I'd win no matter what, and it wouldn't be very fair." I said.

"...Are you sure? I'm offering you unlimited power." my mom said.

"Yes. But I would like… just a peak. I'm a little curious of this mystical behind the veil you're always telling me about." I said.

She smiled, looked deep into my eyes...

I looked into hers...

And her eyes turned black.

I looked at the writer who tried to describe what I'm seeing through his eyes.

I saw God smile and wave at me when he saw me looking.

And I looked even further.

Maybe you'll see it too, if you look into my mother's eyes.

Or maybe you'll look into mine, as I am currently looking into yours.

Do you know what color my eyes are?

Because if you do, you've seen past the veil.

I blinked, and looked back into my mother's eyes which were its normal color again.

42

Sara hugged me with her strong muscles at the school after Max brought me back, and I said to her, "I'm sorry for being so dumb…"

"I was so worried, Hana!! We looked everywhere, even though the teachers told us to stay put… The Champions of the Gargoyle were eager to find their grandmaster!!" Sara said.

"Oh, it's alright. You can call the club anything you want, and I don't need to be our grandmaster… Thank you for caring, though. You guys are my best friends." I said.

Sara wiped the tears out of her eyes, squeezed me again, and said, "You mean a lot to me, Hana. And I think of you as my best friend here."

I squeezed her as well, and said, "You were my first friend here, and were always the best."

She let me go, smiling, and said, "We really were just fighting about what to call the guild anyway, and it got out of hand. That whole party we had was a mush, as we all hoped you would come back sometime and drink and smoke with us, but you didn't. The beer got us too drunk, the pot was too heavy, and we just sat around after using it too much, in a fucking silent circle, throwing up occasionally. Mr. Loren and Mrs. Loren enjoyed their beer, though, and I could hear them laughing and singing all through the night in the teacher's building."

"Again, I'm sorry for being such a dumb, idiot, stupid, bi-" I said.

"Don't insult yourself, Hana. You don't need it, and I won't have it."
Sara said, crossing her muscly arms.

"Ok." I said and smiled.

Sara took me by the arm and walked with me, explaining what was
new, silly gossip and little things about the school that she somehow was
in tune with, and she said, "The new boy looks like a *god* or something...
I swear he must've come down from Heaven."

"That's nice. Are you and Dill still going out?" I said.

"Well, Dill and I really like making out, so we're going to just do
that sometimes. We really aren't sure if we are going to keep going with
each other, but it's nice to have someone to smooch who's such a kind
friend. Anyway, that new boy... He came in here with nothing but some
sort of short, skimpy, white skirt on, that really showed off his muscular
thighs... and no shirt! It was quite a hassle for the teachers to get him
something real to wear, because he said he wanted to 'make a good
impression...' He sure made one, I think! The girls and I were practically
ripping the rest of that garment off! And somehow, he survived in the
wastes, looking really healthy and fit, with nothing but a *bow*... You
think he's some sort of wild man like Tarzan? Or maybe he's just a savvy
stripper. There he is, over there. Let's go ask him." Sara said.

I looked over to where Sara was pointing, and saw the new boy
dressed in a pink hoodie and jeans, crowded in a cloud of girls. As soon
as he saw me, he shouted out, "Hana!" and the girls parted for him like
the Red Sea.

I gasped, and said, "Set!! What- How-"

We ran to each other, and he lifted me up in a big hug.

"I'm so happy to see you again! I had this whole big thing for you set
up, to surprise you as my girlfriend, but then everything fell apart, and
you were even missing! I was so worried!" Set said.

"You're a cheater!!" I said, smiling at him.

"...Huh? No! I never spent time with any other girls, I actually have been trying my hardest to get them to leave me alone by smiling nicely at them and politely telling them I had to continue my studies in love, but I came here only for you!" Set said.

I laughed, and said, "You probably shouldn't say you want to learn in love, Set, or else they'll all want to teach you... first hand, in hand. I meant that you cheated at existence! You're not supposed to be alive!"

Sara was gawking at us, cleared her throat, and said, "...So the witch chick has the new boy... Great. And I've only got Dill. See you at the next meeting, Hana, I'm going to go work out..." and she pushed past me and Set, pushing right through our hug, and fumed down the hall.

"...What's the problem with her, Hana? Sara has really been a very welcoming person to me, as I hear she has for everyone in this school..." Set said.

I sighed, and said, "You're going to have to learn about a feeling called jealousy, Set. I felt that way about her relationship, and I think she feels that way about ours."

"Want me to talk to her? I can explain that jealousy is a very twisty emotion, but if dwelled on in love it can only bring everything apart." Set said.

"I think if that came from you it will only make things worse. I'll talk to her alone. Try not to get groped by the girls too much." I said, and winked. He blushed, as I left after Sara. Set tried to defend himself from the cloud of girls who quickly enveloped him again, seeing their chance to attack, like seeing a calf separated from the herd. I'd be back to defend my boyfriend soon, but I had to placate my best friend first.

I found Sara grunting in the gym, curling weights alone. The boys just let her work out in peace, and actually seemed to have a sense of comradery with her. She asked one of the guys to spot her as she bench pressed, and got under the bar and lifted probably an actual ton of weight, with a frustrated, angry look on her face.

I waited for her to be done lifting weights, and she said to the muscular boy, "Thanks Joe. I was thinking you and I could-"

"Sorry, Sara. Me and Meg have been really warming up to each other. It's not that I don't think you're pretty… but aren't you going with Dill, anyway?" the muscular boy said.

Sara grumbled, and charged off to the locker room. I followed behind her at a distance, and crept after her.

I waited patiently for her to finish taking a shower. She sang a song as she bathed alone that had cheerful lyrics, but sounded sad as she sang. She sang,

"Cockadoodle doo, and the cow goes moo,

It's time to wake up, and go to school.

There's friends to play with, lessons to learn,

There's people to see, and I have butter to churn,

So set off to school, dear daughter,

I'll be here at home, dear daughter,

For as long as the cow goes moo,

I'll be here, dear daughter, for another cockadoodle doo."

She got dressed, and she finally noticed me as she sat on the bench in front of her locker, and she said, "What, Hana?"

"I just want to say sorry. It seems like you had your eyes set on Set-" I said.

"Ohhh, ok, just come to rub it in? Flaunt your new boy toy in my face? Go back to Hell, Hana…" Sara said.

"…I never thought I'd get that reaction out of you." I said.

She slammed her locker door, and said, "Sorry. I just am extremely pissed how you can just disappear, let us spend a week looking for you, and then you come back and you just get the guy without even trying. He just- Like I wasn't even there!"

"I'll tell him that was rather rude and inconsiderate. But we *have* agreed to be boyfriend/girlfriend, and I think he was missing me as I was him." I said.

"But- How?? That guy looked like he just poofed onto the Earth from somewhere magical! It don't make no sense, and it's a little suspicious! Yeah! I bet he's some secret spy to disband the school, or even like you and came up from the bowels of Hell to destroy the Earth!" Sara said.

"...I didn't come here to destroy the Earth. I just came to learn, and live a life that wasn't in shitty Hell." I said.

"Fuck, sorry! I don't mean to offend you! It's hard believing any of your crazy shit, but still, you show us an evil fucking book that's actually the Devil, and it turned my whole life upside down! I don't know what to fucking believe, and in our meetings you tell us just to not believe anything anyway!! It just makes me pissed!" Sara said, "You're nice, and kind, and obviously have some sort of good heart to make that guy fall for you, but I don't get it, and I really wish someone would just be able to tell me what to do! I don't want a guy like Dill as my boyfriend, who I tell what to do and he fucking listens politely and actually obeys! It's just- I don't know!!"

I said, "I think he's only listening to you and doing what you wish because he cares for you, Sara. You even told him you liked that, once, and he listened and heard. I don't mean to be cryptic in our meetings... I only thought it would add a little mystique to forbidden lore, because really, it's just a bunch of bullshit, concocted by evil people to get others to do what they say."

"...Why are we even learning about that crap then?" Sara said.

I shrugged, and said, "We don't have to, but it was a sweet aroma to draw you all in to be my friends, and then clutch you in my embrace like a Venus fly trap. We don't have to continue studying it, as I think we've all evolved past that as a group of friends, instead of some cult. I did name it the Champions of the Gargoyle for a reason, so that we can be stronger than evil, and wouldn't be hemmed into studying any one sort of knowledge."

"...You're just some lonely bitch, who wanted friends. I'm... I'm sorry. I... I won't be so mad at you anymore. You deserve to have a good friend, a boyfriend, who will listen to you too. Heck, you've been alone all year, and I was starting to think you were like Lita and just had a secret love for the same sex, or even just some weird, twisted fetish that you didn't want people to know about." Sara said.

"Nah, I've just been trying to learn about love my own way, with a fantasy to only fall in love if someone wishes to marry me, but I realize that's actually quite childish. Love just sort of happens, and can't be planned exactly. Hey... that's actually a good line. I'm gonna tell Set that. I think he'd like to hear some words of wisdom from his girl-friend." I said.

Sara smiled, and said, "You gonna teach him how to love, like he's always saying he wants to learn how? That's gonna be quite a sight, but it'll be interesting seeing what you both try to figure out yourself. Dude's like a babe in the woods when it comes to the ladies, which is partly why we were all after him. Easy love is tempting."

I smiled to her, and said, "I will teach him all that I can, then! First off, to not go for easy love, because that most *definitely* will lead to regret... Did I tell you I was offered marriage by someone other than my boyfriend? And I accepted? It was like, the worst mistake of my life."

Sara said, "...No fucking way. That sounds crazy- That sounds un-believable. Are you still going to follow through with it?"

"God no. The guy only wanted to get in my head, and was a complete pussy when he met my mother. I suppose I should've expected the Devil to be so disappointing... but I didn't want to doubt such an infamous figure. I'm glad I can just date an angel of love who will treat me much nicer." I said.

"...Again, I'm not sure what to believe here, but... I'll just have to take your word, because I have faith in you, at least." Sara said.

I walked over to her, and gave her a hug. I said to her, "Call Dill Chip instead. He rather likes that name, as it is drawn on a happy memory and previous love. It's all symbols, and I was going to talk about that at our next meeting, as to how they can be used to take sway over the minds of lesser mortals..."

She stopped hugging, held my hands, and said, "...I think I'll call him this other name I've been giving him instead. Love. It always feels silly when I do, but it makes me sort of happy to get my hopes up with my love. Y'know, I just say, 'ey love, get me a beer,' or something like that... but he doesn't know I like calling him that, so I'm going to keep doing it. You think we can just hang out and drink instead of getting all metaphysical? You know, not try too hard?"

"Sure! And very wise using the symbol of love itself to grow love. It's straight to the point, and quite poetic." I said.

We walked out still holding hands, and she said, "We already got 'straight to the point...' It was cool being his first, but he definitely needs some more lessons in love from me..."

I laughed, and said, "Ok, now *I'm* jealous. Tell me all about it!"

She grinned, and said, "Well, I started off, just because he was stuck in make out mode forever, to nip down to his neck..."

I gasped at every new, lovely thing she did for her love, and what he did for her, and listened intently. If it wouldn't have been rude to take out a notebook and jot stuff down, I would've, but I tried to memorize her lesson for me, and if I forgot, it would always just be nice letting things happen naturally and make stuff up as we went along. Just called love!

43

Hmm… This sounded terribly inappropriate, but it was nagging at me, so I whispered in Set's ear, "Um, Set… did Nevaeh… teach you about sex?"

"It's really not so simple to answer that question in either a yes or a no, because I know you're probably thinking about it in a certain way, and not what she actually did…" Set said.

"You can't give me a mysterious answer when I ask if you are making love to your teacher!" I said, "She teaches *love* for Christ's sake! How can she not teach you sex?"

"Because I'm supposed to learn with you, instead of going down the *well travelled* road that Miss Shinto knows." Set said, "If you truly want to know, she said she *could* teach me about bodily love, er, in a more hands on approach, but if I decided to learn that from her… Then I would have to give up on learning with you. I understand that sex is sacred, and by using it in a manner unbefitting to love, to the feeling, manner, and action *of love,* it isn't called making love at all. It is called lust. I would like to make love with you."

That made me blush.

I tried to say it back, but my throat felt very constricted, my heart beat faster, and my muscles tensed up.

He looked at me quizzically as to why I was doing that, and he said, "Do you need some water?"

"I WANT TO MAKE LOVE WITH YOU TOO!" I shouted, and some other people in the library looked at us.

I blushed redder.

"Shh!" the librarian whispered, "Go talk about that in private! I'm trying to read a romantic story, and I don't need it spoiled by two horny kids shouting!"

The librarian put back on her glasses, and smiled into her book, which happened to be another one of Nevaeh Shinto's books. The book's title was Ultimatum of Love.

I went up to the librarian, and asked her what the Ultimatum of Love actually was. She said, looking up from her book, "Hm? Oh it's just a story about a naughty teacher, who falls in love with her student. It's got a lot of drama and sexy stories, as she tries to balance the love between her husband, and her star pupil."

"So… she has sex with her student right away?" I asked.

"Actually, she gives him a choice. The Ultimatum of Love." she said.

"…Which is?" I said.

"You seem quite interested! I'll let you read it. I just need to read… The End! Perfect. Here you go, don't lose it, or I'll bill you as many tokens I can get out of you. Our books are precious, and it took a long while to get all of them in one place like this." the librarian said.

Set walked up next to me, as I stared at the book, and he said, "Oh! That's a good one. I love it when at the end-"

I kissed him, just to shut him up.

"-at the end of her life Miss Shinto puts all her combined life experiences into books, and lets other people enjoy them for a spell. All I did at the end of my life was squirm in my own guts." Set said.

"Oh. Ok. I'll talk to you later, Set. I'm going to read." I said.

"Don't lose your glasses again! It's cool our teacher actually found and repaired them for you. Mr. Lux, right?" Set said.

"Yep! He's pretty great." I said.

"I'm curious how a robot… hmm… Never mind, you'll probably think I'm saying something dirty again, but I'll see you around, Hana!" Set said, and raced out the door, to fulfill some sort of burning curiosity.

I went back to my room to read in private, and only shut the book at the end of the day, finished and satisfied.

It was a very twisty turny romance that the naughty teacher had… She loves two men, and tries to balance it with both of them, one, her husband who had always been faithful, or the other, her star pupil who would do anything to please her.

In the end the teacher gives her student a choice to be with a beautiful young woman his own age, his girlfriend, or her.

But the young man chooses the teacher.

They immediately roll around on the desk… unbuckle belts…

And he actually teaches her a lesson in love instead, with his young body and fresh mind.

Although they had each made a choice in this ultimatum, really, a forbidden love… or everything else. They both lose absolutely everything they had in life, their families, her job and his scholarship… but they each had love. And then it was the end. This was a satisfying story, explaining the nature of love and its give all or take all choices, but it did not relieve my feelings of what Set could've done with his angelic teacher of love.

Then I read the biography at the end of the book…

It said, "Nevaeh Shinto was a first class teacher, professor, and writer of romance. She lived in a small town with her husband, teaching English classes for college and high school students alike. She will be dearly missed in this life, but we know that she will continue to sow the seeds of her love throughout the ages, as a teacher and lover of the written word."

I suppose she had made a choice far before love could give her an ultimatum. She loved books, just as much as I did, and loved teaching, just as much as the teacher in the story did. But she had chosen her true love, her work, and not the young student.

I realized I shouldn't have been so doubtful of myself, or jealous of who Set could love besides me. Set had made the right choice anyway, and if he didn't, he probably wouldn't have been anyone I would want to love. That ultimatum Nevaeh gave Set actually reminded me a little bit of Max's tests...

Nevaeh's picture winked at me above the biography.

I found Set in the hall, and he said, "Mr. Lux told me all about his old love he had, who he's going to see again soon! At first he was reluctant to talk about it, but he really needed to open up to someone, I think. I didn't ask him anything indecent!"

"Good. Try to keep that only with me, from now on." I said.

Set smiled, and said, "You're the only one I want to keep that with."

"Lux even feels love?" I said.

"I didn't think he could either. But I'm sure when he next sees his boyfriend this full moon, they'll be able to have full love like they've been waiting for. He said he was rather nervous, and actually asked me for some advice. I told him that longing makes the heart grow fonder, and if he listens to what he has to say, then he can stare deep into his eyes... and then they will both probably be in the mood to kiss and then- I never got to keep going, because Mr. Lux told me to leave." Set said.

I giggled, and said, "Cool. I'll try that next time on you, then. Although I'll let you keep going, and won't tell you to leave."

Set blushed, I stared deep into his eyes... and we kissed.

44

It was a full moon, and a bit of a holiday for the school. Like when my mother had conquered Hell and officially built her realm, this was the day Lux first started the school. Set and I wandered away from our group of friends, our guild called the Champions of the Gargoyle, Champs for short, kind of stoned and a little tipsy, and Set and I laughed with each other walking down the path to the garden, a path that frankly just sort of showed up because we used it so much.

We looked out across the plains. We saw Lux and a big man sitting out on the makeout hill, an arm around each other so far. We could faintly hear Lux say, "Amare amor, Amare."

The other man said, "I love you, Lux."

And then they started kissing!

We watched for a while, a little curious as to how a robot and the big man were going to continue, but gave them privacy and walked back into the school.

Everyone was having fun, with very loose supervision. People were playing games, eating the snacks saved for this special day, and all around having a great night! It was a very special time, I learned, for the kids and the teachers.

We passed through the halls with couples making out in a lot of secret corners. Fire escapes, secluded benches…

And we kept walking, and got to my room, where everyone in it, my now all friends and members of my guild, Sara, Lita, Micah, and even Sharina, were still hanging out in the garden. Rasputin passed us to go catch mice or something out in the halls, but I think he winked at me.

I set Set on my bed, and took off my glasses.

He was not blushing, and looked very courageous. I suppose being a child soldier growing up taught you how to deal with fear, or maybe he just overcame it for me.

We kissed on the bed, making out and touching each other slightly in pleasant parts of the body, a slight brush on the arm, a feel down to the waist...

I was taking off his shirt, waiting for him to take off my low cut blouse and undo my fantastic skirt that I traded a whole bunch of tokens with Sharina for... but he said, "I would like to make love with you. Would you like to make love with me?"

"Yes." I said.

He paused in our love, and said, "...And you... You, uh..."

"Oh! Would you like to make love with me, too?" I asked.

He smiled, and *then* blushed, saying, "Yes. Nevaeh taught me that consent is a very powerful force, it opens the floodgates in each other's passions, without a doubt, accepting love with each other."

"Ok. Now teach me, my angel of love." I said.

"I love you, Hana." Set said.

I blushed, because he had never said that to me before! I said, "I l-love... I *love* you, Set."

We then undressed fully and got in my bed.

I admired him, and well, angels sure must have a great gym up in Heaven or something.

I was feeling a little self conscious of my own body and didn't know-

He said, "You are beautiful, and I accept you as you are."

I said, "I think you're really hot, and accept you too."

We both blushed, and kissed one more time very close together. He said one last thing before we started, "God accepts you into Heaven as well. He wanted me to tell you that, and sorry if this isn't a very good moment, but I thought you should know. You can always come visit your father and me."

"I can?? What do you mean, and you?" I said.

"...This won't be a permanent stay for me. I'm an angel, Hana. I'm dead." Set said.

"What?! B-But- I love you! Yule stays around for eternities, or some shit! Why can't you??" I said.

"Yule's duty is more pressing than mine. But like I said. You can always come visit... Let me give you a sort of a key to Heaven, or really... just wings." Set said.

He kissed me as I was frowning at him, the most passionate short peck ever, because I was so frustrated with him and he could tell, and then, after that short peck, an act of love...

Wings burst from my back, as I lay in bed.

It scared the shit out of me.

I stroked my soft feathers. They were white, and I saw his wings come out of his back too, and it just added to his gorgeous, good form.

"You can kind of... retract them? Or something. It may take some getting used to-" Set said.

I poofed the wings back in, then out, giggling to myself. I could go angel form!

Set smiled, and said, "Shall we continue?"

I giggled, and rolled with him in the bed, and we continued.

It was very good, in a way that was very awkward. But we were two awkward angels, and our *wings* covered our naked forms as we made love. This experience, this certain, once in a lifetime experience, was very special, and could never be repeated. It was our first time together, and my love that I had with Set could never be replicated by anyone else, or even just each other, as I soon wanted to have another round and it felt just *slightly* different, if more comfortable with each other. This love I had with Set would continue to be different, and it would continue to grow and adapt, as we did as well.

We laid in each other's arms for a while, just enjoying someone playing music outside.

I played flute for him, nude with angel wings coming out of me sitting on my bed, and he listened in love.

The magical feeling had passed, but it would be back again, so we decided to get dressed and go hang out with our friends and have more fun!

45

Set was palling around with Vincent, Dill, Miller, and Devon, playing their own not very organized form of football after classes, and I sat with the rest of the girls, well, besides Sara who had just tackled Dill and joined in on their fun.

Sharina said to me, "Ok. You seem different. Like really effin' satisfied! What's new?"

"Um... Oh you know... Set and I..." I said.

"You did it!! Oh my god, this is like, wow. I believed in you, yep." Sharina said.

Lita said, "...Was it anything like me and Sharina?? I doubt you could come *close!*"

Sharina held hands with Lita, and whispered in Lita's ear, and Lita giggled.

Micah said, "...You did? Together, on purpose? How so fast?"

"It took a long time, actually, if you want to put it in perspective to other couples or whatever. But it just felt right at the time." I said.

Micah said, "...I keep grabbing Vincent, like- But he just seems scared..."

I put a hand on Micah's shoulder, as her stalwart eyes looked kind of sad, and said, "Try to be a little gentler. It sounds like it won't be easy for you, and you should let Vincent know."

Micah smiled, and said, "I just- I thought that- I should do what other people- in the tribe- did to me and I- I realize that is very foolish..."

Sharina said, "You could do what Lita and I did, and just use your hands. Just start with something gentle, instead of full on intercourse."

Lita said, "We've kinda gotta learn this way of love ourselves, because even though there's that sex ed class, it don't teach *actually* how to have sex, just the functions, and we only hear of rude rumors from other people who fantasize about what we do. Still. None of you can come close!"

"Oh, quit being a showoff, Lita." I said, "I'm not going to tell you everything, because it was so good and you wouldn't believe me, so let's not compete at how great our love is."

Lita smiled, and said, "You should try being a lesbian sometime, if you want to see what I mean. I really haven't grown to love that word, though... and Sharina also likes boys."

Sharina said, "Yep! So we're just going to be girlfriends, and worry about what other people call us later."

Miller sat beside us, wiping the sweat from his bangs, and said, "Hooboy, those guys and that girl really know how to tackle."

"How did you and Devon make love, Miller?" Micah said.

Miller said, "Oooh gossipping? I think you may just find what we do sort of crude, since you're all so new at this, but hmm... It took us a while to get to that point, and we make sure *no one* is around us when we do. It's much better being a secret moment of passion, unlike you two, Lita and Sharina. You two are sticking your hands down each other's pants wherever you can! Try to use some composure."

Micah said, "Again. How did you two do it?"

Miller just said, "Well, you can do a lot with an experienced mouth, for starters... but... there are lots of very special places in the body, and that's all I'm going to leave you with. Also, remember that a good bit of hygiene really goes a long way."

Micah sniffed her shirt, and said, "I smell like fries."

Miller said, "That's not your fault from working in the kitchen all day, but... It's good to smell nice, just clean if anything, and if you have the choice... you don't have to douse yourself in raspberry perfume like Sharina."

Sharina said, "What? Is it too strong? I think it smells nice."

"It's a little like you're taking baths in the stuff. Just a spritz, dear!" Miller said.

Lita laughed, and said, "Even a guy is better at being a girl than us."

"A homosexual guy, don't you forget. Although I used to, before I accepted my penis, *did* wish to be a lady, one day. Frankly that is impossible in today's world, and really would make me feel sad for the member that I would be giving up. I'm glad I accepted myself, because really, once I did, I felt much more comfortable in my body as well, and things came easier for love." Miller said.

"I like just watching sunsets with Vincent, and being his dashing princess as he is my shining knight. We have the best meals together, and he always accepts when I give him food." Micah said.

Sharina said, "...You sure he's just not using you to get another snack for his belly?"

"What? No, it is a great gift to give another food, because that is what we survive on, and it comes from someone- from a plant, that is so necessary." Micah said.

I said, "Hmm... I always thought Vincent was a little bit of a trouble-maker, even though he's a good friend now and grew that great weed, but I'll talk to him."

I caught Vincent alone, as the rest stopped playing football and were just joking with each other before we went back to the school and dispersed, and I asked Vincent, "So what do you think of Micah?"

"She's cool, yeah." Vincent said.

"...I mean... Are you doing what she likes? Is she doing what you like, too?" I said.

"Um... Are you asking me if I want to bang my girlfriend?" Vincent said, "...Shouldn't that be obvious, because she *is* my girlfriend?"

"Oh! Er, sorry. I just think it will be tough for her-" I said.

He was crying gently, not boohooing, just a few tears here and there, and he said, "She told me about what happened to her. How her *fucking rapist cannibal father*- How she was abused. I want to make it very special for her, and even though my stomach is exploding and I've never had so much ruffage from all those veggies, I always accept that food she gives me, because for some reason that is a super generous act of true love for her."

"Ok. Good. Please don't be offended by my question. I know she went through a lot of pain, and I'm just looking out for her." I said.

"...Well... Ok. I guess it's good she has more support. Please don't question my feelings for her again." Vincent said.

"I won't. Whatever you do, even if you two lose interest in each other... just be very gentle." I said.

Vincent sighed, wiped off the slight tears, and nodded.

46

I was expecting Zeus... but got even better! Cass and Jake came from the ranch to come visit Lux and I! They were super worried that I just ran off again, but sent out Zeus to find me, and Zeus was rather quick witted and went straight to the school, where Lux told him everything was alright for me. I can't believe I missed him in class! Dangit!

Jake, Cass, and I sat in front of Lux behind his desk, and Jake poked a new skull on Lux's desk, and said, "Where'd you find this, anyway?"

Lux said, "Oh, this whole school is actually situated on an enormous burial ground, another past school! I wonder how many schools are down below this one in the dirt... It would be a fantastic lesson in archaeology to go exploring them."

"Tha's fuckin' creepy shit, man. You got a better place than sittin' hunched up in your office? We wanted to see the little lady and you again... not like we're in trouble and 'bout to go down for something."

"Oh! Let's take a walk outside, how about, to be in fresh air." Lux said.

"Sounds good, Lux." Cass said, "I'd like to visit Zax's grave Hana told us about as well."

We walked through the halls to go outside, and for some reason Lux and Jake were talking about Christ. Jake said, "Hell yeah, the fuckin' guy is like, magic! Cass has been wanting- and even though I didn't- We put a kid in her belly as soon as we put an album on. Guess I just forgot about using protection in that passion, I was so enthralled by Christ's sweet voice."

Cass winked at me.

"What do you mean Christ was singing to you? And protection from what?" I asked.

Cass patted my shoulder, and said, "You'll understand when you make love with someone. Gotta use protection, otherwise you'll be like me… and get pregnant! I'm so happy!!" and she giggled in glee.

"…Get pregnant?" I said.

Jake said, "Lux, you really gotta get some anatomy classes or somethin' for these kids."

I started panicking, and realized I didn't even think about using a contraceptive. They even gave those to you for free if you asked for them! I was just so focused on making love, I had forgotten about what it could lead to!

I felt very faint, and said I needed to sit down. Cass sat beside me on the bench, and said, "Something wrong, Hana?"

"I'm pregnant. I must be pregnant." I said.

"…Are you sure? When was your last time?" Cass said.

"W-Well Set and I made love last full moon-" I started saying.

"I mean when was your last period, dear." Cass said.

"…Last week." I said.

"Oh! So no problem. The full moon was already a couple weeks ago! If you're having periods, you're not having babies, Hana." Cass said.

I sighed, and said, "It's not that I don't think having a baby with an angel of love wouldn't be the biggest act of love ever, it's just- I don't think I want to make *that* big an act of love, yet."

"No, you're much too young. Angel of love? You should teach your dear angel to be more cautious." Cass said, "Unless, of course, you mean he's like Yule or something. Poor angel can't reproduce… and it makes me sad."

Jake said, "I think Yule's one fucking lucky duck. She can have all the sex she wants, and still not worry about it. Beats me why she's *still* with Lucius, but… Lucius does play a nice tune, and I guess it gets 'em both in the mood pretty fast and a lot."

"Oh. So angels can't make babies? I suppose that would make sense… unless one of them breaks the rules… and they do something they aren't supposed to…" I said.

"I'm not sure what you exactly are talking about, Hana. But just be thankful you avoided this marvelous opportunity for now, and take it as a lesson." Cass said, and lifted me up with her strong cyborg arms, and we went outside.

We paid respect to my father, kneeling before the grave. Cass taught me the Lord's Prayer so I could say it for my father, and I prayed with her. "Our Father who art in Heaven…" we both said and continued. I actually liked this prayer, since it did remind me of my father in Heaven.

Cass gave me a couple of gifts to remember my time with them, a blacksmith's hammer that I had used when working with them, and a pocket bible. "You can always build great stuff in the world, and not break things down. Jesus Christ can help guide you in doing that." I thanked her, and put the hammer on my belt by a handy strap and holster that came with the gift, and put the pocket bible in my pocket.

Lux and I waved them goodbye later, as they galloped back to the ranch on their magnificent stallion, Cass behind Jake as they rode off down the plains.

I was tempted to use this hammer on Set and break him down, because he was such an idiot angel of love who didn't even know what love led to, but I just remembered Cass's words and thought what Jesus would do, and continued to build love.

He saw me eyeing him wielding my hammer, as he sat in the garden with Dill and Vincent, and Set said, getting up to face me, "...Something wrong?"

"I think you're really fucking beautiful, lovely, nice, but still need to learn a lot of things. Like using protection!!" I said.

"...I thought it would be more intimate and special if we made love like natural people do-" he said.

"I was so fucking scared that I had gotten pregnant!! I didn't even think about it, and then wham! It hits me in the face like this hammer!" I said, wielding the hammer in the air.

Set looked at the hammer, then back at me, and said, "...But I knew I couldn't get you pregnant. I was dead, and there's no way the dead can reproduce-"

"But what if something happened?? How could've you been sure?? I've seen that not everything makes perfect sense in this world, starting with me being in love with an actual angel of love!" I said.

Dill and Vincent just stared at us with wide eyes, and Dill whispered to Vincent, "Is this real? Or am I just smoking too much?"

"...I think we both need to lay off the grass, because something wicked weird is going on." Vincent said.

Set looked at them for a second, and back at me and said, "...I'm sorry, Hana. I really was just trying to make it as special as I could."

"Then fucking don't act like a jackass and tell me what you're doing next time!!" I said.

"...Alright, Hana. Should I leave?" Set said.

"No, no... I just need time by myself for a while..." I said, and put my hammer back on my belt.

"I meant if I should go back to Heaven now, or later. I was going to leave without saying goodbye, so we wouldn't try to ruin our relation-ship by putting it on a timeframe. I want to tell you that that is what I thought of doing." Set said.

My face went pale, and I said, "...You were just going to ditch me in the night?"

"Not- Not like that! I would've left you with a kiss on the lips after we slept together, and left a kind note or something!!" Set said.

"...I don't want to see you right now, but I will be very pissed if you abandon me after we have sex again. So we're not going to have sex again, until I'm sure about you." I said.

"I didn't mean sleeping together like- Ok. I understand. I'll give you some space." Set said, and passed by me. He was so dumb sometimes, and yet so romantically smart... and at least he was smart enough not to kiss or hug me right then.

I just fumed, sitting next to Dill and Vincent, as they smoked weed. "I think God is like, something in this plant, and we can, like, see him, when we smoke. Because now Hana's talking about having sex with angels of love, and Set is talking about coming back from the dead." Dill said.

"I think the crazy witch chick just found someone just as crazy as her." Vincent said, as Dill passed him the joint.

"Nah, she showed us a book that was the actual Devil when we first met her, well, Sara, Micah and I. We're like, her apostles or something." Dill said.

"Pffft. You're too stoned, and I'll believe it when I see it." Vincent said, passing me the joint.

I took the joint, inhaled, blew out the smoke, and said, "Believe this?"

I then poofed my angel wings out of me, not even ripping through my clothes, and Vincent stumbled back, and Dill laughed his ass off.

Vincent was slowly sitting back down again, and said, "Th-The fuck... I'm hallucinating."

I said, "I thought they were kind of odd too, but Set kissed me, and now I've got wings."

Vincent poked one of my wings, and said, "Wowww... They're so soft! How do they even come out of you like that? Is it like some secret wing cavity in you? And now you have wings because you *kissed* him? I kinda want to kiss him too now, but I'm not sure if I want to mutate like that."

I passed the joint to Dill, and Dill inhaled, and said with smoke coming out of his mouth, "Toldja weed is holy. The only thing I don't get is why they look so pretty. I mean, no offense, Hana, but you have a book that is the actual Devil, claim you've lived in Hell, and teach us dark magic. And yet you look so pretty, with pretty wings."

Dill passed the joint to Vincent, and I shrugged, and said, "I suppose beauty is always different, and inner beauty isn't always shown in outer beauty. Thanks, though."

Dill said, "You're welcome. I always thought you were pretty, and do have that inner beauty as well, even through your unholiness. I think it's like, despite the grasp of evil, you just have a pretty soul."

Vincent inhaled, laughed, and said, "You still have a thing for Hana... better not get your hopes up, because despite her obviously having *such* a fitting romance... Sara would kick your ass if she knew."

Dill said, "Sara knows I think Hana's pretty. She thinks you're pretty too, Hana, and tried wearing sexy high heels like you do all the time to be like you, but she tripped and landed on her butt. But I don't care if Sara would want to kick my ass, I like that she could. She's tough. Heck, she could probably kick anyone's ass in this school."

"Without... Without killing them, right?" I said.

"What? Why would she kill anyone?" Dill said.

"...I want to learn how to be tough like her. Because I want to help protect someone I hate, so that he can live in horrible suffering for the rest of his long life." I said.

They looked at me with their stoned eyes, and Vincent said, "...Still think she's so pretty? That's fucked up, Hana."

"What?" I said, "No it's not! He killed my father!"

Vincent said, "Why don't you just kill him then?"

Dill said, "Now that's fucked up, Vincent. I don't know why, that is the natural response... but it just seems mean."

Vincent said, "Yeah... I just heard it myself after it came out of my mouth."

"I thought of doing that, which is why I left you all for a week... trying to hunt him down... and kill him, with only a sharp rock I found." I said.

Dill said, "Shit. That's why? I thought it was because you just had some feminine issue. Man... A sharp rock? You *do* need to learn how to fight."

"Yep! Although I'm only going to fight if I can save lives, and still not end lives. And you shouldn't immediately assume a girl's got 'feminine issues' if she's upset..." I said.

Vincent said, "But you totally just had a feminine issue with Set. If that dude is right, and he is some magic dead guy that gave you wings, I think he'd be confident enough to know what he's doing in bed to not get you pregnant. I don't even know how the anatomy of angel wings work, but he probably does."

"...I guess that's true... I guess the shock of thinking I was pregnant was still shocking me. I'll tell him I'm sorry. Only if he promises not to hide anything from me anymore. Try to get some work done, you guys, because sitting around and smoking all the time isn't good for you." I said.

Dill said, "Oh, it's alright. Lux gives us a lot of time off after we finish our studies, even if we're painting this mural for him."

"What mural?" I said.

Vincent said, "What? You don't see it? Open your eyes, Hana, see the big picture…"

I looked behind them, and I saw the picture they were working on, a *huge* mural on the wall facing the garden. A beautiful, fantastic piece with Lux out front accepting you and everyone with every person I knew behind him, with some special fantasy touches for each of them. It looked very difficult to do something so nice for each one of the students and teachers, but somehow these guys did.

Dill said, "Set's been gathering info about everyone, making sure we don't leave anyone out. Dude's got a big heart, and he double checks his little list to make sure we got them all. He can't make art with a paintbrush for shit, but at least he cares."

Vincent got the paint back out from the shed, and started working on the mural. He painted big angel wings on the depiction of me, and said, "There… That's better. We didn't know what to do for you, and were contemplating giving you demon horns, but this is nicer."

I smiled and cried in happiness, and said, "I love you guys. Keep it up."

I then went to each of them and gave them a big, strong hug.

47

"...He did that? Isn't that like cheating or something?" Max said, as he looked at my new wings as we drove through the night sky.

"I don't really know. I think either Set is making stuff up as he goes along in the afterlife, or God is really changing what game we play." I said.

Max grumbled, and said, "If I knew *I* could come back to life... Yule only got out because she snuck out of Heaven, and was lucky enough that she had St. Peter to open the gates for her..."

"Does that really make sense, though? That God just let someone sneak out of Heaven, an important angel in his battle against Hell? I'm feeling like free will is just an illusion, and really God is making up a damn show with us." I said.

"...All I know is that he's the best boss I've ever had. We golf together sometimes, and he's a very tough player. I swear I came close to beating him once... but he's God, y'know. If he lost I'd just feel like he was throwing the game, anyway." Max said.

"Man. Having unlimited power must be tough, when you don't have an equal to play fair games with. Maybe that's why God likes my mother, and hasn't smitten her even lower than Hell yet. Or maybe my mother just finds God a worthy adversary, and she would get lonely as the ruler of absolutely everything. Anyway, I *know* they both got bored of the

Devil, because now the Devil is stuck talking to my cat. The Devil even seems to lose against Rasputin's mental battles..." I said.

"Anyway, let's see if... I don't really know what kind of test a guardian angel should even take..." Max said, rubbing his chin.

"Please, please, *please* no tests. Just show me what I need to do, and I'll do it." I said.

"Alright. I guess we'll go find the guy you want to guard... Oh! There he is, down there, about to get the crap beaten out of him, maybe killed. Just, you know, guard him." Max said, and we flew down to a bar in the middle of the country, and saw the shaky man about to get attacked by three muscled thugs, one wielding a knife, one with a bat, and another wielding a broken bottle. I was starting to shake too, looking at them cornering this man I despised against the bar wall, so Max put a hand on my shoulder and said, "Just think of it like doing your job. Or I'll have to do mine."

I looked at Max, and he just smiled nicely. I got out of the car, wielding my blacksmith hammer and raising my shield in defense. I flapped my wings, creating a strong gust of breeze, and said to the thugs commandingly, "Leave him alone."

The thugs looked at me, surprised, and I was *sure* I put the fear of God in them...

But they just started laughing, and laughing, and in the endless moment of their laughter, the shaky man ran off, leaving the thugs laughing at me.

The thug with a bat said, "WOAH! I think I'm fucking drunk! Some hoe came down from Heaven for us! Look at that crappy outfit! With those ridiculous heels, and fuckin chicken wings too!!"

The one with a knife said, "I think God blessed us. I'll give you a gold piece if you suck my cock first, hoe!" and they laughed some more and the man with the knife threw a piece of gold at my feet.

My face was red, and I tried to regain my composure by saying, "I am the guardian angel for shaky man, and you will not hurt him agai-"

They all laughed some more, roaring uproariously, and the one with the broken bottle threw the bottle to the ground, where it shattered, and said, *"Shaky man?? Fucking… pfrfft… Shaky man has a guardian hoe!"*

And they all kept laughing.

I just got back in the car, and the men stopped laughing. "She's fuckin gone." one said.

"I think we need another drink… because… something spooky is happening out here." another said, and they went back in the bar.

Max revved up his engine, and drove off down the road.

I was red in anger and embarrassment, and I said to Max, "…Is there something wrong with how I dress?"

Max said, "Um… No! It's just an acquired taste. First, all that black metal spiky clothes… And now… I don't really know. My only guess is that you tried to become a rainbow. But don't worry about those guys! They obviously have no fashion sense."

"…How come you look so good in casual white? I thought angels all wear big white robes." I said.

"I do? Thanks! A lot of the angels *do* like those robes… but they've been around for millenia. I used to wear one too, until I found out there was no uniform! It was the best feeling ever, learning I could go to work in a hoodie and jeans." Max said.

"A pure white hoodie and jeans. Shouldn't you be dressed in black like how I used to do?" I asked.

"Eh, you'd be surprised how scary it is when some black cloaked, hooded, shadowy guy comes to take your soul. I tried that once, really getting excited for the job… but I had to chase the guy all through the world as he was a ghost, and he nearly escaped me and was nearly claimed by Hell… It sure was a close call, and was a really big mistake on my part." Max said, as we slowly ascended to the sky.

"Should I try to dress for my job as a guardian angel? Put the fear of God in them and make anyone who messes with shaky man run fleeing from me?" I asked.

"I wouldn't worry about it. You saved that guy anyway, so you did your job well." Max said.

"…I saved him as the guardian hoe with chicken wings…" I grumbled, crossing my arms.

"Hey, those guys were just jerks. Don't let their words drag you down. You've been by far my best student yet, and guardian angeling isn't really my specialty, anyway. I'm sure you can figure out how to save shaky man yourself. All you gotta do is just keep practicing, and he'll have the longest, worst life under you… Ahem." Max said.

"I'm your best student?" I asked.

"Only student, too. I never did like working with children, so I never took one under my wing, or even had any with Yule. It's been a nice change of pace, teaching, so I think you passed my course with flying colors." Max said.

"…But… I failed all the time, did everything wrong… and it's over? I have to learn so much more, just to be an angel of death, let alone a guardian angel!! You haven't even taught me the most important part, how to take someone's soul!" I said.

"You really can't take souls when you're alive, Hana. Everything I've taught you is only applicable when you're further on in the afterlife." Max said, smiling to me.

"…You taught me all this, when you knew I could never use it?" I said.

"I think the accumulation of knowledge is more important than the application of it. But yes. I thought it would be the best, most lasting lesson of them all, teaching a child of Hell… that she cannot mess with

God or people's souls. But I think I learned something from you, too." Max said.

"Which was what?" I asked, "That you are the worst and best teacher ever? I'm so pissed right now, but… that does make sense. I applaud your evil holiness."

"I learned I need to lock my doors when I take a good daughter's father to Heaven." Max said, smiling.

I laughed, and said, "The simplest lessons often escape us. I'm glad you didn't escape me."

"Well, since you're all breaking the rules, getting in my car and giving each other wings, I'm going to give you a graduation present! A hoodie from Heaven. Wear it with pride." Max said, and while he was driving he took off his hoodie, and I grabbed the wheel as the car began plummeting, and kept control.

He offered me his white hoodie, wearing only his favorite music band t-shirt underneath. I took it, and said, "It's not gonna stink like death, will it?"

"Uh, I just had it washed! In Heaven! So I hope not." Max said. I shrugged, put on the white hoodie, and felt it around me. It felt like God's beard, it was so soft, and was just a little big, but felt perfectly comfortable.

Max drove me back to school, I waved him goodbye for the first and last time, and he said from the driver's seat, "I'll always be watching out for you as your guardian angel, Hana, and when your time comes… I'll offer you a ride, wherever you want to go."

I smiled and nodded, and said, "Thank you for the lessons, Max. Have a good rest of your eternity."

He waved to me, smiling sadly, and drove off down the road, disappearing from view.

I went back to my room where I found Rasputin talking with the burning book. The book was getting frustrated by Rasputin explaining that no one really knows what happens after they die, and the book said, *"But you've died, I don't know how much, and I've been to Hell. I think that's enough proof, after seeing all the dead sinners I've tortured eternally."*

"But that ended. People die, and they never know what will happen even in the afterlife. Your eternity didn't last eternally, really, and you could die perhaps as well. Maybe if people stop heeding you, slowly forget your name, you'll die just like the rest." Rasputin said.

"...I don't like what you're getting at, and I don't believe it. I am a constant monster in the dark of people's minds, and they'll never forget me." the burning book said.

"Some people don't even recall you by your real name, which I don't know, was Lucifer, correct? As you were an angel in Heaven? Then you became Satan, unless I'm wrong, or the Devil if they feel like giving you an even more diluted name, and now you're the burning book, or just book for short." Rasputin said.

"People will remember me! Someone will always keep a copy of my name alive..." the book said.

"But it could be only as a clown called Lucifer instead. You sure didn't expect to be a clown when you fell, and people's eternities don't last. Death is not only the end of life, but the end of a grand idea, or simply just the end of a slight notion. You could die, book." Rasputin said.

"You better not start calling me 'it...'" it said.

Rasputin said, "That is much too confusing, and no one would know what we are addressing if we called you that. I think you have a part to play in Hana's story, if only as a silly burning book that gets flustered when talking to a cat."

"But- Stop it, cat." the burning book said.

"I am a cat, and I take pride in being one. Well, good night, burning book. I'm going to bed, because my human is here and she is so nice and warm." Rasputin said, and cuddled in bed with me.

48

"That's… different." Set said, as I kissed him good morning in the halls.

"Oh, I just think I'm going to stop giving a shit what I look like. Just a white hoodie with my old black pants from now on, if I can get away with it." I said.

"…In high heels?" Set said.

"What? They're comfy." I said.

He shrugged, and held my hand as we walked to class, and said, "I really liked your color before. It felt like I could touch the rainbow, when I held your hand."

I squeezed his hand tight, and we went to our classes. Set was having a difficult time in most of the classes, as he had only been taught how to take commands and kill while growing up, but I tutored him well whenever I could.

He furrowed his brow at his homework, and said, "But pi… It does not make sense! The only one who should keep going forever and ever is God. This pi can never be exactly calculated, because I'll never know what the end is!"

"The homework isn't to calculate pi, Set. Just that one circle's circum-ference." I said.

"But if I do not know the full picture of pi, I will never know the full measurement of this circle. This circle is just as mysterious as pi, because we are working with knowledge that is incomplete." Set said, "Even this calculator isn't smart enough to know the answer, and only rounds off to ten digits! Even Mr. Lux, a full fledged advanced machine, doesn't know the full pi!"

"Um. It'll be pretty close... Some things you won't know exactly-" I said.

"I will continue to calculate this value until I am satisfied, no matter if pi takes me a thousand million eternities, I shall defeat this evil pi that blasphemes God-" Set said.

"How about we take a break. C'mon, let's get some air." I said.

He looked down at his archnemesis, the eternal circle with its eternal pi, but set his pencil down to take a break with me, his girlfriend.

We looked at the finished mural by our garden, and held hands as we were doing in the mural. Our love would last until this school collapsed to dust, and someone built another school on top of it, probably Lux, because he seemed to already know first hand a lot of the end bits of history we were learning...

I had learned so much in this school, probably the most I ever had, and I would be sad to leave it, but I was looking forward to the adventure that beckoned to me from the outside world.

I said to Set, "There's something I have to do today, instead of tutor you more. I have someone I need to protect. Would you care to join me?"

"I'll always be by your side, even though I would like to know more about what you're doing, as we promised to be more honest with each other from now on, no matter what our good intentions." Set said.

"Let's talk on the way." I said, we poofed out our angel wings, and flew on the wind.

I told him my entire life story, even through walking through the portal from Hell, and into the living world, where my dad was killed by this shaky man.

"...You want to protect him to let him suffer? That sounds horribly... I don't know. In a way it is showing mercy to your enemies, but doing so in ill will doesn't sound like a thing God would want." Set said, as we flapped through the sky.

"I haven't really made up my mind how I feel about him, but I saw which direction he went last time I saw him, so let's watch him for a while." I said.

We landed in a tall tree, and saw the shaky man scavenging in the forest, searching for any bits of food, mostly maggots and worms.

We saw the shaky man take out a locket, with someone, I couldn't tell, on the inside. He cried as he looked at that picture, and continued to shamble through the forest.

Then we heard the shaky man scream at the divine, in a rasping voice, "You took her away, GOD! YOU TOOK MY DAUGHTER AWAY!! You will *never* have my soul, as it belongs to SATAN anyway!!

"But you'll never catch me, Satan. You'll never get my soul. I'll run from you for as long as I can... I will continue to live... in this tortured agony which only death will relieve.

"YOU WILL NEVER HAVE ME!!! BOTH OF YOU SHALL NEVER HAVE MY LIFE AND SOUL!!"

"This man is in horrible pain." Set whispered beside me, as the shaky man continued to limp away.

"Don't you think he deserves it? If he killed my father, isn't it only right that his daughter died?" I said.

"...That is not a loving response to suffering, Hana." Set said.

"...But... I cannot forgive him, and let him come back to some good life. He's dangerous, anyway." I said.

Set said, "This man looks weak, pitiful, and the only way he would've killed anyone is if he got a lucky shot using a gun with that shaking hand."

"I suppose… Let's see where he's going." I said.

We watched the shaky man cross a bridge, stop halfway, and look down. It looked like he was contemplating suicide, as he stood on the very edge.

So I stepped into action, as a guardian angel.

I said, "Stop, shaky man. You're not going to die… yet." I said.

He started shaking even more, trembling in fear of me.

"Y-You're an angel. I must've killed you too. Th-The bullet went through him, and hit you. Please don't hurt me." he said.

"I don't want to have to hurt you. Just step down from the ledge." I said.

He screamed in terror, and jumped off the bridge.

"NO!!" I cried, and jumped off the bridge as well.

I flew with my wings, speeding faster and faster, flapping to fall faster and grab him.

We nearly hit the rocks underneath, because there was no river underneath this bridge, it had long ago dried up.

I caught shaky man in my arms, as he cried in fear.

I set him gently on the ground, and he cowered before me. "Please, just kill me. Get it over with… Please." shaky man said.

Set flew next to me, and said, "It sounds like you're going to have a very busy guardianship, if the man you're trying to save wants to end his life whenever he sees you."

I frowned at Set, turned to shaky man, and asked him, "…Why did you kill my father?"

"I-I jus-just needed to buy her back. I needed to buy her back… I knew they had her. I knew. I spent so long trying to find her… but they took her, and I knew they wouldn't let me take her back unless I had money." shaky man said.

"Take who back?" I asked.

"H-Here. Take it. I'll never see her again, anyway." he said, and pressed the locket into my hand.

I opened it, and it was a girl from my school.

"...What do you mean, took her away?" I said.

"Sl-Slavers. They stole my daughter, killed my family... and I ran. I kept running. But I know she's there." he said.

"Y-You're wrong. There's no one like this there. Just go away, and don't come back." I said.

"They took her, they sold her, they took her again... I know. She's somewhere... I can feel it." he said.

Set looked at the locket, and said, "I think she would like to know her father is alive."

I started grumbling, then screaming, "I *hate* you, shaky man! I *hate* you! You took my father away, and he'll never be back!! You don't deserve to see her, or anyone again!! *I absolutely hate you!!*"

Shaky man said, "Please. Just let her know I tried, then. If you kill me, please let her know I tried. That's all I ask."

I looked at Set who was looking at me gently, as I was in absolute utter fury, and I said to shaky man, "I'll do better than that. I decided I never want to save your soul again. I'll bring you to Lux, and maybe he'll just crush your skull instead, but I'll let you see your daughter."

"Th-Thank you. That's all I ever wanted. Thank you. I've missed Hannah for so long." he said.

"Her name is Sara now, so get used to it." I said.

49

The next day, I sat next to Sara, as Lux sat next to shaky man, only us four alone in the cafeteria while everyone else was in class.

"My name is Sara, and I don't have a father." Sara said.

Lux said, "How can we verify your tale, Mr…"

"Toby. My name is Toby. I only have that locket… But I know you are my daughter. Y-You look exactly like you were when you were a child… I'm sorry that I could not save you… It is my biggest shame, but I kept looking. I knew you were somewhere, and now you're here. Mr. Robot, I will offer you my life as your servant, as a slave, if you allow my daughter to go free." Toby said.

Lux said, "This is not a slaver's camp, Mr. Toby. This is a school, and Sara came here of her own free will."

Sara said, "Hana told me you killed her father with a gun."

"That was the other option. Either buy you, or kill your capturers. I was so close, I could feel it... I was about to charge in and kill everyone in here to save you… but I heard a voice whispering in my head… to do the other option… so I demanded money from them-" Toby said.

I said, "And you killed my father anyway."

"I-I didn't mean to. You pulled that gun and I- I didn't-" Toby said.

I pulled a pistol finger at him, and said, "Bang."

He jumped back.

Sara said, "...So what if you somehow know I was a slave? I worked, I scrubbed dishes, pulled plows. I did everything I had to, and one man looked at me chained up next to the others, and he unlocked the chains. And I ran. I got to this place, and it's been my home ever since."

"Please tell me how you got here. I thought you were gone forever. I thought I was chasing just a feeling. If they abused you I'll-" Toby said, shaking angrily.

Sara sighed angrily, and said, "I was only a little girl when I was enslaved, and I do not remember my parents. I had a very difficult life, being bounced around from master to master, some better than the others. They all thought of me as only muscles to use. The one who freed me was as bad as the rest, but I think he was just too drunk, and felt sad for me. If you're asking if they forced themselves on me, well... I can only say I got very lucky. The other little girls felt the pain a woman feels, but I pulled a plow, instead of getting plowed. I thought about trying to free the others... but I was just a scared, little girl. "

"I'm so sorry. When they took our home, I ran. I couldn't save you-" Toby said.

Sara said, "I don't believe you, and I think you sold me to them."

Toby said, "...No, Hannah. I can make up for running. I can give you another life-"

" I *told* you, my name is Sara. I don't care what your story is, and I don't care if you really were trying to find me. I don't want to find you, and I'm not going to leave with you. I don't have a father." Sara said.

The man slumped his shoulders, and said, "Take this, and at least remember that you came from some sort of family." and he gave Sara the locket. Sara looked at it, and just stared at it for a long time. She shoved it in her pocket, and left.

Toby looked at her leave sadly, and Lux said, "She is a great student, and will be able to make whatever life she wants on her own. I understand your pain of watching a child leave, but you should allow her to live her life as she goes out into the world."

Toby, the once shaky man who had now stopped shaking, said, "I think that's best."

I said, "So you gonna kill yourself now? You better not, because I don't want to have to save you again. I realized I *never* want to be your guardian angel. It'd be pointless volunteer work for someone who doesn't appreciate it, and I think I can better use my time elsewhere."

Toby said, "No... I think I will go far, far away. I wish I could've done this sooner. I am very sorry for taking your father away."

"Whatever. We can't do anything about it now. Leave, because... I don't want to have to hurt you."

I pointed my pistol finger at him, aimed it at him, and he got up, and walked out the door. I holstered my pistol finger, and let him live another day, my last act as a guardian angel.

Lux said, "I think you should go talk to Sara, and give her support as a friend. I will excuse you both from classes for the day."

"Ok, Mr. Lux. I'll go find her. She's probably out by the garden." I said.

Lux nodded, and left to continue his duties in the school, but stopped on his way out, and said, "And Hana... I like that you and your friends are really becoming so self-sufficient... but don't let me catch you drinking and smoking in school again. It's only a while before you go out into the real world, so practice some temperance, please. It's not a good example for the other students, seeing you shamble around with bloodshot eyes."

"...Er, sorry. I think you should teach the skills we learned ourselves. It could save a lot of hassle for young minds." I said.

"I will consider it, even if it is unnecessary and harmful to pollute young minds with such products or the learning of their creation... I suppose I could teach a few students to specialize in drug making, and open up my vast, stored knowledge of that subject... But only for medicinal purposes. Good day, Hana. Try to comfort your friend without the use of drugs or alcohol." Lux said, and went off to his duties.

I did find Sara by the garden, drinking the last of our beer and smoking pot with the other hand. She just stared at the mural, sitting in the garden that was quite empty after we harvested it. I sat beside her, and she passed me the joint, which I put out on the ground, crumpling it to bits.

"Hey!! Why'd you do that??" Sara said.

"It's really not going to make you feel better right now, and I know I won't with it either after hearing that damn shaky man- Toby, tell us his bullshit." I said.

"I know!! He actually was contemplating shooting up the school!! And 'hearing a voice in his head...' It just makes me shiver, there's people out there like him." Sara said, slurping her beer.

"Yep. This place is all messed up, this place called life. Toby was quite an apt introduction to it, because as soon as I walked into it, I lost a father." I said.

"I never had a father, and I don't plan on adopting one. Fuck that guy, even if he had a picture of me. I'm glad his twisted fantasy, after he probably found this locket in a ditch that my real family had lost, is over. Fuck that stupid, evil, awful, crazy person. Fuck him to death. I don't need a past, and I'm not a scared little girl anymore..." Sara said, and got up, took the locket out of her pocket, and threw it at the mural in rage, letting it shatter to pieces against the school wall.

The photo flew out from the pieces, and I went over to it, picked it up, and said, "You should hold onto some piece of the past. You have a family somewhere, and maybe you'll find them one day." and I handed her the photo.

She looked at it, but noticed something on the back, something scribbled on the back of the photo.

Her eyes went wide, and she started crying.

"What's wrong?" I asked.

"Cockadoodle doo... the cow goes moo... My f-father... My father taught me that song, this song, *on this picture*, and that's all I can remember. M-My father..." Sara said.

She ran down the garden path, and I chased after her.

Sara called out, "Cockadoodle doo!! Come back! You said you'll be there for me!! Come back!!"

But no one answered.

I said I would look for him, and burst into the sky with my wings.

I looked for Toby, scanning from the clouds, but... he seemed to have run away again, disappearing like he never was there.

I flew back down to Sara where she asked me if I saw him, but I shook my head.

She cried, and I hugged her.

"I-I'll find him again, one day... I know it. I am Hannah." she said.

"I'd stick with Sara. You still don't know for sure, but hold onto that hope." I said.

"When I was a slave, I was only called 'slave.' I got the name Sara from a book I found in a ditch... but you're right. I'll just stick with Sara for now... but I'll find my father, one day." Sara said.

We walked back, and she sang her song,

"Cockadoodle doo, and the cow goes moo,

It's time to wake up, and go to school.

There's friends to play with, lessons to learn,

There's people to see, and I have butter to churn.

So set off to school, dear daughter,

I'll be here at home, dear daughter,

For as long as the cow goes moo,

I'll be here, dear daughter, for another cockadoodle doo."

I held her hand as she cried, and I smiled to her.

Sara said, "And your wings really freak me out."

I laughed, and we laughed into school.

50

I offered my shield to Mr. Loren, who said it was a fine piece of craftsmanship, in trade for an old, dull hatchet. At first he said he didn't want to give me a weapon, and said that the hatchet belonged only in crafts, but I said, "It's just a tool. The most dangerous thing about weapons is the hand wielding them, and not the object itself." He said that was a good point, looked fondly on my shield, and accepted the trade.

I put my hatchet on my belt, along with my blacksmith hammer. I decided instead of having my head in the clouds trying to be an angel in life, I would live my life on Earth and work to live. And I needed tools to do that. Soon, the hatchet was in good condition after I worked hard on it, sharp and sturdy, and I worked hard with it as well.

I signed up for any extra hours along with Sara, learning useful talents like chopping trees, fixing roofs, and other handyman skills. Sara was glad to have another set of good muscles work beside her. "Well, little shrimpy muscles. But they'll get bigger over time." she said.

I soon had a big bag of the school tokens, our currency, and saved them up, even though they would be valueless after I graduated.

I looked at my high heels, and thought there was never such a useless piece of workman clothing, and was going to offer them to trade with Sharina for some thick boots she had that would go great with my new work gloves I had earned, but she said, "Are you kidding, girl? Those are gonna get you a husband who can do all the work *for* you. Keep them, and don't offer me another one of your most prized possessions again, or I may have to accept your trade so they can be on someone's feet who will truly love them."

I smiled, and thanked her. I said, "How's everything going with Lita? I know you two didn't really get off so well at the start but now you're... having fun with your hands."

"Oh, I always thought she was just a tomboy who thought she was too good for everyone. But now I know I'm the *only* person she's been with, even just as a girlfriend. At first we just did that to explore, but it actually feels... comfortable! Like I'm having secret fun with my best friend..." Sharina said.

"Er, it's really not that much of a secret." I said.

"I *know!* Isn't it great?? The bitches all freak out when they see us making out, and the boys fall down and faint! It's no fun having a secret if you can't spread it around." Sharina said.

"I'll keep that in mind in case I ever want to tell you something confidentially." I said.

Sharina said, "If you ever need to talk, I'm always here." and then she winked.

I decided to only wear my black high heels for very special occasions to have them last longer. I just wore my walking shoes usually, the ones I first walked to school with my father in. But I wore my heels today, because today was a very special occasion.

This was the day I was going to break up with my boyfriend.

My boyfriend that I loved with all my heart...

He kept on looking up at the sky at random times, staring at it longingly, and I knew I was just keeping him from his afterlife. He said he really enjoyed being alive again, and even got permission from Nevaeh to be alive to continue his training, but… it wasn't the right thing to do to keep him here.

I hated that I came up with this conclusion myself, and wished I could just selfishly keep him forever, even if he'd prefer to be dead again…

I didn't know what to do, because whenever I tried to say the lines I rehearsed in my head to do so, they would fall apart under his smile. I didn't have the heart to have sad sex with him one last time, because if I did, I'd probably say it was the last time, and then the last time, over and over again and keep him as my lover until we were old and shriveled.

I didn't want to break his heart, and I wished he would just break up with me, but he loved me too, and would put off eternity to spend just another day with me. But I knew I had to do it.

I waited outside of the gym, and he came out from physical education smiling and waving to his friends he had accumulated very quickly. The girls all adored him, the guys all respected him. I'd say he was one of the most popular kids in school. He was so kind to everyone, and had time for them no matter who they were. The only thing he wasn't great at were classes that didn't involve his muscles, but he had me for that, and was really starting to get a hang of them himself. It was too good to be true to snag a guy like this, and I told him so when we were walking down the hall hand in hand.

He turned to me, holding both my hands, and said, "I think you're even better than my entire past life. This little bit of life I am having with you can never be replicated, and you gave me a feeling I never ever had. You gave me true love. I had no one growing up, and I had no one when I left life. I have to leave you, but I will always hold you close. Our time together was better than Heaven."

"…Did you just break up with me?" I said.

"…Um… If you want to put it in a simple phrase like that…" he said.

I let go of his hands, and said, "Why couldn't you have let me do it?? Why didn't you say it in a bad way, or even just rudely?! Couldn't you have just ripped off the bandaid, said, 'I'm breaking up with you, Hana,' instead of this fucking bullshit romance?!"

"I… uh… I wanted to soften the blow and I knew-" he said.

"Well *here's* the picture! I'm breaking up with *you!* Take that! Doesn't feel good, and it's not supposed to!" I shouted out for everyone to hear. A few people looked at us.

"-I knew you wanted to break up with me, but didn't want to as well, so I wanted to save you that pain of being torn apart. It does hurt. I didn't know it would be better to hurt someone in love…" he said, and looked sadly at me.

"I didn't mean to hurt you- I just want- I want to kiss you now. I don't care what I said. Kiss me." I said.

"I want to make love with you until we're both sore and broken. If I'm going to go to Heaven, I want to leave passionately in your arms." he said.

We kissed, in a heated embrace.

People were really staring at us *now…*

But we snuck off to be in private. "Quickly, in here." and were about to go into the girls' locker room…

But Vincent came out, smiling very cheerfully.

"…What were you doing in the girl's locker room, Vincent?" I asked, holding Set in my arms.

"Hm? I was? I don't know… I, uh… Man…" Vincent said, with that happy smile, and woozily walked away.

"Whatever. He's probably stoned. Let's go." I said, and pulled Set into the locker room…

We walked through the door, I dragged him to a hidden corner, turned to him…

And he wasn't in my arms anymore. He wasn't there.

"…Set?" I said.

I looked around, and saw Micah putting back on her shirt. She turned to me, smiled, and said, "Knew I could do it. I took your advice and was a little gentler, and he melted in my arms. Then... Oh man. Sometimes it's really good with a rough finish..." Micah said.

"He's gone." I said, knowing that Set and I... had broken up with each other, said our true feelings of passionate love, and he left in my arms, just like he said he wanted to do.

"Yeah... Leave 'em wanting more... That's how you keep that good feeling..." Micah said, stretching her arms.

I burst out crying, and Micah came to me and asked me what was wrong.

"I- I'm so... sad..." I said, and continued to cry.

51

After I had spent a day crying in my bed where Set and I had first... I explained to Lux that Set had left of his own free will, and that they shouldn't go looking for him.

"I'm going to need more of an explanation than that, Hana." Lux said.

I sighed, and told him all about angels of love, angels of war, seraphim, caretakers of Purgatory, angels of death, guardian angels, all I had learned from skirting with the afterlife, and even poofed out my wings, shouting while standing up in his office, "See?? I'm a fucking angel now, my angel boyfriend is gone, and I just want to... I just want to die so I can start my real life, with my real love, and not feel so bad!"

"...I see, Hana. And I understand."

"How could you... You don't even have a soul! You're just our robot teacher, teaching us to live a life on Earth! Well, I hate Earth, I don't want to go back to Hell again, and everything I ever wanted is in Heaven!" I said.

"Is that not a reason to continue living?" Lux said.

"No, it's not! It's just bullshit *life!*" I said.

"You've been blessed with something only two other people I've met, your mother and Yule, are as fortunate to have. You've seen what is after the end, and it is up to you to use this glimpse of afterlife to continue life, and help others to do so as well." Lux said.

"It's just a *curse!* I've even seen what's after the afterlife, with a glimpse behind the veil! I'd prefer it if I was blind!!" I said.

"I'd prefer if I was alive, and had actual eyes." Lux said.

"You're just lucky. You don't have to deal with any of this shit, you just be done, poof, when you die..." I said, sitting down and crossing my arms.

"I once thought that way. Then Jake told me about Christ, Cass taught me the meaning of family, Lucius gave me an appreciation for nature, Zax showed me what can happen when Heaven and Hell merge in unity, Dina showed me... well, things I can't even explain or ever will see or feel again, and Yule, the angel I brought back to life... showed me how to show true love and friendship. I had none of these things before.

"I do not know for certain what will happen to me when I die, and I know Heaven may help you find these things... but if you don't actually try to find them, you will never really have them. Heaven does not just appear on your lap. True Heaven is finding true value in life, and maybe the Heaven in the clouds is simply a place to enjoy and recollect the things you've found in life, but I do not know. Maybe it's just a place to dream, and find the things you wish you had.

"But if you do not try to find value in your life, even without a glimpse of this afterlife, you have wasted a marvelous opportunity, and even if you get to Heaven, it will still feel like a waste. You have the opportunity of a lifetime, Hana. You can show people the beauty and love you've experienced, and show them what it means to be in Heaven, in life, on Earth." Lux said.

"Set said I could go there. He said I had a key to Heaven with my wings." I said.

"God has opened his gates for you... probably so you don't feel left out. You deserve that freedom to be in Heaven, because you've spent your entire life in Hell. But it is up to you if you want to go to Heaven, stay in Heaven, or just let the time pass and go there later anyway. You have free passage." Lux said.

"...I guess if the road is clear for me... it isn't *so* pressing to try to go there..." I said.

"I prefer to think we all have a clear road to go to Heaven, at some point. I don't know what will happen when *I* die, but I know I would probably like to go to Heaven. But since I do not know, I will do my best to show others Heaven on Earth." Lux said.

"Ok. I suppose... it would be nice to show others what I've learned." I said.

"And you still have so much to learn as well." Lux said.

"I do. Thank you, Mr. Lux. I'm going to miss this school when I go out in the world." I said.

"Well... You don't have to leave just yet. I could use someone to train as a vice principal, or even just another teacher, just in case. I could teach you how to take my place in time." Lux said.

I opened my eyes in surprise, and asked, "Why? Are you going somewhere? It seems like you'll always be around."

"I could leave, at some point... I never know what uncertainties life will throw at me, and it doesn't hurt to be prepared." Lux said.

"Oh. Why me?" I asked.

"You show a constant hunger for knowledge, you have an unstoppable drive, and I wanted to offer you another life, over an afterlife. If anything, think of it as another job opportunity, an open opportunity, and a chance to build your already astonishing resume." Lux said.

I smiled, and said, "I do have a pretty good looking one, if unbelievable in some areas. Started a club, a garden, grew my own pot and brewed my own alcohol, took responsibility of a cat, play and practice the flute, have great grades besides average chemistry, even though I know how to make a good bomb, worked handyman jobs around the school, and apprenticed under an actual angel of Heaven. I will think on your open offer. I would accept right away, but I have to finish my school year first, anyway."

"We're always here for you, in this school, Hana, no matter what direction you take in life." Lux said.

I shook his hand, smiled, and left his office to continue my day.

It was going to storm outside, with dark, scary, black clouds. It looked like either Heaven or Hell's wrath, probably both, and you could feel the lightning in the air.

But I didn't care. We were going to have a party.

I spent every last one of my tokens, on food, games, anything that could be fun. I invited all my friends, who invited their friends, and so on. Even the loners who somehow missed out on our friendship were invited, as I had given them an invitation to the Champions of the Gargoyle blowout party.

It was a Sunday, and soon we would be out of school. I wondered why I never saw winter like I had heard about, but it seemed there was only rarely snow in the world these days, because the world had heated up so much in global warming.

But everyone was ready for the party. I was outside alone on this perfect dark clouded Sunday… looking at the mural in our empty garden.

Then it began raining, *and* snowing. I felt delight at such a beautiful occurrence.

The sun even shown down through a crack, straight on me, like God was winking.

Then he smiled, and I saw the rainbow and lightning in the clouded sky.

I gasped. There was one thing I still wanted to do, that would evade me no matter what.

I decided I'd at least try.

I burst out my wings, and went to catch the rainbow.

The rain and snow pushed me back, keeping me from the rainbow which always was one step ahead. I flew faster and faster, as it ran even faster.

I was alone in the dark, and the light was closing again.

The rainbow would soon be gone, and only could be seen from far away.

So I looked past the veil so I could see it correctly.

My eyes went black, I could feel it strangely enough, and then I saw *every* color of the rainbow, even the colors humans can't normally see.

And I somehow knew... I could be faster than the speed of light escaping. It was so simple... and all you had to do was look at the light just right to be faster than it...

I raced to it, faster than the speed of light, reached out my hand...

And I caught the rainbow.

I screamed out in triumph and pain, with the rainbow in my hand, being burned alive by pure, colored light.

I decided I'd keep this rainbow forever, but it escaped through my clenched together hand in a tiny opening, and its light went straight into my eyes as I looked at it.

I went blind, and fell.

52

I heard voices all around me, but nothing was in sight.

"She fell straight to the ground like this! It was the strangest sight I have ever seen. She *caught* the rainbow in her hands, is what it looked like." a voice said.

"Will she be alright? Can you do anything for her?" another voice said.

"Her eyes seem completely damaged..." another voice said.

"We need to pray. We need prayer now more than anything." another said.

"I jus' feel so bad for the kid... She had everythin', and then she loses her sight..." and another said.

"Why can't I heal her? Why can't I let Hana see?" another- my mother said.

"M-Mom? Wh-Where are you?" I asked.

My mom hugged me, and said, "It's ok. I'm right here. I love you, Hana. Yule, Lucius, Lux, Cass, Jake... please let me have a moment with Hana."

I tried to look at her, but her voice came from a different direction, so I looked at that. She said, "If I take you back to Hell, I believe I can give you your sight again. I'm not allowed- or something, to be able to use my power here. I thought God was bluffing, when he said I couldn't in the living world... I'm already encroaching on our terms just by being here. But if I take you back, I think I can get you your sight. But you will have to stay in Hell to keep it."

"O-Ok. I'm so scared right now. I want to see." I said.

"I will take you back home immediately... but first, let my friends, people I consider our family, tell you what you will be giving up. All the rest of our family are dead, and you are my only offspring. But these people have been my friends through thick and thin... And they all live here, in life. Let them make you their offers." my mom said.

"I don't think there's anything more precious than being able to see... I can't read a single book now. I can't see rainbows. I can't even see... *you...*"I said, and cried.

My mom held my hand, and called out to the rest of our family to come back inside this room, this blank room to me.

I immediately felt Yule hug me, I could tell by her strength and comfortable embrace. The first thing she said was, "We all love you, Hana. We all think of you as sort of a niece, and never want to see you go through this suffering. We will protect you, and it is specifically my duty to protect you."

"Because you're a seraph of God? You protect God's throne, not me." I said.

"I protect God's throne, yes. But where do you think God is seated? Up in Heaven? Well, yeah, he does like to relax in his super big, super comfortable throne, but only occasionally. The rest of his time the throne he sits in is usually his favorite lawn chair by the sunset, his favorite reading spot on the couch, or one on the judge's bench, where he judges us eternally, and rests our sins in his palm, weighs them, and then lets them fall away from us. His favorite throne is his seat in creation. I just protect it, from anyone, everything, even themselves." Yule said.

"That sounds like a very difficult task. So you want to protect me for your duty to God, as a seraph?" I asked.

"Well, I was thinking more as your aunt. I was kind of an aunt to Paul, your ancestor, and I was a friend to your father... even a very brief lover, for a dream. I would feel honored to be a guardian to you, and will help you live your life with your new condition, however I can." Yule said.

"Oh... That does sound very nice. But I will never be able to see anything God has made." I said.

Lucius hugged me next, he just felt so pleasant to touch, and felt like he knew exactly what I wanted, when I started to cry again. Lucius said, "You don't just see nature in life. Be silent with me, one more time."

I was, and I felt our hearts beat, as he hugged me, along with the motion of our breathing .

"We all live on the beats of the heart, and the rhythm of our breath. You will be able to see the life of the world in other ways. We *do* have five senses just in case one of them goes missing. You never see the actual wind, but you will still be able to feel it." Lucius said.

And suddenly... as if on command, wind rushed into this room. Was I even in a room? I felt the breeze ruffle my hair, and caress my body.

Lucius said, "And you will still be able to play music, for as long as you can breathe."

I smiled, and Lucius let go of me to play me a song, a happy song that went through my entire body. I was bouncing my head to the music, and in a way I wanted to dance... So I did.

I got up from the bed, or table, or couch, or something, I think, and danced.

A man took me up in his strong arms and danced with me, taking me out of the room. I felt the scars on his arms, and I knew he was Jake, as we danced to Lucius's tune.

"I fuckin' love music, man. Christ plays like magic, and you'll always be able to listen to 'is albums too. We were going to jus' come here to congratulate you, Hana, and we had a gift for you. A dark mare, jus' your size." Jake said.

"A horse? How will I ride a horse?" I said.

"She's a wild beastie, jus' like you, and I ain't sure you'd see where you're going… but she can. I can show you how to tame that wild mare even more, and you'll always have some companion with you, a companion that can take you wherever you need to go." Jake said.

"What's her name?" I asked.

"Er, I was thinkin'… Nah, that's jus' a crude joke to us guys on the ranch. Here, reach out your hand, and touch her mane. Be careful, she's a biter." I said.

I thought I was in a building? Jake gently brought me to a… a horse, and she sniffed my hand, and allowed me to pet her nose. She lowered her head, and I pet her mane. It was the softest feeling in the world, and I could practically imagine how she looked.

"Shit. Tha' black maned bitch is bein' nice. I guess she understands." Jake said.

I continued to pet her, and said, "I want to call her my Nightmare, because she will help me through this nightmare called life."

"…Weird fuckin' name, Hana. But it's up to you." Jake said.

Cass hugged me next, as the horse was nibbling my hand gently, I could tell by her robotic arms and pregnant belly. She said, "We will all pray for you, so life won't have to be a nightmare. I think it will be so fantastic to have a cousin for my child. Maybe you can help teach her, too?"

"Her?" I said.

"That's what I'm praying for. You could be like sisters! It's so exciting. I offer you a place on our ranch, to live with us for as long as you like. Yule and Lucius are going to settle down with us, too! We're only a short ride from the school, and you could pick up right where you left off, teaching the kids or doing whatever you feel like! You have so much life to live, and can do so with us, your family." Cass said.

"I... I only ever lived with my mom and dad. In Hell. But... living with all of you... in that awesome ranch... That... really makes me feel accepted." I said.

"You got that right, dear! We accept you, same as Lux accepted you into his school." Cass said.

Lux said, "You don't need eyesight to teach, and you don't need eyesight even just to read."

"...How?" I said.

Lux offered me something, guiding my hands to his gift, and I took it gently out of his robotic hands, and it was a book. I started crying, thinking I could never read the words... but Lux said, "Open the book, Hana, and feel the words."

I opened the book, and it was covered in a bunch of strange bumps.

"That is called Braille. Besides one of us being able to read to you, you will be able to interpret these bumps into symbols and words. I know the language fluently, and I could translate whatever book you desire to read into these bumps, for you to enjoy whenever you like. All you have to do is learn the language. Easy, really." Lux said.

I smiled, and said, "Learning isn't so easy for us humans. I'm going to have to take lessons, painstaking tests and learn through trial and error... It will be a long road for me. But I am willing to learn."

Lux said, "And all of us are willing to teach you how to live in the world without sight."

"Thank you. Everyone, thank you." I said.

My mother, the Queen of Hell, took my hand gently and said, "So what will it be? You can always visit me and Cerberus in Hell. The way is easy. Just ride your Nightmare into the abyss, and soon you'll be in Hell. But you can still live with your family and their gifts of life for as long as you wish."

"I don't think I could give up on such fantastic treasures my family has offered me, even for such a thing called sight. I will stay in life. But I will definitely visit you, Mom. How are things going down there, anyway? Won't it collapse without you?" I said.

"Things weren't perfect in Hell for a reason. If they were... everyone would get greedy, and want an even better existence. We lived in a normal sized house, as a normal family, and I only went to work in the morning, judged sinners and found them jobs in Hell, went to bed in the evening, and 'life' continued. Beleth is doing my job now, even though he wants the whole thing for himself... but Hell is a perpetual machine thanks to me, that doesn't even need an eternal ruler. I do have to get back to work though, and grease the wheels..." my mom said.

"Why don't you just live with us here? It'll be a longer commute to work, but you're my mom, Mom, and I want to have my family with you too." I said.

"Hmm... I suppose I could. It wouldn't be a bad thing to live in life again... God doesn't *seem* like he wants to smite me down yet... Ok. I accept." my mom said.

"You've always got me, Mom. I love you." I said.

My mom said, "I love you too, Hana."

I could feel the sunlight on me... and I prayed for a miracle that I could see the sun again...

But God doesn't answer every prayer exactly how we wish it.

I didn't see anything, I just felt the sun's rays, felt my family all hug me around me, and danced with them to the music that Jake put on from... the van. I had been laying in the van, and they had all converged on this spot, finding me in an accident on their way to the school, as Lux looked for me himself. My mother just knew where I was, I guess.

"Ain't fuckin' Christ somethin' else?" Jake said.

Christ? I just heard Elvis singing. I suppose Christ is in all of life, love, and music.

I felt like my father was looking down on me. He would be waiting for me in Heaven, as my mother from Hell danced with me, in this place called life.

53

I put Rasputin on a leash, not so I could guide him, but so he could guide me. He walked me through the halls, avoiding corners and walls. People stayed far away from me, so they wouldn't get in my way, but my best friend came to my side, however, to help me with whatever I needed. Sara said, "You look good today, Hana. Just a white hoodie, black pants, gargoyle tabard on… No heels, though."

"I didn't want to trip and have a hard time getting back up." I said.

"That's alright. You look beautiful today. Don't even need glasses anymore, I guess! But I wanted to ask… Why the white sash over your eyes? It would be simpler just wearing dark shades or something." Sara said.

"I didn't feel like hiding my disability, and have people be awkward as they question if I'm blind or not. And I don't have any shades." I said.

"Well… You are being walked by a cat, so I suppose it's not too big a question… I think people will just wonder why the fuck you have a sash over your eyes, so here, take a spare of shades. I never use 'em anyway, cuz they're too dark." Sara said, then offered me some shades. I unfurled my cloth, opened my eyes as Sara gasped, and I put on the shades. "It's like, your eyes… I didn't expect any eyes to be that color."

"See? I didn't want people to freak out because of that." I said.

"But- But- I don't know if I just looked into a rainbow, or the absence of one." Sara said.

"I caught the rainbow, and I paid the price. I'll never know what you see when you look into my eyes, but I get that response a lot." I said.

"...Ok. Are you sure you want to go to crafts with me?" Sara said.

"Yes. It's the only class that people don't need to change everything just for me, and I'd like to do something physical with my hands. I just sort of guesstimate the measurements, but it feels sort of right in my grip, so I like building stuff." I said.

"Use the ol' measure with your thumb trick. That'll get you far enough with smaller objects." Sara said, and Rasputin guided me into the crafts room.

I worked on a birdhouse with my hammer, cut the wood with my hatchet, all under my hands that had caught the rainbow.

Mr. Loren said, "Wow. Good job, Hana! It's like... I don't know, like you're cutting as smooth as light."

"Really? Are you just being too nice, or something? I can take it, tell me how my birdhouse looks." I said.

"...Well, it looks sort of like an abstract house for some crazy artist bird... But everything looks like it would work for a bird to live in. You've made a nice home for a bird who thinks out of the box." Mr. Loren said.

I smiled, and wished I could've seen my house, but it felt right, nice and smooth, so I think it was good.

I had lunch with my friends, and we all reminisced about the great party we had, dancing, singing and laughing.

I went to Lux's class last, took a test orally just for me, and then my school year was finished.

We still had one more meeting of the Champions of the Gargoyle, however, because our friendship would last even over school.

All the last years like me and kids who had other homes were packing up to leave, and I contemplated which spot would be a good place to have a last meeting... We had spent time in the library, a secret basement, the garden, the cafeteria… These would all be great spots to have one more meeting, but I don't know. I wanted the last one to be memorable.

Rasputin said, "Why don't you take them to your father's grave? You could show them all what is after the grave with the last meeting."

"I was really going to explain the burning book to them, and I don't want to bring something so evil to my father's grave." I said.

"Then don't bring it. In fact, you can just leave it behind if you like. Donate it to the library, and let someone else take a gander." Rasputin said.

"…Are you sure? But it is literally the Devil." I said.

"I find it to just be a silly book." Rasputin said.

"But it will burn all the other books…" I said.

"Then put out its flame." Rasputin said.

I didn't really know what he meant, but I took out the burning book, which tickled my scarred hands, and said, "You gonna be a good book if I donate you?"

The burning book said, *"You're really giving me away?? But… I'm the Devil! How can you just let me go??"*

"I think it'll be nicer for your eternity to corrupt new minds with your evil lies, don't you think? I basically finished you, and I'm really disappointed that you don't have an end, but I suppose that makes sense. It's kinda cool that you don't, because you're an eternal book with something new to give always, even if it is new evil. I suppose there is always new evil in the world…" I said.

"New good, too. New minds to snuff out and devour… I'll… Oh, you've fucking heard all my threats before. I'll be the most evil book in existence, but I will be enjoyable. And I won't be the only book on the shelf… People will find me much more pleasant, when they see me next to Shelley and Shakespeare, and then choose me for something 'new.' If I was the only choice people would read

me out of necessity, and the temptation of evil would be gone." the burning book said.

"I'll make sure they put you right next to the Bible then, so people have the temptation of good as well." I said.

"And the eternal battle continues. I'll be more popular than any silly Bible, New Testament or Old, because my story doesn't end at Revelations... My story and my eternal battle continues throughout the ages."

"I still don't believe that you won't try to burn all the other books down." I said.

"Take my word, then... because really, that's all books are. You will never know if I am a liar or not, or even if I am really the Devil..." the burning book said.

"True. I suppose a liar doesn't lie all the time, though, because otherwise that would just be telling the truth backwards. I'll take your word, book. I'm sick of questioning you, anyway. Have fun with the other books, and try to offer something worthwhile." I said. The burning book tried to stutter out another lie or truth, but I just threw it in my bag and took it to the library, led by my cat.

I gave the burning book to the librarian, and the librarian put the book on a dusty shelf, actually far away from the Bible because she categorized it as fiction after reading the first line that said, *"I am the Burning Book."* and knew readable books didn't burn. I think the Devil decided he'd rather be a readable book, rather than a burning paperweight which was no good to anyone at all.

54

I walked with my cat and my friends, my club called the Champions of the Gargoyle, Champs for short, and we paid reverence to my father who was dead. Micah brought an offering of food for the dead, some natural, uncooked potatoes, and placed them at the headstone. Sharina and Lita brought flowers that they had gathered all day beforehand, and placed them at the headstone. Devon and Miller said prayers with me, as these two gay boys, now gay men, were both deeply religious actually. Miller came from a homestead of heavy religion, but was still accepted for his lifestyle by his family, eventually, and Devon always thanked God on the farm for their yields and their dinner. Dill and Vincent offered paintings they had each made depicting how my father would've looked to them. It was a shame I couldn't see them.

Sara sang her song for us and my father, with an extra verse at the end,

"Cockadoodle doo, and the cow goes moo,
It's time to wake up, and go to school.
There's friends to play with, lessons to learn,
There's people to see, and I have butter to churn.
So set off to school, dear daughter,
I'll be here at home, dear daughter,
For as long as the cow goes moo,

I'll be here, dear daughter, for another cockadoodle doo.

I'll be here in Heaven, and I'll wait up just for you."

We sat in a circle beside the grave, and I told them all about the angels in Heaven. I poofed out my angel wings, just so they wouldn't wonder, took off my shades so they could look into my eyes, and allowed them to see the real me.

It was a long conversation, and a very intense one. They all questioned reality, theology, and the very meaning of life. Even the cat, Rasputin, joined in the conversation and clarified some things for them.

"Your eyes are… something, because you caught the rainbow, you have angel wings because you loved an actual angel of love, you learned how to be an angel of death, even though you can't be one now, guardian angeled my maybe dad… and… I don't know what else. I suppose I'd have to see your life looking through your eyes to understand it all. Sorry, that's not a very good saying for you, because you're now blind…" Sara said.

"I'm hoping my words will suffice, and you don't need to really walk a mile in my high heels. I'm keeping them just in case someone I love and who loves me would like to see me in them, one day." I said.

"…Like who?" Sara asked.

"Oh, someone who'll listen to my stories and just be a real good friend to me. I won't see Set again until I die, but I'm sure I can find another unique love in anyone." I said.

"…I like seeing you in high heels, but just because they seem to make you happy, and that makes me happy." Sara said.

I looked into her eyes, I think, with my something eyes, and I winked. She laughed, and held my hand. Soon we were all holding hands together in a circle, with Micah holding my hand on my other side. All of these people were like my family.

Vincent broke the circle first, reached into his pocket, and said, "Well, I've got one more joint left. Will hardly do anything for all of us, but it's more the ritual of it, I think. Let's toke."

Lita broke hands next, got a bottle of something from her bag, and said, "I have one last bit of… radish wine. I know, you hate them, Hana, but I just had to try distilling them."

"I accept our evil vegetable, in our last holy drink. Let us drink the blood of radishes, and be happy that they aren't drinking ours instead." I said. My friends laughed, and we passed the booze and the joint around.

We laughed, we joked, and our last meeting ended at sunset. Micah told me, "It's beautiful, and I wish you could see it. It's like, orange, red, gold, purple… all streaming from that big sun." I held her hand, and she squeezed mine tight.

We walked back to our school, our once home, and went on to continue our lives in the real world.

In the morning, Rasputin was packed up with Yule and Lucius in their van, Cass and Jake rode their stallion, my mom got in the van, and we all said goodbye to Lux. I shook his hand, said I would be here for the next year to learn how to teach, and then hugged him goodbye. Cass and Jake guided me on Nightmare, and we rode and drove to the ranch.

I hugged big ol' Zeus, ready for him to take me soon as I was single and an adult-

But my mom said, "Woah. Heya, god. We need some help unpacking, mind helping carrying some things?"

Zeus said, "It would be my pleasure, my Queen. There's a few whole guest houses ready for all of you, but that's not even going to be the best part of living here! We'll all build homes together."

"Mmm… I love a man who can make a full home, such a full man too… Come. Slave for me, god." my mom said.

"As you command, my Queen, I shall please you in my full capacity…" Zeus said.

I was getting sharper at hearing, and I heard Zeus bow, and my mom stroke his bearded chin as she passed him into the house.

I was jealous of this, but even more jealous when late in the night I had all been settled up to sleep... and then I heard my mother shriek like she was being struck by lightning, and Zeus moan like he was being tortured in Hell. They both sounded quite happy...

In the morning, us three ate breakfast together, and I was kind of silent as the two seemed so cheerful and good spirited.

She slapped Zeus on the butt on his way out to work, and I said to my mom as soon as the door closed, "Do you still love Dad?"

"Hm? Of course. I love your father with all my heart." she said.

"...Then why are you taking the first man you see into bed with you?" I said.

"I'm enjoying my new life, Hana. It's been a very long year in Hell. A very lonely, stressful year. My bed has been empty since your father left, and I had almost forgotten what a man looks like who doesn't have horns, a tail and disgusting lust filled fantasies..."

"...But Zeus used to be a prostitute." I said.

"Really? That makes a lot of sense. *I* used to be a stripper. I think both our works intertwined into the other's at times, and when we inter- twined last night-" my mom said.

"I don't want to know, Mom... I didn't even know you were a strip- per... But- How come Zeus- How come he won't-" I said.

"Are you jealous? That is quite cute, dear. You are absolutely beau- tiful, have angelic wings whenever you want, and being blind... really, that can be kind of a blessing in bed. I wouldn't worry about what us old folks are doing. You'll meet someone nice soon, too." my mom said.

"...Ok. It frankly seems very difficult, as yeah, I'm blind." I said.

"Take advantage of the fact that every person around will want to satisfy you in any way they can. And if they just want to take advantage of you... I'll know, and I'll-" my mom said.

"You need to let me make my own love, Mom. I know that's difficult for you." I said.

"...Ok. Well, I'm off to work too. I'll see you around, dear. I love you." my mom said.

I said I loved her too, she kissed me on the cheek, and she poofed down to Hell. I'm not really sure how, and I couldn't see it to describe it.

I walked around with Rasputin a lot, had coffee with Lucius and Yule, learned to ride a bit with Jake, helped Cass in the forge as best I could, and it was a rather nice day. But I too wish I had someone to help me get over this long, stressful year...

I heard running come up to me from afar. And I thought... could this be the person I was waiting for?

I couldn't see who it was, but we held hands and I knew who it was immediately... and I knew I had found my love, who traversed all this distance just to be with me instead of going on with their own life. We would make our new life and love together, because my love kissed me immediately, and I responded in turn.

My love said, "You are my love, Hana. I love you."

Adding one more line to the end of my love's song and my story, I said, "Cockadoodle doo, I love you too."

Sara's Song

Cockadoodle doo, and the cow goes moo,
It's time to wake up, and go to school.
There's friends to play with, lessons to learn,
There's people to see, and I have butter to churn.
So set off to school, dear daughter,
I'll be here at home, dear daughter,
For as long as the cow goes moo,
I'll be here, dear daughter, for another cockadoodle doo.
I'll be here in Heaven, and I'll wait up just for you.
Cockadoodle doo, I love you too.